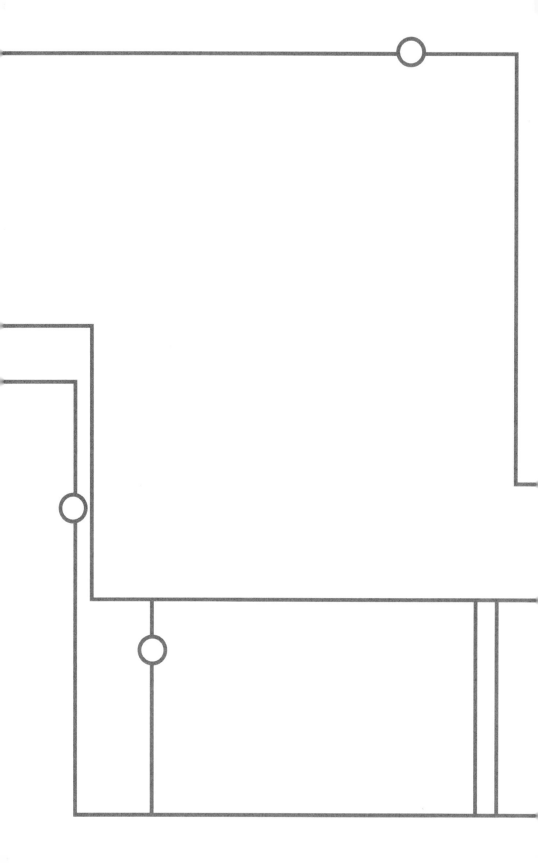

HAZZARDOUS UNIVERSE

JULIE WRIGHT & KEVIN WASDEN

Covenant

Covenant Communications, Inc.

Cover and interior artwork © 2011 by Kevin Wasden

Cover and book design copyright © 2011 by Covenant Communications, Inc.

Published by Covenant Communications, Inc.
American Fork, Utah

Printed in the United States of America
First Printing: March 2011

17 16 15 14 13 12 11   10 9 8 7 6 5 4 3 2 1

ISBN 978-1-60861-206-2

Praise for *Hazzardous Universe*

"Aliens, mobsters, magic, action, and humor—everything a reader could want!"

—Jessica Day George, author of *Princess of Glass* and the Dragon Slippers series

"Hazzardous Universe is the perfect book—a fun mix of humor, compelling plot, and action. I really loved it!"

—James Dashner, *New York Times*–bestselling author of *The Maze Runner* and *The Scorch Trials*

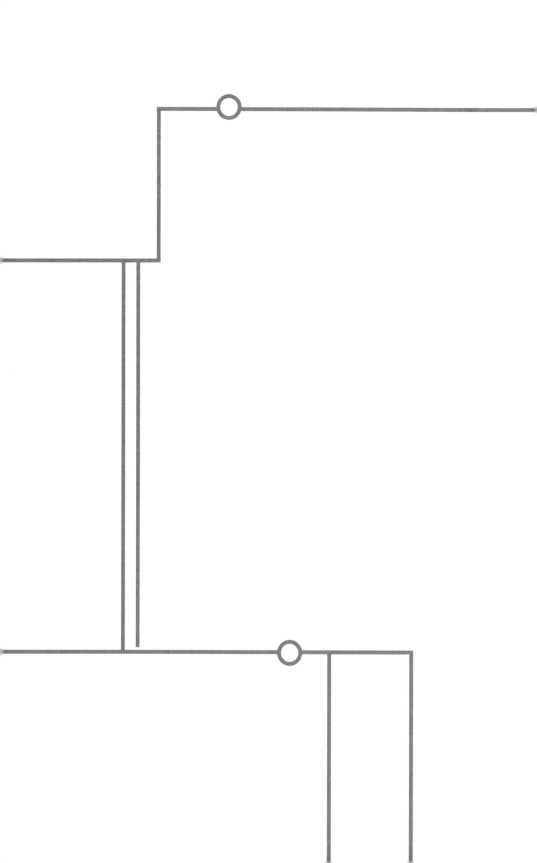

To Merrik, Chandler, Ethan, Cameron, and Alex—because the universe is in short supply of heroes and could use a few more boys who are willing to stand up and be men of honor.

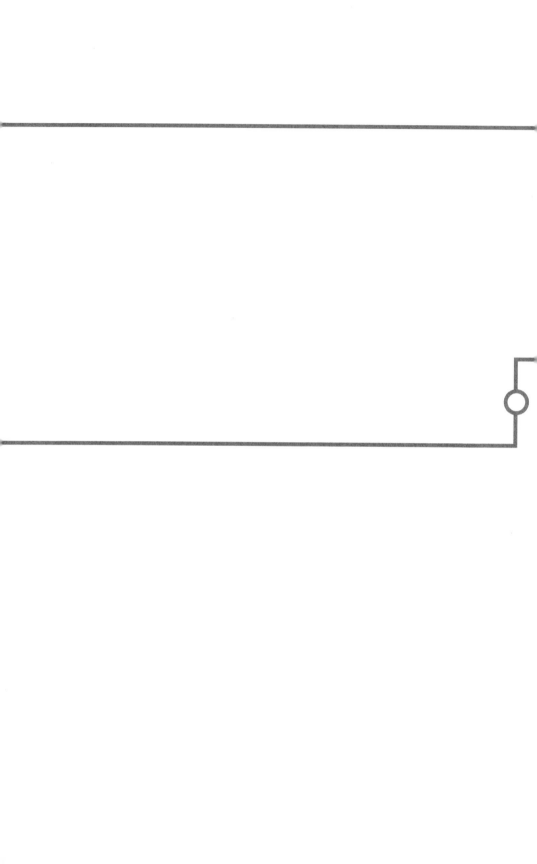

ACKNOWLEDGMENTS

HAP'S STORY STARTED A LONG time ago, in a galaxy so close, you're probably sitting in it. It began the day Hap sneaked into Kevin's imagination in 1993. Over the years, Hap repeatedly found his way into sketchbooks and short stories. He brought his friends from all over the universe with him. Kevin drew Hap's adventures with his friends but never really knew what to do with the stories he'd created. At a convention fourteen years later, Kevin met Julie. They talked briefly, Kevin sketched a dragon and an ogre for Julie, and she signed a book for him. Kevin read Julie's book and decided she might be the one who could tell Hap's story. They met for lunch, discussed ideas, argued over who would pay for lunch, and a beautiful partnership was born—because only a fool would turn down the idea of a character named Hap Hazzard.

And now that Hap is here, Julie and Kevin would like to thank the following people:

Josi Kilpack, Alex Choules, Nathan Davenport, and W. Gerald Peterson for their insight and help in refining the story.

James Dashner, Jeff Savage, Howard Tayler, and Jessica Day George for their unending support and friendship.

Kirk Shaw and Kathy Jenkins for their vision and absolute faith in us and for their solid belief that this journey was worth taking.

Robby Nichols, Mark Sorenson, Margaret Weber, Ron Brough, Kelly Smurthwaite, and the rest of the Covenant family who approved, designed, and marketed Hap's Universe to the world.

The Wright and Wasden families, who put up with us during the creative process. Scott and Michelle have been our first line of support and our strength to move forward. None of this would be possible without our spouses and children cheering us on.

And thanks to you, our readers, who will continue giving Hap life every time you turn the pages.

1. Mysterious Magician

THE BELL JINGLED AS A gnarled man stepped into the magic store. He ducked his head, but his top hat still brushed the door frame. His cape fluttered at his heels like a shadow as he swept off his hat and leaned heavily on his cane. He scanned the magic shop before locking eyes with Hap.

Hap didn't mean to, but he gulped.

"Fredrick Eugene Hazzard?" The voice sounded like stones grating against each other.

Hap flinched at the name. In all his fourteen years of life, no one ever called him by his full name—except when he was in trouble. He quickly stowed the *Technosaurs* comic book under the counter so he didn't look like he'd been wasting time. Hap raked his fingers through his hair to flatten it down. Sometimes his hair stuck out from his head and looked like flames—one disadvantage of being a redhead. "Yeah . . . how can I help you?"

The man's cane clicked against the wooden floor as he closed the distance between the door and the counter. Hap recoiled slightly, feeling grateful to have the counter between him and this weather-beaten wizard. Lots of *eccentric* types came into his grandpa's magic store, but no one had darkened the door of Hazzard's Magical Happenings so *literally*. The guy seemed to suck all the light from the shop into the folds of his black cloak.

"I must speak with Fredrick Eugene Hazzard immediately."

"You're talking to him. But everyone calls me Hap." Hap's gaze slipped toward the back room, but he decided against calling to his grandfather until he saw whatever this overzealous salesman might be showing off. Hap tried at a smile.

The old man *didn't* smile. His right eye twitched as though he'd bitten into a Sour Zapper—the latest in candy gags. His lips puckered as he leaned his cane against the counter. His thin, blue-veined hand slid inside the top hat and, with a flourish, flew out again, holding a rusted metal ball.

Hap's smile widened. Having always wanted to be a magician, he appreciated the theatrics some salesmen used when showing their merchandise.

The man's skeletal fingers placed the ball on the counter. It shifted on the countertop, revealing the venting holes along the diameter. It shifted again. Something was alive in that ball.

"Cool!" Hap leaned closer to get a better look. A smaller rabbit or dove would be able to fit in such tight quarters. This guy might actually be selling something worth looking into.

With the grace of a practiced magician, the man reached a finger toward the slight depression at the top of the ball.

Before his bone-thin fingers could touch the ball, both the man and Hap leaped away from the counter at the sound of what seemed like an explosion outside the front door. The sun catchers rattled against the window panes. Hap hurried to the window display to peer outside and groaned.

"What happened? What was that noise?"

Hap turned to see his grandpa hurrying through the red curtain that led to the office and storage room in the back.

"Someone kicked the garbage can into the door." Hap jabbed a thumb to where the can rocked on its side near the front steps. He looked back out the window to see if the culprit lingered by the crime scene.

Grandpa Hazzard moved to join Hap by the window but stopped short when he saw the man who seemed to take up all the space in the front of the store.

"Tolvan?" The alarm in his grandfather's voice made Hap turn away from the window and pay closer attention to the man whom his grandfather seemed to know.

Tolvan palmed the strange ball and rubbed his fingers together to show his now-empty hand.

Grandpa Hazzard's gray eyes widened in disbelief. He pointed at Tolvan's empty hands. "Surely you didn't mean to use a disrupter *here*?"

Under heavy black eyebrows, Tolvan's eyes twisted to glare at Hap. "I've put it away, haven't I? He claimed to be you. He may have your eyes, and that devilish hair from your youth, but he clearly *isn't* you. The boy lacks respect for the elderly." Tolvan had regained his cane and now used it to thump the ground in irritation. He looked anything but elderly. Terrifying, yes. White-haired and weathered, yes. But *not* elderly.

Hap fidgeted under his grandfather's gray gaze. "He looked like a salesman. I was just running interference like I always do. He said he needed to talk to Fredrick Eugene Hazzard, and that *is* my name. You were busy doing inventory."

Grandpa Hazzard closed his eyes and scratched at the sparse remnants of gray hair at the back of his head. He suddenly looked old and frail. "The boy meant no disrespect. Usually, I'm grateful when he diverts attention away from me. It's been a long time, Tolvan. Let's go into my office." Grandpa Hazzard pulled the curtain back and gestured for Tolvan to pass through. "Something tells me we have much to discuss."

"Can I come too?" Hap asked. Many magicians had visited Grandpa Hazzard over the years, though none with such archaic clothing. Hap had always been included in conversations and had even been given lessons on some of the best magic tricks—the ones you can't buy or learn in books. This guy could probably teach some great magic.

"No, Hap. I need you to watch the store."

Hap had already started walking back with them but halted at the words. He blinked in surprise. "What about Mom? Or Alison? She could watch the store for a few minutes."

"Your mother and sister are taking the mail orders to the post office."

Most of the store's real business came from Internet sales—making post office visits a daily chore.

"Couldn't you two talk out here? There's no one else in the store." Hap hated the whine in his voice.

"Not this time, Hap. I need you to stay here."

"But—"

"No!" Grandpa Hazzard coughed and said more gently, "No."

Stunned by his grandfather's sharp tone, Hap watched the two men disappear behind the curtain. He couldn't believe it. He'd never been left out before, not once in the year and a half he'd been working with his grandpa at Hazzard's Magical Happenings. And *never* had his grandfather raised his voice.

He edged closer to the curtain, his ears straining to listen, his heart thumping hard against his ribs. He'd never eavesdropped on his grandpa before. He'd never needed to.

Tolvan's gravelly voice whispered with an urgency that heightened Hap's curiosity. "She has the pyramid. Once she delivers it, he'll search for the books. If he gets it, everything we hold dear will be like candle flame to parchment—nothing but ashes. The trust is in danger. Fredrick, you say you're done with the trust and ICE, but now you must help—"

"Excuse me, one moment," Grandpa Hazzard said.

The curtain swept aside so fast, Hap nearly fell into the office. "I was just . . . looking for . . ." He grabbed the broom leaning against the wall near him. "The broom." Hap nodded as though he could make them agree with his declaration of innocence.

Grandpa frowned at Hap. "What a good idea." He rested a heavy hand on Hap's shoulder, leading Hap away from the back office and its odd occupant. He led Hap all the way through the magic shop, past the practical jokes and pocket tricks, past the racks of obscure gourmet candy, and out the front door.

Grandpa Hazzard pointed to the garbage can, still rocking in the breeze. Styrofoam hamburger packages from Big Bite Burger next door spilled down the front steps and over the sidewalk. Half-full cardboard cups had leaked cola into huge sticky puddles that would require scrubbing to clean.

Grandpa Hazzard squinted into the mess before picking up what looked like burned shrapnel. "The aliens have been busier than normal today. Old Noory on *Coast to Coast* said they would be."

Hap rolled his gray eyes. "Yeah. Aliens . . . in Ridge Creek. If I were an alien, I'd definitely come to Utah to knock over some random garbage can."

"Lots of people come here."

"You mean lots of people come *through* here. No one wants to stay. And why can't I hang out with your magician friend?" Hap used the term "friend" lightly. Tolvan seemed more like a visitor from a nightmare than a friend. Something felt *wrong* with the whole situation.

Grandpa Hazzard set his mouth in a firm straight line, making the gray hairs bristle on his chin. "This isn't about pulling a dove from your coat sleeve, boy. Magic is about keeping secrets." He held out his hand and the piece of shrapnel melted right before Hap's eyes. It re-formed into a quarter-sized polished blue stone. "And sometimes there are secrets I cannot share, not even with you."

And with that declaration and bit of magic, Grandpa Hazzard disappeared behind the door, the little bells jingling after him.

Hap wanted to call him back—to keep him from returning to the strange man with his strange magic—but couldn't think of any way to do it without sounding paranoid, and without ending up with Grandpa yelling at him again.

Grandpa had been especially soft spoken since Hap's dad got sick. His dad had become too sick to stay at his job, and their family had moved in with Grandpa so they didn't have to worry about household bills as much. The whole family had pitched in and helped earn their keep by working at Hazzard's Magical Happenings, and Hap suspected Grandpa was grateful they had come. But from the sad, long looks Grandpa gave Dad and the lowered, hushed tones Grandpa used when talking, Grandpa ached as much over watching Hap's dad get sicker as Hap did.

Life was grossly unfair.

And now Grandpa Hazzard had yelled at him for the first time ever.

Hap kicked lightly at the garbage can, making it grind over the cement, before he sighed and set it up straight. How could his grandpa know a trick like that and never teach it to him? How could Grandpa Hazzard keep secrets? The outright betrayal of holding back something so cool as that shrapnel melting into the polished stone made Hap want to kick the garbage can a second time.

He grumbled while he worked; it made him feel better—well, not really, but that's what he told himself.

Hap's mom pulled her car into the side parking lot. Alison hopped out and skipped to the edge of the debris. "You're gonna be in trouble."

"I didn't do this." Hap resisted the urge to swat her with the broom.

His mom followed on Alison's heels. "Heavens, Hap! What have you done out here?"

Hap shook his head in disbelief. "I didn't do this!"

She narrowed her eyes at him and stepped closer, sliming the heel of her shoe through a smear of processed cheese. "You didn't do this?"

He yanked on the bottom of his Hazzard's Magical Happenings shirt in irritation. "Of course not!"

She folded her arms and tapped her toe, making her curls bounce against her shoulders like the googly eyes they sold in the shop. "Then who did?"

"Grandpa said it was aliens." Hap regretted the statement as soon as it left his lips. Grandpa Hazzard loved aliens. He owned every *X-Files* season on DVD and had every book that every ufologist had ever written on the subject.

Mom and Dad . . . well, they *didn't* love aliens.

Her paled face reflected years of strain from this same topic. Mom hated contention. She usually let Dad argue over aliens with Grandpa Hazzard, but with Dad being sick, she did all she could to keep Dad comfortable, and that meant she was the one stuck with telling Grandpa to knock it off with the alien stuff. Mom and Dad didn't want Hap or Alison to get weird ideas. They didn't mind Grandpa Hazzard believing what he wanted, but they didn't want him brainwashing their children with nonsense either.

Mom looked at the front door of the shop with resolve. She planned on fighting this one.

"Oh, Mom, I was kidding. Stupid kids probably did it."

She scowled but relaxed visibly since she wouldn't have to have "the argument" with Grandpa Hazzard after all. "Yes, that's likely."

Some of the kids from school thought Grandpa Hazzard belonged in a mental institution with a padded room and a white, long-sleeved coat. They egged the store, lit firecrackers in the Dumpster, and once hung plastic aliens all over the front of Hazzard's Magical Happenings with a big poster board sign that read NO INTELLIGENT LIFE FOUND HERE!

"But *I* didn't do it." He scrubbed his hand over his head.

She sighed in resignation. "I'm sorry I accused you. Of course you wouldn't. I'll get you a dustpan." Her agreement on his innocence didn't get him out of cleaning. Mom went into the store with Alison following closely behind. Alison likely didn't want any association with the mess so she wouldn't get talked into cleaning too.

"Stupid people are lame. Lame, lame, lame," Hap muttered under his breath. As he ranted, his voice grew louder. "And I can't believe we have to deal with the restaurant's trash! We should file a complaint with the city! ARGH! Whoever did this is such an ape . . . stupid, unevolved, idiotic—"

"Excuse me?"

Hap whirled around to face Tara Jordan staring at him with her big hazel eyes. "Tara!" He took a deep breath to calm himself. "What are you doing sneaking up on people like that? I thought you were my mom." He turned away and shoved a drippy cup into the can. The grime from the trash can's contents caked his hands, the smell making him wrinkle his nose. He swallowed to keep from throwing up. The rancid carbonated beverages and moldy hamburgers smelled like vinegar and tomatoes.

Hap hated tomatoes.

He peeked at Tara. She wasn't a regular at the magic store, though he remembered she had been before her parents split up. She didn't really hang out anywhere anymore, at least not that Hap knew of.

"I wasn't sneaking. I came here to give you an application."

"An application for what?"

"A job." She held a piece of paper out for him to look at. She wrinkled her nose at his filthy hands and tried to pull the paper away, but he snatched it from her.

"You want to work here?" He ran his wrist under his nose and looked over her résumé. "Let's see . . . Tara Jordan, age fourteen. You had a paper route, and you've done babysitting and house sitting. Hmm, you don't have much experience."

"I have as much as you do." She snatched the paper back before he could read her hobbies.

"I've been working in this shop every summer since I was tall enough to reach the register while standing on a milk crate. And I've been pretty much the only one working here since—" He broke off and scowled. *Since they told us my dad was going to die.*

"I know quite a bit about magic tricks." She was talking big, but Hap heard the doubt in her own voice.

"Really?" He smirked. "Prove it."

Her eyebrows furrowed. She seemed irritated and flustered, and the gold flecks in her hazel eyes seemed to pulsate as she glared at him. "Excuse me?"

"Show me a trick." He crossed his arms over his chest, the smell of the garbage on his hands. He sniffed and grimaced, clasping his hands behind his back instead.

With a great breath, she tucked her blonde hair behind her ear and took a small orange scarf from her pocket. In silence, she held the corners at the top of the scarf and showed him both sides. She then scrunched the scarf into a ball with one hand while making a fist with the other. Tara stuffed the scarf into her fist, packing it down using her fingers and thumb. Then, with a flourish, she spread her hands wide to show they were empty.

"Nice. Bring it back."

She wrinkled her forehead. "What?"

"Bring it back. Every magician knows it's not enough to make it disappear . . . you gotta bring it back. You've seen *The Prestige,* right? You can't want to work at a magic shop without watching a few magic movies. Make it come back."

Exasperated, she put her hands together and tugged at something inside her fist. She ended up dropping the false thumb she'd stuffed the scarf into. The false thumb bounced with the little orange scarf hanging out the bottom like tendons. It rolled off the porch steps.

Tara reached for it but missed as it rolled into the grass and settled, sticking up as though a corpse was trying to dig its way out of a grave under the lawn.

"We're not hiring." Hap turned his back on her and picked up some more garbage.

She plucked the thumb from the grass and shoved it into her pocket. "Don't be a jerk, Hap! If you're not hiring, why would you have me do the trick?"

The question had merit. He was irritated because he'd been excluded from the conversation going on between Grandpa Hazzard and Tolvan—felt angry for being put out on the porch step like a bad dog. And something tugged at the back of his mind. Tolvan's panicked voice . . . his grandfather yelling at him . . . the way that shrapnel melted into the blue stone. He shook himself and turned to face her. "I don't know. To see if you could, I guess. Anyway, it doesn't matter. Grandpa's funny about underage employees."

"You're underage."

"Yeah, but I'm family. I totally don't count."

She took a deep breath and looked at her shoes. "Oh."

"Hey, look, maybe in a few months we'll be hiring. Things always get busier around Halloween. Okay?" He held out his hand for her to shake it.

Her mouth twisted as she looked at his smelly hand, but she must have really wanted the job, because she took his hand firmly in hers.

Her mouth fell into an O and her eyes widened. She yanked away from the stinging zapper in Hap's palm and cradled her hand against her stomach. "What? Why?" She sputtered and glared worse than his mom when he was in trouble. She finally straightened and jabbed her finger at him. "Why did you do that?"

Hap chuckled. "Aw, c'mon, Tara. It was just a joke. Besides, everyone who comes in our front door tries to make me shake their hand after they put the buzzer on. If you don't know *that* trick, you don't really want to work here." He turned his back on her again and stooped to pick up more garbage. As he stood to throw the trash in the can, he came face-to-face with his grandpa.

His satisfaction with himself faded with the disapproval in Grandpa Hazzard's eyes. They stared at each other for a long moment before his grandpa nodded to something behind Hap.

Hap turned to look. Tara had already made it across the street, stomping through the field toward the thick overhang of trees that led to the canyon trails. Her movements looked angry. Hap guessed if he could see her face, she might even be crying.

"Proud of yourself, are you?" His grandpa spun the dustpan he'd brought out for Hap in his fingers.

"I was only joking around."

"Looks like *someone* doesn't think you were very funny."

"Well, I can't help it if she's being sensitive." Hap took the dustpan from his grandfather's hands and swept the debris around their feet into it. He hadn't exactly meant to take his frustration out on Tara. But what kind of person comes looking for a job in a magic shop if they can't deal with a random joke?

"You should apologize."

Hap rolled his eyes. "She isn't hurt, Grandpa."

Grandpa Hazzard raised his bushy eyebrows and twitched his shoulders in a shrug. "Maybe not physically. But I think you hurt her feelings. You embarrassed her. You know her parents just got divorced. You know she probably really needs a job. Things have been tough at her house without her father. *You,* of all people, should understand that."

"I still have a father!" Hap couldn't keep his voice from cracking with the fear that overcame him every time he thought about his dad. It was so much easier not to think about the man who used to be strong, who used to play baseball with him, who used to have a job and go to work like other dads. It was so much easier not to think about how he'd gained so much weight and lost so much hair. Everyone still held out hope that the chemo would work, but fear hovered at the edges of their hope. So much easier to not think about it at all.

Hap looked out to the field where Tara had gone. *My situation isn't anything like hers. My dad isn't choosing to leave us. Her dad did!* And that's when he realized how much worse he'd feel if his dad *had* chosen to leave them.

Hap grunted and bent low to sweep another pile into the dustpan. "Fine. I'll apologize at school tomorrow." He lifted the dustpan to the open garbage can and dumped it.

"That's not the Hazzard way, Hap. We're men of honor. If you owe someone something—even an apology—you pay them back immediately. That girl's life has been hard recently. As one of her classmates, and someone who has a bit in common with her, you owe her that apology. Now."

"But I gotta clean up this mess."

Grandpa Hazzard tucked his thumbs in the belt loops of his jeans. Hap liked that his grandpa wore jeans and not overalls like the other grandpas in town. "You gotta clean up that mess too."

"But this mess came first," Hap argued.

Grandpa Hazzard's eyes misted slightly. *Why is he acting like this?* Hap wondered. Grandpa Hazzard never acted sentimental. First raising his voice and now tears? Even with all the stuff going on with Dad, the only one who cried was Alison, and Mom when she thought no one was around to hear.

Grandpa Hazzard sniffed. "Chronology. Humans always worry about the most trivial things. Leave time out of it. Humanity is more important."

"She's probably home by now . . ."

His grandfather took the broom from Hap. "You know as well as I do that the Jordans don't live anywhere near the direction that girl headed."

Hap tugged at his shirt, looked down at his hands that smelled like rotting tomatoes, and ran into the shop. He came out while stuffing his arms into the sleeves of his jacket and trudged across the street to the field. "Fine!" he called back over his shoulder. He could have sworn he heard his grandfather's chuckle on the breeze.

2. Abduction

Hap stumbled along the narrow trail that seemed to disappear in the low light of the setting sun. He squinted to see farther past the scrub oak. *What kind of girl takes off into the woods just before dark?*

"The same kind that freaks out over a little joke . . ." Hap grumbled to himself. He bent down to pick out remnants of foxtail weeds that got stuck in his socks while crossing the field then hurried to catch up to Tara and apologize. He needed to get back to the shop to help close up so he could go home and get the smell of tomatoes off his hands and clothing.

Deeper into the trees, the hard-to-see trail became an impossible-to-see trail. Hap pulled out a mini flashlight from his jacket pocket, where he kept several magic tricks, his EpiPen for allergies, and a few odds and ends. He shook the flashlight and clicked it on. He was supposed to shake it for a full minute to give him sixty minutes' worth of light, but he sincerely hoped he wouldn't be out that long.

It felt like forever when he finally reached a place where the trail flattened out into a small clearing. Tara was perched on a large boulder, looking toward the darkening western sky. She'd have had to be blind not to see Hap approaching, but she ignored him as though he were a tree.

Well . . . might as well get this over with. He wanted to get back to Grandpa Hazzard and Tolvan as soon as possible. He sniffed, trying not to let the tomato smell get to him. "Hey, Tara."

She didn't respond. Hap decided she wasn't ignoring him like she would a tree. If a tree spoke to her, she'd likely make some reply. Nope, she was ignoring him like she'd rather eat rat poison than have to talk to him. All this over a stupid little joke.

That was the bad thing about girls. Girls held grudges. Guys weren't like that. When guys insulted each other, they'd punch each other a few times, laugh about their bruises, and go off to play video games. Guys were so much simpler.

"I know you can hear me." He started once more, stating the obvious. At her persistent silence, he added, "I came to say I'm sorry." He flipped off the flashlight and stuffed it in his pocket so he could bend down and rub his hands in the dirt for a minute to clean them off. Hap preferred dirt to tomatoes any day.

She turned to him, her hazel eyes piercing. If she'd had the superpower of heat vision, he'd have been nothing but a pile of ash.

"What exactly are you sorry for?" she asked.

What? Was this a quiz? Wasn't it enough to apologize without having to consider the details? He shrugged. It was the best answer he had. The fewer words, the faster he could get back and discover what Tolvan and Grandpa had talked about.

"I'm asking . . ." she said, while climbing down from the boulder. "I'm asking because I want to know if you're sorry for making fun of my magic trick, or my application qualifications, or if you're sorry you made me look stupid in front of your grandfather, who might have given me a job if you hadn't been there slapping buzzers on my hand."

Hap blinked and scratched his hand through his hair. "Um . . . I'm sorry for *all* that." He almost said he was only sorry for the buzzer but felt pretty certain she expected him to be sorry for all of the above.

She now stood in front of him, her arms folded across her red shirt. "Are you really?"

"I wouldn't have said it if I wasn't. I really am sor—" A loud crack from overhead interrupted Hap's second apology, which he knew would have been far more brilliant than the first if he'd been given the chance to finish it.

They both looked up to see what had sent the birds sputtering from the scrub oak and cedars.

Three airplanes cleared the mountain top. Hap's mouth dried up instantly as it hung slack. He tossed a quick glance to Tara. Her mouth hung open too.

What first seemed like airplanes were really something Hap had only seen in his grandpa's alien newspaper clippings. They looked like something out of a science fiction movie—like *spaceships*.

The first wedge-shaped aircraft raced across the sky. The beat-up silver triangle seemed to have two levels—a smaller wedge on top of the bigger one.

Right behind it, two smaller planes raced to catch up. They didn't look beat up at all. Silver metal glinted in the light from the last rays of the sunset. When the sleek darts opened fire on the first aircraft, Hap felt pretty sure they'd succeed in shooting it down. And when that happened, it would land right on top of him and Tara. "We need to go." His voice was a hoarse whisper. He couldn't get his voice box to repeat the words. He'd never seen anything like the weapon fire from those ships. Not even in the movies. Blue lasers like lightning blazed from weapons he couldn't quite see.

He reached for Tara's arm to pull her back down the trail with him, but he wasn't able to stop looking at the dogfight in the air. Hap just stood there gaping at the sky and clinging to Tara's arm.

The wedged ship spun into a roll, avoiding the fire from the sleek ships. It banked suddenly, missing the canyon wall and climbing into the sky, leaving one of the fighters to crash in a fiery blaze into the mountainside. The second fighter clawed for height, trying to continue pursuit.

For as bulky as the wedge looked, it moved like nothing Hap had ever seen. It banked and rolled and pulled out of each maneuver as if it were anticipating its adversary's every move. The wedge stopped and hovered midair above Tara and Hap. Hap wanted to run—every part of his being screamed for him to run—but fear rooted his feet to the ground.

Hap and Tara stared into the belly of the wedge as a small hole dilated, shooting a beam of light directly over their heads. The heat rolled over them in a wave like the blast of an open oven. In the next instant, a huge crate rocketed toward the earth—right on top of where they stood.

Tara screamed and yanked her arm free from Hap's grip. Hap yelped and tried to jump out of the way.

The ship returned laser fire on the approaching fighter ship. Bright violet beams shot from the right side of the wedge. The incoming fighter ship spun out of the way. All this happened while the crate rushed toward Hap and Tara.

Then everything stopped exactly where it was. Hap was stuck mid-leap; Tara looked as though she were doing the splits in the air. The crate hung over them but no longer fell toward them. Nothing in the light moved. Inside the beam of light, it sounded like a giant's heartbeat . . . slow and heavy. The light felt like it was burning Hap's clothes right off him. He felt the dirt and tomato dry up and flake from his hands. The light baked him clean like his dog's chew bones left out in the sun too long.

Hap wished he could close his eyes against the brightness which every second seemed more blinding.

The heartbeat noise came louder and faster until Hap thought his eardrums were going to split; then it stopped. Even with the crate not moving, suspended in the air just feet above them, Hap felt the need to duck for cover. Not that he could duck . . . he just really, really wanted to.

Then the light overtook everything within his vision until nothing existed but light.

A zipping noise like static snapped over them. The light winked out.

Darkness.

3. NOT-SO-HUMAN BEINGS

HAP'S EARS RANG AS HIS whole body crashed facedown against something hard and cold. He didn't move for several seconds, wondering if his body had shattered to pieces on impact. It certainly *felt* like he'd broken every bone. He blinked several times in the darkness, but his eyes never adjusted.

A groan next to him reminded him about Tara. He lifted himself on shaky arms to a crouched position. In the dark he felt like his equilibrium was off balance; he couldn't get his legs to stand up straight.

"Tara?" He felt in the dark to find her. "Tara, are you okay?"

After another groan, he located her foot, finding comfort in the familiar outline of a tennis shoe. "Tara?"

"What happened?" Her voice sounded like his arms and legs felt—shaky.

He didn't answer right away since . . . well, he didn't know what happened.

"Maybe the crate landed on us and we're inside of it now." Hap knew his statement would go down in the hall of fame for dumb things said, but he didn't have any other answer.

When Tara harrumphed at his words, he blushed, grateful for the dark. The sound of her jeans whispering over the ground indicated she had tried to get up too. "You had a flashlight on before that lame apology. Do you still have it?"

My apology wasn't lame. But Hap felt in his pocket, sifting through the tricks he kept on hand to impress customers at the shop. His fingers felt over the fake vomit, scotch-and-soda coins, and his

EpiPen for his allergies before he felt the hard plastic tube of the flashlight. He pulled it out, gave it a brief shake, and flipped it on.

For the second time that day, his jaw slackened as though on hinges that needed their screws tightened. Tara gasped audibly and moved closer to Hap. Hap had no idea where they were. "Holy Houdini . . ." Hap whispered.

The crate sat only a few feet away from them, though it didn't look quite so big and terrifying now that it wasn't falling on them. Nothing else the beam of their weak flashlight fell on looked familiar at all.

The metal walls looked old and rusted into a deep copper color. Etched into the walls were letters from some foreign language, like Egyptian. The light flashed and reflected off several jewels embedded in the writing. They reflected prisms of colored light that danced and spun as Hap moved the beam of his flashlight over them. Hoses and coiling hung from the walls—coming from and going to where was anyone's guess.

Under the floor, the whirring of an engine hummed. If Hap felt dizzy and disoriented before, it was nothing to how he felt now. It was like being in an elevator on super-speed and heading straight to the top of a mountain.

His whole body felt like it was being compressed into a puddle on the floor. He couldn't have stood if he'd tried. Tara let out a low wail and forced her hands up to hold her head. Hap did the same, wondering if his head was going to explode. His ears ached under the pressure and then popped. The pop came as both a relief and another source of pain since, as soon as they'd popped, they were under that same intense pressure again.

With a jolt, the compression ended. His ears popped several more times—each time feeling like minor explosions. He put a finger in his right ear to check for blood, sure that his eardrum had ruptured.

With another jolt, Hap and Tara slid, smacking against one of the cold walls in a tumble of arms and legs. They hurried to scramble to the side since the crate was—once again—coming straight for them. The way it grinded against the floor indicated it was heavy enough to squash them like bugs.

Hap struggled to maintain hold of his flashlight since his palms were slippery from sweat and panic. He managed to get his hand through the flashlight wrist strap in time to slap his palm down to catch himself from rolling when they slid the other way.

Tara shoved her body around so when she hit the wall, she caught herself with her feet. Hap allowed himself a moment to feel dumb for not thinking about that himself as his head thwacked the wall.

He only had a moment to feel dumb, though, since the crate slid his direction fast. He dove out of the way and ended up skidding on his face until he hit the corner.

Then everything righted again. The tilting stopped, and the crate no longer ground against the floor to crush them. Tara's breathing sounded ragged and forced—or was that Hap's breathing? He wasn't sure since his ears still rang.

"Where are we?" Tara asked. "And *don't, don't, DON'T* tell me we're in that ship!"

Hap only shrugged, nodded, shook his head, and shrugged some more. If they weren't in the ship, then they were both crazy because no other explanation made sense. He didn't believe in ali—no! Hap couldn't even think the word in his own head. He'd almost thought of an intelligent way to answer when voices and the clanging of heavy footfalls came from behind what might have been a door.

Hap scrambled behind the crate, dragging Tara with him. He fumbled with the flashlight until his quivering fingers finally found the switch and turned it off. Tara's rapid breathing rasped loud in his ear. He put a finger to his lips to quiet her, even though she couldn't see him now that they were in absolute darkness again.

A clank, followed by a sucking-hissing noise, filled the room. A bright band of light streamed in from the doorway. The light felt blinding after having been plunged into darkness. Hap squinted around the corner to see if he could catch a glimpse of who was coming in.

When he saw the hulking mass, he drew back and pressed himself tighter into the crate. Tara drew her eyebrows together as though asking him what he'd seen. How could he explain that he'd just seen a monster? Hap shook his head at her and closed his eyes, reverting back to his childhood belief that if he couldn't see it, it couldn't see him.

A slow, garbled voice rumbled from the large monsterlike creature he'd seen. A higher-pitched voice that garbled just as much followed.

They took turns rumbling and squawking until they were doing it at the same time.

"Stop it!"

Hap opened his eyes, surprised to hear a female voice speaking English. He looked at Tara and offered a lame smile, trying to comfort her. Dumb to try to comfort a girl when he was the one in need of comfort.

"I sent you in here to tie down the cargo, not to fight. We'll be hitting the wormhole soon, and I can't have that thing banging all through the spiral drop. If it breaks, it's worthless. I didn't risk my life coming back to Earth for nothing, so *stop* arguing and get to work!"

More garbling from both the rumbling and the squawking voices.

The woman heaved a deep sigh. "You know . . . busting you guys out of ICE may have been the biggest mistake I've ever made."

More garbling from the squawking voice.

"I could have found it on my own." She sounded defensive. "And the time it took to bust you out nullified any time you may have saved me in searching, so get over yourselves. You didn't do me any favors."

More garbling from the rumbling voice this time.

The woman grunted and with exasperation yelled, "No one is in here but you idiots. See!" She darted about the room pretending to be looking for someone. She ran past them and called out to the wall in front of them. "Is anyone there? Hello-o?" When she turned, looking smug and satisfied for mocking the ape and whatever else was in the room, she stared right at Tara and Hap—and blinked.

"Mosh!" she yelled, and the huge creature lumbered into full view. He was entirely hairless; at least the parts of him that hung out of his clothes were hairless. His chin looked more like a huge bullfrog pouch, his top lip disappearing into his huge underbite. He wore a leather kind of flight jacket that didn't quite cover him, leaving his basketball-shaped belly hanging out. His arms were thick, meaty extensions that ran almost all the way to the floor. He looked at both Tara and Hap and grinned, showing yellowed, stumpy teeth.

Tara gasped and pressed herself even tighter against Hap's side.

Hap could only gape.

The woman pointed at the two kids. "Grab them!"

A huge, beefy hand plucked Hap up by the shoulder and another hand grabbed Tara.

Hap was finally truly sorry he'd teased Tara.

4. Catastrophe

Aliens . . . these things were aliens! If his grandpa could see him now! Hap was scared, well, *excited* and scared. At the moment, definitely more scared than excited. Having a mountain-sized bullfrog with arms that could span the state of Texas grab you in one fist dampened most thoughts of being excited.

Tara wasn't too excited either. "Let me go!" She swung her arms but hit only air since the big Mosh thing kept her far enough away from him that her swinging made no difference.

Hap blinked in the hallway's strong light.

Tara blinked too but kept on yelling. "Let me go! I'm warning you! I'll—"

"You'll what?" The woman jerked on the bill of her baseball cap, which sported a logo that had the letters ICE inside a shooting star. She waved her hand to indicate the hallway. "You gonna scream? You gonna call for help? Go ahead. Scream 'til your lungs burn up. No one around here is gonna care . . . got it?"

Tara fell silent, though she looked like she contemplated screaming. Hap couldn't have screamed if he wanted to. The one time he tried to ask a question, his voice came out like a squeak. Guys should never squeak.

The big thing garbled.

"Throw them in the detention cell."

More garbling that seemed to end in a question.

The woman pointed down a narrow hallway. Black hair fell sloppily out of her baseball cap. She pulled the cap down harder over her head when the little creature, the one closer to Hap's size, squawked and waved his arms up and down—all *four* of his arms. His eyebrows were more like thin, feathery antennae that poked out over round, black eyes. His silver flight jacket had an exoskeleton look to it. The jacket clung to a darker sort of suit that looked like a cross between the spandex outfits ice skaters wore and a superhero outfit. Hap doubted the little four-armed thing ice-skated *or* did acts of superhero magnitude.

"I can't leave them in cargo. The grav stabilizer doesn't work very well in here. They'd be killed as soon as we went through the spiral drop. And the air compression doesn't work right either. If they didn't get smashed, their lungs would dry up."

The thing waved his four arms again and sounded angry. His pointed ears flattened back, and he hissed through his wide mouth.

She rolled her eyes and crossed her arms over her chest. "Why should I? What did they do wrong? They wouldn't even be here if you hadn't decided to drop our load. That makes this your fault, Gygak. That makes *you* the nursemaid for our toddling tagalongs."

Gygak followed her down the hall, seeming to be arguing with her, but Mosh stopped at a door. It opened without him doing anything—no retinal scans or thumbprint verifications or saying "open sesame" or anything. Lights flickered on as the door opened. He set Tara and Hap down on their feet deep inside the room. Before they could say or do anything, the door swished closed again.

Tara's wild eyes roved over the detention cell, which looked more like a janitor's closet to Hap than any kind of real detention cell. Tara ran to the door, banging on it with her tiny fists, screaming for them to let her out.

Hap inspected the items on the shelves, thinking back to all the Harry Houdini tricks he knew and wondering if he could find a clever way to escape. There had been an article in *MUM—Magic, Unity, and Might*—magazine about great escapes, but Hap hadn't taken the time to read it yet.

Escaping aside, Hap wanted proof this was happening to him. He knew alien abductees never came home with physical proof of their abduction. He might as well make his abduction useful. If he were Houdini, he'd escape in mere seconds and the audience would shower him with thunderous applause. Thunderous applause and proof of his abduction to stop the fights between his parents and grandpa sounded like nothing short of awesome to Hap.

Hap took a deep breath and looked down to find that his hands trembled. He tried to say something to calm Tara down, but his voice box still refused to take commands. He forced his shaking fingers to slide open the see-through doors on the shelf in front of him. He assumed the doors helped hold the shelf's contents in place when the ship made sudden maneuvers. He felt a little bit of panic at the thought of the ship making sudden maneuvers without him being seat-belted into anything.

But Hap couldn't help being curious too. His insatiable curiosity accounted for many visits to the emergency room and many phone calls to poison control. He'd been forced to consume more ipecac than any human he knew.

Tara finally exhausted herself at the door then turned on him. "I am locked in a broom closet! There are things on the other side of that door that *shouldn't* exist! Aren't you going to do anything?" she demanded. Her voice sounded hoarse and high pitched with hysteria.

"Yes." He wasn't sure what he meant by that answer, since he had no idea what exactly he should do. He searched through the things on the shelves, desperate to find something that would help, but nothing looked very promising. He pulled out a shiny black box from the nearest shelf. He turned it over in his hands and moved his fingers to the latch.

Tara threw her hands in the air and turned away from him.

"I truly do not suggest this course of action, young sir," a voice said, but it sounded like it had come from everywhere.

Hap nearly dropped the box. His eyes darted all over the place. "Who said that?"

Tara cried out, "Who cares who said it? Just put that thing down or you'll make it mad!"

The voice sighed. "Listen to the girl. Though I'd be far more concerned with what the results of your actions would be than with my emotional state."

"What would the results be?" Hap asked.

"An infestation of undesirable beings in a very small space."

Hap frowned and looked closer at the box. On the side were markings he couldn't read that were similar to the ones in the cargo hold. He turned the box over and over in his hands, careful to not touch the latch in case something horrible came out. He gave up trying to figure it out and decided the voice was pulling a joke. "It's too small to hold anything too bad."

"It's a ship washer for when you're 'on the road,' so to speak. I'd put it down if I were you. Anything strong enough to chew crettles off the hull of a ship is strong enough to chew the skin off your bones."

"Who are you?" Hap asked defiantly, although he *did* put the box down.

"What does it matter who it is?" Tara snapped. "We're prisoners! We have no idea where we are. We have no idea how to get off this airplane. My mom is all alone . . . I have stuff I gotta get done . . . Hap, are you even listening to me?"

Hap listened but only partially. A noise outside the door caught his attention. He picked the box back up and could have sworn he heard a tsk.

His hands shook and perspiration gathered at the back of his neck, but he held the box out toward the door as though it were a talisman protecting him from evil. If it was as dangerous as the voice said, then maybe it would scare whoever hovered outside their door. Hap put a finger to his lips, hoping it would calm Tara down.

It didn't.

"You're an idiot!" She picked up several tin-looking packages from inside the bin and threw them at Hap.

He didn't mean to . . . it was an accident . . . his finger slipped on the latch and the lid popped open.

5. Scourabs

The ethereal voice had been right about the box. A stream of black shot out in violent spurts, covering everything in its path. Tara dove for cover behind the huge metal mop bucket. The force from the box nearly yanked Hap's arms out of their sockets. His eyes widened as he tried to take control of the box and close the lid. Tara screamed, "Close it, Hap!" over and over.

The voice seemed amused. "You should have at least read the instructions."

The stream stopped. But a sea of wriggling black already covered the ground—expanding and multiplying every moment.

A sea of bugs.

Shiny, black, beetle-like bugs crawled and skittered everywhere. They clung to every part of the room. Tara screamed behind the bucket. Hap would have screamed too if he wasn't afraid a bug or twenty would crawl into his open mouth. They gathered around his ankles . . . then to his knees, crawling on both the insides and outsides of his pant legs. He kicked against the pinching feeling of their tiny legs on him. Razor-sharp teeth moved up his legs, biting against the top layers of his skin in a way that felt like a million paper cuts. Fear and frustration surged his mind. They were going to drown in bugs!

The bug army climbed the walls and hung from the ceiling until the room looked like it had been swathed in midnight.

"Hap, help!" Tara yelled as the sea of black moved up to her waist. She stomped her feet as hard as she could, but nothing seemed to be squishing under her black tennis shoes.

Hap's own feet felt like they were involved in some psychotic dance as he stomped. No squishing under his feet either. The beetles were practically indestructible. Nothing could stop them. Hap worked every muscle he had to take a few steps toward her, but the force of the bugs held him in place. He swung the box, trying to knock the floor of writhing black out of his way, but no matter how many he scooped aside, there were at least that many to take their place, if not more.

They marched over his hands, between his fingers, and up his arms.

Tara looked like she'd been overcome with seizures the way she jiggled and danced trying to get them off her.

The door swished open and the black bugs surged out in one huge shiny wave. The wave would have knocked Hap off his feet if he hadn't been bracing himself against that force so he could make it to Tara. The outpouring swept Tara toward the door, looking like a fish caught in a whirlpool. Bugs wound themselves in her hair, and covered almost her entire body.

Hap scooped and swiped, again and again—anything to clear a beetle-free zone.

Out of the corner of his eye, Hap saw someone pushing through the wave. A hand shot out, tapping a finger over a little gold button at the top of the box.

The crawling horde stopped immediately. The room fell into silence except for Tara's final scream of, "Hap! Help!" Then a loud whine blared through the box, and the mass of shiny black flowed into itself, seeming to dissolve into a much smaller mass. They flowed out of his pant legs. He shook and stamped his legs trying to help them along. Even after the sensation of things crawling on and scouring his skin had gone, Hap still felt like he needed a shower.

The remnants of crawling bugs marched swiftly to the box and hopped in until the room was empty. The lid snapped shut.

Horrified, Hap dropped the little roach motel and on trembling legs ran over to Tara. "Are you okay?"

She stood on her own shaking legs and nodded. Then she punched him in the arm.

"Ow! Hey, why'dya do that—"

"She's angry because you didn't listen to Nana."

Hap turned to their rescuer and saw a girl a little shorter than him. Her wide, lavender eyes blinked at him curiously. The antennae on top of her head twitched like they were sniffing him out. Her ears ended in sharp points. Her hands smoothed over her purple dress, which was more like a miniskirt over black tights. She opened her mouth into a wide grin, showing perfect white teeth. "So you're our guests."

Tara flipped her blonde hair back behind her shoulders. "Really? Guests? That's a funny way to put it since we're being treated like prisoners. I've seen movies. I know an alien abduction when I see one."

"Abducted? 'Abducted' would indicate we *wanted* to take you, which we didn't. You were entirely accidental and not prisoners at all. A bit of an inconvenience, certainly, but nothing to be done for that now. Your name?"

Tara's voice filled with uncertainty and bewilderment. "I'm Tara."

"What *were* those things?" Hap interrupted.

"Scourab beetles."

"What?" Tara brushed at her arms and her stomach as though making sure she was the only thing in her clothes.

"They clean—scour. We keep them to scour the ship's exterior. It's near impossible to make sol with crettles hitching rides on the hull."

Tara's face was a mass of confusion, and she seemed more than a little weirded out to be talking to a girl who had antennae sticking out of her head. "If we aren't prisoners, then let us go."

The girl fidgeted. "We can't do that right now. Nothing personal, but we've got our own issues to be worried with."

Hap couldn't tear his gaze from the girl's slight frame and delicately carved features. "Are you a fairy?" he blurted out.

The antennae straightened into quivering rods. "I am *not* a fairy," she shouted, spinning around and twitching her shoulders. She jabbed her thumb toward her back. "Do you see any wings—any silvery, iridescent things that flap?"

Hap didn't see wings but found himself terribly disturbed about the long, sinuous line of her tail. It ended in almost a fork shape. The fact that she shouted over a pretty harmless question disturbed Hap too. Not that the whole situation wasn't disturbing. She seemed so nice just a second before . . .

"Do you see any wings?" she demanded again.

Hap shot Tara a look to which she shrugged, seeming as bewildered as he felt. "No wings," Hap said.

"None at all," Tara agreed.

The girl spun around again to face them. "Earth-siders know nothing about twin-souls. All those cutesy fairy tales handed from generation to generation without any thought to reality. Don't you people value truth?

"But now you've seen for yourself! No wings!" She stopped her tirade and smoothed her hands over her skirt.

Immediately she faced them with smiles and sweetness again. "And I hardly ever fly, anyway."

"You fly?" Hap asked, slicking his hand over his hair to brush away bugs that weren't there.

"Only when I'm surrounded by joy. I can't fly unless true happiness abounds." She cupped her hand and whispered, "I'm never able to fly on *this* ship."

"I heard that, Tremble," a voice said. It was the same one that warned Hap not to open the scourab beetle box.

"I meant you to hear," Tremble said back to the voice.

Tara raked her fingers through her blonde hair. Hap guessed she too felt like bugs were still crawling over her. "Who are you talking to?"

"Nana. The ship. They designed her to be nurturing for long voyages . . ." She cupped her hand and whispered again. "But instead of being maternal, she's one of those crabby mothers, more likely to eat her young than not."

"You'll be jettisoned if you're not careful." The tone sounded so much like Hap's own mother's that he almost felt like he was home.

Home . . . Hap's mother was going to be furious he didn't finish cleaning the garbage up . . . and soon she'd have missing posters up all over town with his picture on them. His grandfather would tell her Hap had been abducted by aliens, and then they would fight about it. Hap felt a little sick over all the arguments he'd be the center of if he didn't get home soon. And what if this Tolvan guy meant harm to

Grandpa Hazzard? And his dad . . . what if Hap's absence caused him to become sicker? Hap had to get home.

"Tremble, do you know where we are?" He spoke carefully, afraid she'd do that weird personality switch and start yelling again.

"We're heading to the edge of the spiral. We'll be going through the spiral drop soon." She brightened. "That's why I'm here! Gygak is supposed to be doing this, but he's a little angry Laney wouldn't drop you out into space. He refuses to take care of you. He sent me. Nana said you were causing trouble in here and would be better off in the control room where Laney can keep an eye on you . . . and you'll want these." She shoved her hand in the pocket of her dress, her bright pink lips pressed tightly together while she rummaged. "I know they're here somewhere . . . oh, here!" She pulled out two miniature discs that weren't much bigger than the fingernail on Hap's pinkie.

"What are they?" Tara tilted her chin up and looked suspiciously at Tremble.

"Translation crawlers."

"What do they do?" Hap didn't think they looked like much; they were too tiny . . . too much like miniature dimes.

Tremble blinked her huge lavender eyes and stared at him as though he were dumb. Her ears twitched in what might have been frustration, but Hap had no idea how an alien species showed frustration, so he hoped she just had twitchy ears and wasn't planning on screaming at them again. "They translate."

"They translate what?" Hap asked.

She made a click noise deep in her throat. "Language. You only understand *me* because I was trained in communications before I was allowed off the planet Delat. I speak English better than Laney does. But how do you plan to understand Mosh or Gygak?"

"Who?" Tara asked. She looked completely frazzled and exhausted with her hair hanging in sweaty, clumpy strands around her face. Hap didn't feel too far different. He didn't really want to understand anyone. He wanted to get home and sleep off the craziness.

"Nana's crew. Mosh and Gygak are new and won't be with us long if Svarta has anything to say about it. Svarta's our engineer and isn't very nice. She actually speaks English too, though I wouldn't talk to her if I were you."

Tara snorted softly, as though Svarta and Tremble had more in common than Tremble thought.

Tremble held out the translation crawlers. She had only three fingers and a thumb. Hap wondered what happened to the missing finger but decided it would be rude to ask, especially if her species wasn't supposed to have four fingers and a thumb on each hand.

Hap couldn't help but be curious about the discs; he plucked one from her palm and held it between his fingers.

"What do we do with them?"

"Hold it in your palm. The crawler knows what to do."

Hap opened his palm and placed the disc in the center. He had to talk Tara into doing the same with hers. Then they waited.

Tiny, hairlike legs sprouted from the discs' sides. Hap's eyes widened with fascination at the same time Tara's widened in fear. She whispered, "A spider!"

"No," Tremble corrected, "it's a crawler."

And true to their name, they began to crawl. After the whole beetle incident, Hap wanted no part of any more creepy crawlers. Tara stiffened and her breathing became erratic and panicky. "Get it off me!" She flicked her arm back and forth as the crawler made its way past her elbow. No matter how wildly she twisted, the crawler held on. Once it moved up onto the sleeve of her red shirt, she started dancing all over the small room while trying to swipe the crawler off her shoulder and screaming loud enough to surely be heard throughout the ship.

Hap didn't have anything against spiders—at least he hadn't before he'd opened the roach motel—but he wasn't all that excited to have one crawling up his arm and over his neck. Would it bite him? Did the thing have tiny metal teeth? Hap shook his arm right alongside Tara, totally unconcerned with the fact that he looked kind of silly. Then he felt a tickle just behind his right earlobe. Hap shook his head like a dog shaking off water.

He'd been afraid of the black bugs too, but there were so many of them that it was hard to focus his fear. This solitary spider seemed far scarier than the mass of black scourabs.

His breathing sounded as choppy as Tara's. Then he felt a tiny pinch, like the kind you get when they take your blood at the doctor's office. Hap instinctively slapped his hand behind his ear, but nothing was there.

Tara let out a wail, and Hap knew she'd felt the same pinch.

After the pinch, Hap felt nothing at all.

Tara rubbed at the place behind her ear, her eyes wide. "It bit me!" She rubbed her hand over her neck furiously. "Where is it?"

Tremble leaned against the shelving. "It's done." She inspected her three fingers. She didn't really have fingernails, so Hap couldn't tell what she found so interesting about her fingers.

"What's done?" Tara demanded.

"The crawler." Tremble's tail lashed behind her, and her ears twitched again. She seemed annoyed to be repeating the same thing.

"Did it inject poison into my blood? Am I going to be an alien experiment?" Tara's fear awakened a few fears in Hap as well. Hap had spent his whole life with his grandfather telling him about the horrible things done to humans who were abducted—mutilations, amputations, probes . . .

"Yeah," he agreed with Tara. "And where did the crawler go?" He rubbed at his ear yet felt nothing. He looked at the floor, wondering if the crawler had leaped off his neck somehow.

"It didn't go anywhere. It's in your skin."

"No!" Tara yelled. "You did *not* just implant a mind-controlling device into me!" She jumped around and clawed at her skin behind her ear.

Tremble blinked, her face darkening. "Yes, I did! How else do you think the translation takes place?" Tremble was shouting again.

Hap's heart pounded against his chest. The little fairy girl with the devil's tail and bad temper just admitted to implanting a mind controller in his head. He felt sick and then wondered if feeling sick was a side effect of having an alien creature living in his body.

"Take it out!" Tara demanded at the same time Hap yelled, "Get it out of me!"

"Control yourself," Nana said as though she were talking to a small child.

Tremble took several deep breaths, her face going from red back to pale. She waved her hand as though shooing at flies once she'd controlled her temper. "Humans are so dramatic. You're fine. Nothing is damaging you. The minerals and metals that make the crawler work are absorbed into your physical body and become part of your body, but they add new synapses to your intelligence. They link you to the many sounds and tones of other languages; they tap into your brain and upload the knowledge base that understands all these languages. It's perfectly harmless. It's like taking a vitamin. Well . . . except for the nasty rash you'll get—"

"Don't tease them, Tremble; they aren't evolved enough to handle that," Nana said.

A sound of air releasing into the hallway made Tremble look up. "Look how you've distracted me! We're to be buckled in already! Come on, I'll take you to the control room."

Hap almost took Tara's hand. The need to touch something real, identifiable, and human almost made his eyes well up with tears. Was this how everyone reacted when they got their first alien implant?

He didn't take Tara's hand, though. She'd think he was flirting or something weird like that. She'd either slap him, or when they got home, she'd expect him to take her to movies or to dances or whatever it was that girls expected from boys. He looked over at Tara.

From the way her mouth firmed into a tight line and her fists remained clenched into white, little balls, he figured she'd definitely slap or punch him again.

They went into a huge closet. Tara looked around expectantly, as though waiting for the closet to cave in on her. The closet didn't cave in, but after a moment their feet left the floor and they ascended upward.

"What's happening?" Hap asked, casting nervous glances up and down. He tried to stomp his feet but hit only air. Tara moaned. A scourab that must have missed roll call when they all filed back into the box *fell* out of one of the folds in the back of Tara's shirt. Hap reached out and flicked it away so Tara wouldn't see it. The bug continued to float, though it spun in a different direction.

"It's an airlift tube. Laney wanted to install stairs when she first took control over Nana, but Nana refused to be part of such a primitive method of ascension."

"Of course I did!" Nana said. "And I was right to have kept things as they were designed. Imagine Mosh trying to get his big feet up those tiny stairs made for humans. The very idea is a mockery to my programming. I was built to accommodate species in almost all varieties." Nana's voice sounded prideful. Hap imagined that if he could see her, she'd have her nose in the air.

They floated to the top where a platform jutted from the wall and settled underneath them. Hap felt a tugging at his feet as they reconnected with the solid surface. The scourab beetle scuttled toward the edge and disappeared over the side.

Hap looked around. He looked for a way off the platform—a way that didn't involve falling—and saw that Tremble stood next to a door. It swished open.

For what seemed like the millionth time that day, Hap's jaw dropped.

Tara let out a cry.

The familiar blue planet, Earth, hung against the dark backdrop of the universe just outside the windows of the control room.

6. ICE

"WHERE IS THE GROUND?" Tara demanded to know.

The blackness of space showed through the multiple round port windows. Out those windows, Hap could easily let himself believe he was looking into the nighttime sky of his hometown. Space and stars and darkness in between were visible through all the windows except for the one in front.

One long oval window took up the whole front of the control room. Earth glowed bright blue and white. Spots of green filtered through the swirls of white. Hap's whole body went numb as his eyes widened to take in the view of his home planet.

"Holy Houdini," Hap whispered. He whirled around to see out every porthole. "We're in outer space!" Being abducted by aliens was one thing. Getting hauled into outer space was another altogether. He'd known he was in the ship, but he hadn't known they'd actually left Earth's atmosphere. "Uh-uh." He shook his head violently. "How do we get down from here?" He looked at the earth, which seemed more sideways to him than downward. His entire sense of direction fled in that first glance out the front window.

"Dump 'em space side, Laney. They asked for it," the four-armed thing squawked from his seat in what looked like a beautician chair. Only now Hap understood the words inside the squawking.

Laney, the dark-haired woman who'd ordered them locked up in the broom closet with the beetle box, sighed from the chair on the end of the small row. "One more suggestion like that, Gygak, and *you'll* be getting dumped space side, hear me?"

Laney eyed the two teenagers as though she wished she *could* dump them out. She rubbed at the bridge of her nose.

Hap's head ached. Grandpa Hazzard never mentioned headaches when he talked about abductees. Hap wondered what the crawler might be doing inside his brain. He wondered if it was reproducing and if he'd have a bunch of little baby crawlers eat their way out of his skin. He shuddered and tried to focus on the earth as it cast a blue, comforting glow into the control room, rather than think of the alien implant.

Earth.

He found himself walking toward the front window. *Oh, holy Houdini . . . Dad, what have I done?* He reached out to touch the window, to somehow call Earth, and his family, back to him.

Laney jumped up and snatched his hand away before he could touch the glass. "Are you insane?" She pointed to the window. "You can't put your bare hand on a plasma window! The energy would fry your body to burnt hamburger!"

Hap folded his fingers into his palm as he pulled his hand into his chest. "I just . . ." He whirled around and focused his gaze on Tara. "I don't believe any of this is happening." Denial seemed to be the easiest way out of this. Denial had served him well throughout his life, from actually believing in magic and finally learning the tricks behind the illusion, to claiming ignorance when his parents asked him questions like, *Didn't I ask you to clean the garage today?* or *Who drank the last of the milk and put the carton back in the fridge?*

Laney grunted and threw her hands up in the air. She moved back to her chair; she obviously trusted that he believed her about the window. "Believe it or not, kid, you're here. Welcome to the universe." She tugged her ball cap down as though he was anything but welcome.

He stared out the window for a long time, looking at the planet he no longer felt beneath his feet. Hap looked down on the patch of green he recognized from the globe in his dad's office. "This is the closest I've ever been to Australia."

"Are you kidding me?"

Hap once again found himself grateful Tara didn't have the superpower of heat-ray vision from the way she glared at him.

"You're farther from Australia now than you've ever been! You're not even in the same atmosphere!" Tara waved her arms wildly at the window and jutted out her chin. "We want to go home!"

Laney rolled her eyes and slapped her hand down on the armrest of her chair, bringing up an odd display of lights. With a cluck of exasperation, she slapped at her armrest again—on purpose this time. The display of lights winked out. She tugged on her hat. "Believe me, I want you to go home. But I can't take you back yet."

"Why?" Both Hap and Tara said, the word coming out like a surround-sound whine.

"They'll be searching the fly space around Earth for the next four months. If I go back, I'll get ICE-d."

"They'll kill you?" Hap was pretty sure the justice system didn't work like that.

"Maybe. More like prison if they can take me alive—which they can't. ICE stands for the Intergalactic Culture Enforcement. They keep outsiders from communicating with earthlings. We go back, and they'll shoot us into unidentifiable pieces, since I refuse to go quietly. You're safer here."

"But my family—Dad . . ." Hap trailed off. *ICE!* Tolvan said Grandpa Hazzard had been part of ICE in that snippet of conversation Hap overheard. His mouth dried up as he stared at Laney. She was the one Tolvan had come to talk with Grandpa Hazzard about. She'd stolen something . . . Hap couldn't remember. Something about books . . . about trust . . .

Hap took a quick inventory of the control room, but nothing looked stolen or out of place. Not that he had any idea what had been stolen, but everything here looked attached. The white chairs looked pale blue in the backlight of Earth's glow.

Hap narrowed his eyes at Laney. "You're an earthling. If earthlings aren't supposed to know about outsiders, how is it you're out here with a spaceship?"

Laney looked surprised to have him question her—surprised enough she actually answered him. "My father used to work for ICE. This was his ship. My sister and I took control for the short time we were actually dumb enough to work for ICE too. We earned this ship." She hesitated at the word *earned,* which led Hap to believe that

ICE hadn't exactly given the ship to her.

A low wall that appeared as though it had been carved from stone stood between the oval window and the row of chairs. The top of the wall glittered with several jeweled buttons. Sketches like graffiti covered the whole length of the wall. One was a spider, another a monkey with a curly tail, several spirals, birds, funny-looking people, lizards, and even what looked like a rainbow. Then there were just shapes, triangles and squares all zigzagging through each other in a way that reminded Hap of the first time he'd ever seen a street map.

He looked at the lady who'd had them thrown into the janitorial closet, who had very likely stolen something from a company his grandpa worked for, and asked, "Is that a map?"

Laney glared. "Who've you been talking to?" She turned on Tremble. "What have you been saying?"

"You're so paranoid, Laney. I didn't tell him anything. And like it would matter if I did. He's a *human* child."

Laney stiffened in her chair. "That doesn't mean he can't think. Remember your captain is human."

Tremble twitched her ears and lashed her tail. "How could I forget? You remind me all the time." She sat in one of the boutique-looking chairs and bands flipped themselves over her shoulders and around her waist.

"Very good, Tremble," Nana said. "You controlled your other self very well just now."

"She doesn't need babysitting, Nana." Laney jabbed her finger onto a blue jewel.

"Of course she does. Positive reinforcement creates good behavior."

"Shut up, Nana." Laney fixed a hard stare on Hap and Tara.

"I demand you take me home! You can tell whoever's after you that you have kids on your ship. They won't shoot you then." Tara flipped her hair back and straightened her shoulders in a no-nonsense way.

Laney snorted. "So naive . . . Even if the bad guys aren't really bad—which they *are*—your little plan won't work."

"Why not?" Hap spoke up to try to defend Tara a little. Bad guys? If his grandpa worked for ICE, then *they* definitely weren't the bad guys. Hap had the feeling that he was looking at the bad guy. She said she worked for ICE but that it had only been for a short time. She likely got fired.

"We have an errand to run." Laney looked away when she said those words. Her movement looked like guilt to Hap.

"So take us home first."

"We can't without getting shot at."

"Okay. So do your errand and then take us home."

She shook her head, making several dark strands of hair fall loose from under the cap. "It isn't that simple. Kid, do you understand space travel?"

Hap shook his head. Tara shook hers too, though Laney wasn't asking her.

"Do you understand travel at the speed of light?"

More shakes of the head.

She grunted. "Well, let's just say that even though we're moving fast, and even though we're going through several spiral drops, or wormholes—do you know that term?"

More shakes of the head. She rolled her eyes. "What are they teaching in school? The point is, we still can't get you back home for several months."

"What?" Hap felt sick.

"Why?" Tara looked sick.

"It's a big universe," said a nasally, high voice. Hap turned to the little four-armed creature with leathery, pointed ears. "It takes time to get through that much space, even when you use the drops."

Hap wanted to punch the little know-it-all. Hap stepped toward Laney. "My dad might not be alive that long. He's sick and—"

An alarm went off, interrupting Hap's plea for intervention, and Nana's voice boomed through the control room. "We've been tracked!"

Mosh lumbered in from the airlift tube and took his seat. Everyone bustled and shouted, forgetting all about the two kids until Nana told them to find seats and buckle in for the drop.

Mosh had a different kind of chair. It looked like a huge leather recliner like Hap's dad used in the TV room. Mosh turned and showed his teeth at them. Hap couldn't tell if the huge, hairless ape-frog was smiling at them or not. Mosh opened his mouth and the garbling sounds, though still gruff, actually made sense. "Better for you to be belted here. The supply room has bad grav sensors, almost as bad as the cargo hold's." He lifted his huge, meaty arm and pointed to the only vacant seats, both of which were near him.

Tara looked at Hap and shook her head as if to say, "No way am I sitting by the Hulk."

Hap nodded to the chairs and shrugged as if to say, "What choice do we have?"

She furrowed her brow and tightened her mouth as if to say, "This situation is impossible and I am not happy!"

Hap shrugged again as if to say, "But we can't do anything, so we might as well sit."

He did sit, taking the chair closest to Mosh so Tara didn't have to. She sat too. Belts automatically strapped over them, sucking them tightly to the chairs. Tara turned to glare; only this time, Hap didn't dare interpret what she might be trying to say.

Gygak ignored them both, pretending to see past them and through them, as he busied himself with fiddling the fingers at the ends of his four arms.

"So how big?" Hap asked Gygak. Saying the universe was big meant nothing to Hap. How big was big? A jelly bean looked big to an ant—Hap wanted something he could compare to. Besides, if he could get this thing talking, maybe he could find out more information about ICE and whatever Laney stole from them.

Gygak ignored the question. Hap would have asked the ape with the stumpy teeth, except the ship lurched abruptly, snapping Hap's head forward, his teeth clacking together as his top jaw hit his lower jaw.

"We've been hit!" Laney declared. "Svarta, damage report!"

An angry voice came through the com system, yelling, "Nothing I can't handle! Just fly this thing outta here!"

"I would think after all these years she'd have more respect than to call me *thing*." Nana sounded genuinely hurt. Hap stared around him. Surreal. That's what this was. Everything surrounding him was totally surreal. A ship with its feelings hurt? Some other ship shooting at them? Outer space? A guy with four arms and a girl with a tail? *Was this happening?*

Another lurch and the ambient blue light from the earth-glow outside flickered white, as though a lightning bolt had zipped through the control room.

Tara muttered under her breath and grabbed Hap's hand, latching on tightly enough to cut off his blood supply.

Laney slapped the red jewel in front of her which released a small lap desk, laid out with various images of lit-up lines and grooves. Laney's fingers flew over the desk, and a set of lights appeared in front of her face. The lights sharpened until they formed a screen. The screen displayed numbers and scrolling information that Hap didn't understand. As she ran her fingers over the grooves on the desk, some of the numbers changed, and some of the information disappeared as though deleted. The ship jolted forward, making Hap feel like his brain might melt through the back of the chair.

They turned away from Earth. Hap wanted to reach his hand out and call the blue planet back, but his head felt glued in place.

Hap had no idea how much time passed, though it felt like an hour or more, before a huge orange ball loomed in front of them through the front window. The ball grew until they could see nothing but orange. "We're . . ." Hap rasped. "We're going to hit a planet. Tara . . . she's driving us into a planet!"

"I know! Oh no!" Tara's eyes widened, her pupils reflecting the bright orange ball in front of them.

"Statistically, it's not possible to hit a planet." Nana tried to sound reassuring. The ship banked to the side and skimmed across the planet's atmosphere so all they could see in the front window, and all the little portholes, were orange swirls.

"Laney . . . behind us—"

"I know, Tremble!" she yelled, running her fingers over the grooves. The ship distanced itself a little from the planet. "Nana, give me a multi-D display. I need to see where we are and what's after us." With a swipe over her desk, the screen in front of her shifted to her left.

In front of the wall, a large display of light came to life. Hap recognized the orange ball as the planet they'd almost slammed into. There were several other balls, and Hap recognized his own solar system from years of various science classes. He'd made several mock-ups of the solar system for the science fair but had never won anything. A blue wedge represented their ship and a red wedge followed them. They were moving away from the blue ball that resembled Earth. They'd just passed Jupiter.

Tremble tapped a green jewel, revealing her own little lap desk and screen—only her screen seemed to have pulled up blueprints of the ship following them. Various pictures of the ship and readouts of the ship's abilities flashed over her screen. "It's an ICE Razor!" she announced.

ICE! Hap looked behind him, even though he couldn't see anything but the back of the control room. He hoped with everything he had that the ICE Razor would rescue them.

"How did they track us?" Tremble glared at Mosh and Gygak. "You guys didn't clean your suits before you boarded!" Her face boiled over into red fury. "I bet you're both carrying trackers on you right now! You mindless strall crevices! You led them right to us!" Tremble had a gun in her hand.

It appeared as if by magic, and though Hap admired her ability to pull her weapon from thin air, he worried that this gun's ammo was substantially more than thin air. His worry stemmed from the fact that he sat next to the guys the gun was aimed at.

"Holster your weapon, or I'll have Nana knock you to the next galaxy!" Laney yelled as her fingers danced over the grooves. The ship swung left. A white-hot light streaked past the top portal windows.

"They're firing at us. Hap, they're firing at us!" Tara's fingernails gouged into Hap's hand. Laney yelled some more at Tremble, Nana, and everyone else. Tremble continued to yell at Mosh and Gygak, who argued that they *did* clean their suits as Laney instructed. Hap was pretty sure he screamed, but no one else heard him over the rest of the noise.

He screamed because Laney had aimed the ship straight into what looked like the mouth of a huge snake made out of light.

7. Spiral Drop

It didn't take Hap long to realize they were in a spiral drop. The shape he'd seen hadn't been a snake at all but an opening created by stellar dust. He felt like he'd entered the world's longest free-fall—a *spinning* free-fall. The ship spun around like water swirling in a flushed toilet. Hap felt like his brain would be permanently bruised as it sloshed against his skull repeatedly and the ship spun faster into the drop. Everyone else had stopped yelling and arguing, seeming too consumed with trying to keep from vomiting.

Outside the portholes, the sky ruptured with lights. The only reason Hap didn't throw up was because gravity—or the lack of gravity—wouldn't allow anything to come up. That same force tore the scream from his mouth so nothing but silence came out.

The drop ended instantaneously even though it felt like it had lasted an eternity.

A cold blast of air from the little wall blew straight at him, drying the beads of sweat pouring off his skin. He sucked the cold air into his lungs, welcoming the relief the air had on his burning throat. "Holy Houdini!" Hap yelled, mostly to assure himself that he was alive and that his voice did in fact work. He looked around at the aliens and humans all in their own forms of recuperation.

Laney drew a deep breath and stretched her neck. She inspected the lit-up dots and shapes in front of them. Hap had forgotten the display and even that they were being chased by an aggressive ship until he followed Laney's eyes to the array of light.

In front of him, the display showed they were nowhere near the solar system Hap recognized. And no ship trailed after them. He swallowed his disappointment along with the hope of rescue. *I really have been abducted.*

And yet he was nowhere near the solar system he recognized! How many teenagers could say that? He focused on the display in front of him. The lights showed many brightly colored balls of varying sizes. The blue wedge glided past a shimmering pinkish ball. Hap looked out one of the portholes on the right and saw the planet. He wanted to get out of his seat and get closer to the porthole so he could look out better, but after that drop, he didn't think his legs worked. He swallowed, remembering his queasy stomach. *What if I don't get home in time . . .* He closed his eyes against those kinds of thoughts. He *would* get home before anything happened to his dad.

"Where are we?" Tara whispered.

Hap shook his head, unable to come up with any decent answer.

Gygak scrubbed his four hands over his head as though greasing back hair he didn't have. "Stupak's Circle," he said. He wiggled the center of his forehead where two small holes like nostrils sat. Since the place where a nose should have been was flattened and empty, Hap decided this was the creature's "nose." Gygak confirmed Hap's suspicion when he wiggled his forehead again and made a loud sniffing noise. "I'd recognize that stench anywhere."

Nana groaned. "I'm recirculating the air. If you smell anything, it's just you, and I don't want to hear any whining about the stench when you know perfectly well that we haven't even hit their atmosphere yet."

"Your ship is overly sensitive. I didn't say *she* stinks," Gygak protested.

Tremble pushed forward, and the straps holding her to her seat released her. "You wouldn't notice if she did." She walked around the wall and out to the display, moving through dots and balls of light. Her hand jerked and fidgeted at her side.

"And don't you go pulling out that drubber again. I won't be threatened by you," Gygak said.

Tremble's hand flicked and she gripped the gun again. Hap couldn't believe the little creature dared to challenge a girl with such erratic emotions.

"No temper flares, Tremble. Put your drubber in its holster. I'm too busy to clean blood from Nana's carpet." Laney moved against her straps until they released her. She stood and fixed a stare on Gygak. "And he's not worth the energy."

"Hey! I'm worth the energy!" Gygak complained, though Hap couldn't figure out why. Was the guy insane? Was he trying to get Tremble to shoot him?

Laney turned away from him and moved to the center of the light display. "He said he'd meet us here." She pointed at a ball that looked like a golden cat eye with a milky white center.

Tremble blew out a long breath, and her face relaxed.

"Very good! I think you've proven who's the dominant personality here." Nana sounded like she would have clapped if she only had hands.

Tremble ducked her head and dug her toe into the carpeted floor. "I *have* been working on it."

"Good. Great. Now that you're *you* again, let's try and focus, shall we?" Laney grabbed her hat and pulled it down tighter over her head. She nodded when she saw that everyone had given her their full attention.

"He said he'd meet us here for the delivery." She pointed back to the ball with the milky center. "He's expecting us in two rotations." She pointed to a set of numbers hovering over the ball. Hap hadn't noticed them before and wondered if it was because they weren't there or because he hadn't noticed.

He watched Laney closely. *The delivery.* Tolvan said someone had stolen something and that once she delivered it, some books and the *trust* would be in danger. *What's the trust? What did she steal? And more importantly, what can I do about it?*

"We're early." No one acknowledged Mosh, not even Nana, who seemed to feel personally responsible for making running commentary on the crew.

"Do you want to land in the Orissa?" Tremble asked, seeming to understand whatever was so important about their being two days early.

Laney nodded and pointed to the milky center. "Of course."

Gygak scrambled out of his seat belt and all but leaped to where Laney and Tremble stood. "Orissa's a bad idea. Just contact Nova. He'll set us up somewhere else, somewhere nice. He'll take care of us."

"He'll take care of us, all right, and no one will find the bodies when he's *through* taking care of us. Not a chance, Gy-geek. We land in the Orissa, where we'll still be in charge of this transaction." Laney turned her back as Gygak sputtered and gesticulated wildly with his four arms.

"But we *can't*!" Gygak widened his eyes. "Please! The last time I was in Orissa, I . . . I just can't go back there."

Tremble laughed. "Not a problem. Nana can jettison you right now. She can rid us of you, the brainless mountain, and the *trackers* you're both carrying."

Gygak hissed, showing teeth that looked more like fence posts put in by a guy who didn't understand how to do straight lines. "I'm not going to put up with your foul humor, you wingless fairy!"

Laney slapped her hand over her eyes and shook her head. Nana tsked. "Now you've done it."

Tremble—well, she *trembled*.

Her face darkened into red fury. The gun was in her hand again. She had better sleight of hand than anyone Hap knew. He'd have complimented her on it—and asked for some pointers—but he was too busy forgetting that his legs felt like water as he scrambled out of his seat to duck for cover behind the wall. Tara had already made it out of her seat and had gone for greater safety by running around the chairs *and* the wall.

Hap didn't think he had enough time to follow her lead.

Tremble screamed, her high-pitched voice carrying a deep, resonant quality that Hap never would have expected. Hap scrunched his eyes closed. "Holy Houdini!" he repeated over and over in raspy whispers.

"Tremble!" Nana's voice scolded. "Control yourself!"

But it was too late. Tremble pulled the trigger on her gun, and a bright white light flashed across the room, making spots dance in Hap's vision. Nana groaned. "You just put a hole in my wall! It'll take multiple rotations to fix me after you make me look like some cratered moon off the Vestail."

No one acknowledged Nana. Laney dropped to the floor to stay out of the crosshairs, and Gygak leaped behind the wall next to Hap. Hap didn't see where Mosh went.

"Don't come near me. She wants to kill you, not me!" Hap shoved his foot a little at Gygak to give them both some distance.

"Come back here, you slime off the nose of a Wist!" Tremble's deep-throated demand sent shivers down Hap's spine like nails on a chalkboard.

"Holy Houdini! She's crazy!" Hap looked around to see how he could escape.

"Not crazy, she's just given over to her other self," Gygak said as another white light zipped over their heads.

Nana yelled, "Googool! Stop this instant or you will forfeit the right to remain on my ship!"

"Who's Googool?" Hap asked.

"*She* is Googool," Gygak said. He began to crawl backward to the other side of the wall. It was hard to hear him over Laney and Nana and this Tremble/Googool person screaming at each other.

"She said her name was Tremble."

"It is—when she's Tremble. But right now she's Googool."

The wall between them erupted in a shower of sparks and hissing static. Hap's face burned from flecks of metal that pelted him. He decided Gygak's decision to crawl backward was a good one and scooted himself toward the opposite end of the wall.

He peeked around the wall to see that Tremble/Googool was still focused on the wall's center, and so he took the chance to round the corner to where Tara hid.

Tara's eyes were clenched shut, her whole body so tense that when Hap touched her arm, she nearly leaped up. "Don't do that!" She yanked her arm away and glared at him.

"We gotta get out of here!" Hap whispered.

"You think?" Tara's voice shook. "We're going to be killed in a place where no one will find us to give us decent burials."

Another blast hit the wall, creating sparks that fizzed and zipped in a shower of various colors.

"Not my jewel sensors! Can't you aim, Googool?" Nana said. "You're trying to hit the Gygan, not me!"

"I will hit him," Tremble/Googool said, "as soon as he stops moving." Her deep voice sounded like she was possessed or like she was one of those fraudster fortune-tellers trying to act like they were communing with the dead.

In her higher-pitched Tremble voice, she said, "Let me shoot. I have better aim."

"But you have no nerve," the Googool voice said.

"I have nerve!" Tremble shot back.

But she never answered herself.

"We're not going to die." Hap hoped he sounded convincing. He certainly didn't feel convinced. He peeked around the top of the chair to see Tremble/Googool leaning over the wall directly on top of where Gygak huddled with his four hands covering his head. She grinned, not really even looking like Tremble, and aimed the gun directly at the Gygan.

8. TWIN-SOUL

HAP SCRUNCHED BACK DOWN BY Tara, not wanting to witness someone getting killed. It was one thing to watch that on TV and in movies, where the actors got up—only to be shot again in some other movie—but quite another thing to witness it.

Several seconds of horribly loud silence passed. Hap braced himself for the final shot to blaze.

He jumped when the door behind the chairs swished open. Both Hap and Tara watched as a person dressed all in black leather, with a black helmet covering its face, stepped out from the airlift tube. Hap pressed himself tighter into the back of the chair as the person aimed what looked like a large metal plate at Tremble/Googool.

Tremble/Googool's gun flew over Tara's head and slammed into the plate with a thunk that echoed from the metal.

Tremble/Googool growled and leaped the entire wall and the chairs in one single bound to face down this newcomer and get her gun back. "Give me my drubber," Tremble/Googool said.

"Not a chance. You've just created at least ten rotations of work for me. You need a blackout." And with that, the person pulled what looked like Hap's old magician wand and aimed it at Tremble/Googool, who collapsed into a heap on the floor.

Laney walked over to stand by the newcomer and stare at Tremble/Googool. "She is going to be so mad you did that when she wakes up."

"Tell her if she can't deal with my methods of calming her down, we can send her back to Delat."

"We're not sending her back. Anyway . . . about time you showed up."

"I was outside repairing hull damage from our other misfortunes. I'd just barely gotten out there too. Do you know what a pain it is to suit up, only to hear the ship you're trying to repair is being blasted from the inside?" The newcomer took off the helmet. Black hair spilled over her shoulders. She had dark burgundy lips and skin so pale that she looked ghostly. She unzipped a pocket in her suit and pulled out something small that she used to tie her hair into two pigtails. Her bangs nearly covered her eyes, but Hap knew when she turned to look at him. "Who're the stowaways?"

"No one important," Laney said.

Hap didn't like being referred to as "no one important," but from the way Tara tensed, he figured she liked it even less.

Laney and the newcomer both turned away from Tara and Hap and walked toward the hole burned through the wall near the door.

"I told you not to let a twin-soul on the crew. She's been nothing but trouble."

"She passed all the tests to get off-planet. No one else would hire her." Laney reached a hand into the hole and ripped out a still-sizzling assortment of wires.

"You should take a lesson from that."

Laney looked at the newcomer. "Svarta, she'd have starved."

"You're such a bleeding heart, Laney."

"And yours is a black hole."

Svarta's black suit creaked as she shrugged. "What's the plan for the stowaways?"

"No plan. We'll have to get them back to Earth somehow."

Svarta grumbled something Hap couldn't hear over his relief that Laney was at least considering the possibility of taking them home. "We can't go back there. ICE is watching for you. We shouldn't have gone there in the first place."

"And what, Svarta? We forget Dad? Let him rot wherever ICE has stowed him away? We need the device. The fact that anyone else wants it is secondary. We didn't do it for the payoff—remember that. We did it for us. For our family."

Svarta threw her hands in the air and let out a long breath that lifted the hair over her eyes enough that Hap could see they looked worried and scared. They looked like his mom's eyes did when he came home too late.

Gygak no longer cowered behind the wall. He stood up and straightened his jacket. "You aren't supposed to use the device. You're supposed to deliver it."

In one fluid motion, Svarta had a gun pressed to his temple. "I should have let Googool dust you." Her lips curled in disgust.

Gygak's furry antennae eyebrows fell limp against his cheeks as she pushed her gun harder against his skin. "I was only warning you . . ."

Mosh had ambled up behind him but stayed back enough to not be included in the whole gun interchange. "She didn't like being cautioned."

Laney put her hand on Svarta's arm. "Don't worry about him or ICE or Tremble or the stowaways. Don't worry about anything. We're too close to fail."

Svarta pulled the gun away from Gygak's head, though she seemed to regret the action. He rubbed the circular dent in his skin where the barrel pressed against it. Though Svarta's hair hung down in her eyes, Hap felt her stare fixed on him. He shifted and then held still so he didn't look nervous.

Tara stood, brushing the hair back from her face. "I appreciate that you guys are busy and have a lot going on and all that. But my mom is alone. She needs me. I really need to go home." Tara's eyes glistened and her voice cracked.

Laney looked down at the wires in her hand. "I understand how you feel, but there isn't anything we can do." Laney focused again on Svarta, seeming determined to ignore them again.

Tara's lip wobbled. Hap felt bad when she looked away to hide the tears leaking out the corners of her eyes. Tara and her mom had lived through a bunch of rough months after her dad left. Being away from the only solid thing in her life had to be killing her. He knew how she felt, living every day like it was the last time he'd see his dad . . . what if the last time he saw his family really *was* the last time? "Hey!" he called out. "Hey! Our parents probably think we're dead. You have to do something!"

Laney rolled her eyes. "Can it, kid! They'll know you're not dead when you go home. Think of it as giving them a really great surprise."

Svarta made a noise between a snort and laugh. "And you say my heart's a black hole."

"What? There's nothing I can do!" She turned on Hap. "What is it you think I can do, huh?"

"I don't know." He felt a little dumb that he'd made demands but had no plan for that demand. "At least convicts get a phone call."

Mosh chuckled, his huge, basketball-shaped belly rolling around as though someone were actually dribbling it. "Phone call!" he repeated as though he were a toddler discovering a new noise. "Primitive people . . . with no links—no vids."

Hap stared in disbelief at the frog-ape with the ill-fitting flight jacket. Who was he to call Hap primitive?

Mosh shook his head, making his bottom lip seem disconnected from his jaw. "Lots of credits to link to Earth."

Hap felt Svarta's eyes on him again. "The mountain's called it. We don't have the credits to let you contact your folks. Do you know how many satellites and solar flares it takes to make such contact possible? The cost of linking that far is astronomical."

"I'd pay you back." Hap didn't know why he said such a dumb thing. His entire savings consisted of the bank account his parents never let him touch and the hundred and fifty bucks he was saving to buy himself a real magician's box. When they said a phone call was expensive, he figured his measly funds wouldn't come close. From working at the magic shop and from his constant contact with money—mostly other people's—he had a pretty good idea of what expensive meant.

Laney raised an eyebrow. "Pay me back how?"

"I'll help you do whatever it is you're trying to do. I'll clean your ship, do any chores you need . . . whatever." He looked away to hide his lie. He didn't intend on helping her do anything. Whatever Tolvan had been telling Grandpa Hazzard, Laney sat at the middle of it. He planned on getting home and dragging Laney in to the cops or ICE or whoever.

"So what, you're applying for a job?"

Hap shrugged and pretended not to see Tara glare. Tara had been the one who'd wanted a job today. "Yeah. I guess."

Laney shrugged too. "Well you ought to be working for me anyway, since I have to babysit you for so long. I'll have to pay for your room and board."

"Tara will work too." Hap caught Tara's look and hurried to add, "At least we will if you let us contact our parents."

"C'mon, Laney. You'd have done anything if they'd let us call Dad. Give them a break. They're no different than we were. Than we *are*. If you knew where to call Dad, you wouldn't care what it cost."

"Yeah, but I've been waiting eighteen years. They've only been gone for a day—a few hours. To them, at least."

"To them?" Tara asked. Her eyes were still watery looking, but no tears fell.

"It took some time to make sol." Laney turned to Svarta. "Get Tremble to her room and put her in lockdown in case she wakes up as Googool."

"What happened to her? Is she okay?" Tara asked.

Svarta grinned. "You're sweet to worry about the person who shot up your ride. She's fine. I blasted her with a nerve disrupter. It makes it so the currents flowing information to her brain get jumbled. The brain can't handle the jumble so it goes . . . to sleep. She'll have a headache when she wakes up but will otherwise be fine."

Laney tsked in exasperation at Svarta.

"What? I'm taking her. There's no harm in answering a few questions."

"I could take her." Gygak's eyebrows no longer drooped, but they quivered like the tail of Hap's dog when she was in trouble for chewing up his dad's shoes.

Laney glared at Gygak. "I don't trust you to take her."

Tara interrupted the argument that was sure to follow between Laney and Gygak. "What's a sol?"

"Speed of light. Once you make sol, it takes a little under an hour to get to the drop behind Elara."

When both teenagers stared at Laney, she shook her head. "Elara? You know? One of Jupiter's moons?" She shook her head again and Hap felt the disgust in the motion. "Don't even know the moons in their own solar system. Honestly, what are they teaching in school these days?"

"Just one call, then . . . My dad has cancer. He's dying. The doctors gave him just a few months longer. Waiting isn't an option." Hap felt like his chance to talk her into letting them reach their parents was fading fast. At this Tara shot him a look that clearly said, "Please! If we only get one call, please let it be to *my* mom."

He didn't care whose family was contacted, as long as Tara's mom gave his parents and grandpa the message. Grandpa Hazzard had to be told what happened. He'd be able to arrange a rescue if he knew where to look. At the very least, Grandpa Hazzard could tell Hap how to pull off his own rescue. He'd get home faster than Laney thought.

"Fine. One." Laney nodded to Svarta, who immediately moved to pick up Tremble/Googool. Svarta tossed the limp body over her shoulder into a fireman's hold and headed off toward the airlift tube. Laney followed her sister without so much as a backward glance at Hap or Tara.

Tara rubbed her arm absently as though she were a little cold. "Thanks. I'm sorry about your dad, Hap. That's got to be hard. And I feel selfish insisting we contact my mom, but she won't survive another loss—first my dad, and now . . . now me. You're okay with that, right?"

"As long as your mom gives the message to my family—to my grandpa especially."

Gygak smoothed his multiple hands over his bald head. "You humans are so naive. How is she supposed to keep her deal with you? That cracked sister of hers already spilled that they don't have enough credits left on her card. There isn't any way they can make good on your deal—not that they don't want to, they just can't. But Nova's down on that planet. He'd give you each your own cards with more credits available than either of you could imagine. You could link to anyone and everyone you wanted with Nova's help."

Tara eyed the little creature and gave a sniff of distrust. "What were you in jail for—back on Earth?"

Hap admired the way Tara adjusted to her situation enough to use the phrase, "back on Earth."

Gygak stiffened and his eyebrows lowered a little when faced with the accusation in Tara's voice. "Nothing that should worry you."

"Well, it worried somebody, or they wouldn't have put you in jail."

Gygak jabbed one of the fingers on his lower left hand at Tara. "Naive human girl. In this universe it doesn't matter what you do if someone decides they don't like you. Anyone could end up in jail. Even you. So don't act like I'm space waste."

Mosh lowered his head so that he stared into Tara's eyes. Tara flinched but didn't back away when he jutted his lower lip out even more. "We were supposed to get the crystal pyramid. ICE caught us before we could jump from your world and we were caught. Laney came after us to get the crystal. We are all the same, after the same thing. If you trust her, why not us?"

"You can stop calling me naive. I don't trust anyone here," Tara said, narrowing her eyes at Hap. "You never know when someone who you thought was nice is going to slap a buzzer on your hand."

Hap groaned. "You can't still be mad about that! We've been kidnapped by aliens, for crying out loud! We're on the other side of the universe."

Gygak cleared his throat. "I wouldn't be running around the universe calling anyone aliens."

"Why?"

"It's rude." Gygak's forehead wrinkled as he sniffed.

"Rude might get you killed," Mosh said, his head nodding with each syllable.

"*Alien* doesn't mean anything bad. It just means you're foreign to the environment you're in." Hap felt pretty proud he was able to spout off his grandfather's words with such confidence.

Gygak snapped two of the three fingers on his top-left hand in Hap's face. "That makes you the alien here, pal, not me." Gygak sauntered off and Mosh, after a minute of looking at Tara, lumbered after him. For all his size, Mosh was pretty light on his feet, as though any step might send him bounding through the roof. It seemed like he tried to tiptoe when he moved.

"Did he just call us aliens?" Tara asked.

Hap looked down at the planet they orbited. "I guess we are." He suddenly felt small, and the universe seemed so much bigger.

9. Room Service

Tara stared blankly out at the stars and the planet with the milky cat-eye middle through one of the side windows. She wrapped her arms around herself as though using them to hold herself upright. Tears trailed down her paled cheeks in silence.

It took Hap a long time to speak. "I really am sorry about the buzzer. I didn't do it to be mean or anything. I was having a bad day, and I dunno . . . It just seemed like it would be funny."

"To who?" Her blonde hair hung flat over her shoulders, soaked down with perspiration.

Hap shrugged, knowing if he said it would be funny to him, she'd be mad all over again. He'd seen enough people argue to know that girls never took things the way a guy meant them to be taken. "It's just done, and I'm sorry. We need to work together. You can hate me when we get home, but for now let's call a truce, okay?"

She pursed her lips, never looking away from the porthole closest to her, before finally saying, "Sure. Fine. Just don't ask me to shake on it."

Hap wasn't sure she was joking until a smile tugged at the corners of her mouth. "Do you think they'll let us call home for real?" Hap asked.

"No. The little *bat* thing is right. She's just trying to make us feel better." Tara finally faced him. "I have to get home, Hap. I have to take care of my mom."

"I know. I need to get home too. My dad is . . ."

Tara inhaled sharply. "I know. Your dad. I'm sorry. Is he getting better?" She looked hopeful that he might say yes. More hopeful than anyone in his family had looked for two months. He hadn't directly told anyone about his family situation, but everyone in town and in school knew. Teachers offered pained little smiles at him and patted his shoulder when they walked past his desk. And it had been a long time since he'd gone to his friends' houses to play video games or hang out. Longer still since he'd had any of them over. He knew people whispered about his situation. He knew people felt sorry for him, but it somehow irritated him that Tara, who had her own problems, could look at him with such pity.

He didn't need the pity. He'd show her he was strong and could handle it. She'd understand once he got her back to her mother. "You know, I think my—"

"Laney never agrees to anything she doesn't mean," Nana interrupted before Hap could finish his sentence: *grandpa works for ICE and might know how we can get out of this.*

Hap jumped, not expecting the interruption and grateful he hadn't said anything that might get back to Laney. "I thought you'd left with the others."

Nana laughed. "Left? Everywhere they go, I'm there. But I'm here too."

"What happened to Tremble?" Tara asked, looking around as though trying to find physical evidence of Nana.

Hap had almost forgotten about the weird, fork-tailed girl who didn't like being called a fairy.

"She's a twin-soul. 'Split personality' might be an easier term for humans to understand. She has a pleasant side and a dark side. Everyone from Delat has this condition. They determine the dominant soul fairly young. Those who never gain control of their dark side are cast off to the desert. Every so often, the people war over who should rule the planet. Sometimes the dark souls win and they control the governing body; but their anger gives them short-lived power. Tremble is a light soul . . . mostly. She's like her own planet and goes to war with herself for control of her body. She's pleasant most of the time. You just caught her on an off day."

Hap looked around the various smoldering holes that were left over from Tremble's tantrum. "Off day? Holy Houdini. This place looks worse than just an *off* day."

"Svarta will repair me. And it wasn't Tremble's fault. After Googool takes control, it is difficult for Tremble to win control back."

"But Tremble *is* Googool," Tara said.

"Not really. They are twin-soul. They share the same body, but they are not the same person."

"That's totally messed up," Hap said.

"For you it may be. But for someone from her planet, it is normal life. If you like her better as Tremble, I don't suggest insulting her." Nana's stern voice reminded Hap of his mom. Nana was a fitting name for this ship.

"So what do we do now?" Tara asked

"Wait here. Laney will return for you when she has time," Nana said.

"Do you think we'll have somewhere to lie down? My head is killing me," Tara whispered to Hap as she held her head.

"Laney will take you to your room where you can rest."

"I'm here to do that right now," a voice behind them said. Tara and Hap spun to see that Laney had entered undetected.

Hap darted a quick a look at Tara. Private conversations seemed to be impossible in this place. They followed Laney in relative silence to the airlift tube where they descended to the bottom level.

Laney led them down the hall they'd been in before with Tremble but veered off into a shorter hallway with four doors. Laney finally spoke up. "With all the new visitors, we've had to double up on sleeping compartments. Nana's not a big ship, and most of her space needs to be used for fuel and water resources." Laney opened a door that led them into a closet-sized room with two beds that looked more like shiny silver coffins.

Tara looked at the room then Hap then Laney before saying with a lot of indignation, "No way!"

Hap felt a little dumb over her getting snooty about sleeping accommodations. Sure, they'd be cramped, but they weren't being tossed overboard into space. Hap needed to focus and figure out a plan, but he couldn't think when his body screamed at him for sleep. It surprised Hap that Tara had enough energy to care what kind of room they got.

"I can't share a room with a *guy!*"

So the room didn't bother her—he did. Not that he wanted to share with her either. A guy needs his privacy, after all, but she didn't need to be so insulting about it.

Laney glanced at Hap. "He looks normal enough."

"Says you. Really. My mom'll freak. My mom's sworn off all men forever since the divorce. I'm not even allowed to date until I'm graduated from college with a master's degree."

Hap almost said he wouldn't date her if she was the last girl in the world—in the *whole* universe—but his tongue suddenly felt awkward in his mouth and he couldn't make it work.

Laney looked at the ceiling as though trying to talk to the ship through telepathy. For all Hap knew, she was doing just that. "Well, I guess we could put you in with Tremble. She's still sleeping, but you have a fifty percent chance of her waking up as Tremble so she *might* not strangle you while you sleep."

Tara backed up a step, bumping into Hap.

"Oh, don't look at me like I'm mental. The room divides." As Laney said this, a wall materialized and cut off Hap's view of the far bed, though far seemed to be an overstatement. A door led to this new room, and Laney stepped through it. "You can sleep in here . . ." She hesitated as though fumbling for his name.

"Hap."

She raised her eyebrow. "Right." She turned back to Tara. "*Hap*-py now?"

"But his door leads right to my room." Tara *wasn't* happy and had no issue with vocalizing the fact.

"Lock it, then." Laney had lost patience with them already.

The possibility of getting kicked off the ship—left to float in space—grew larger every moment, but Hap had to voice his own concern. "She can't lock me in. What if I have to—you know . . ." He couldn't think of any right way of saying it.

Laney smirked. "Are you talking about going to the bathroom?"

"Um . . . maybe." He felt his face heat up to the sun's surface temperature.

"There's all the standard equipment in the closet in your room. It states SANITATION right on the box and gives information for usage. I picked it up when I was earthside so it's in English."

Hap figured she meant she'd thieved the sanitation kit from the same place she stole the thing Tolvan mentioned to his grandfather. He didn't think much of people who had no problem stealing.

Laney stretched. "Nana's working out the sequence for landing. Sometimes landings are a little bumpy, so I suggest you stay in your rooms in your beds until I come get you. Sleep well, Hap and—"

"Tara," Tara said.

"Earth." Laney smiled—a first.

"Excuse me?" Tara still glared at the wall and the door and likely wondered how to lock Hap in his room.

"Your name, Terra, means "Earth"—as in the soul of your home world. I hope that counts as good luck for our mission." Without another word, Laney turned and left, the door sliding shut behind her.

Tara looked at Hap and shrugged. "I thought my parents named me after some hill in Ireland where they went on vacation once."

"I wouldn't tell her that." Hap jabbed a thumb in the direction of the door Laney had just exited. "That was the first time she seemed happy."

"Happy? She's a dragon lady! She totally could have told me the room divided before she went off on making me share rooms with the split-personality psycho."

"I think she wants us to stay scared."

"Laney would not want to keep you scared." Nana's voice made both Tara and Hap jump in surprise.

They glared up toward the voice eavesdropping on them.

Hap wanted to tell Tara about Tolvan—wanted to tell Tara about the thing Laney stole from Earth—but couldn't say anything without the ship listening in and tattling on them.

"Well, I need to sleep." Tara looked at him pointedly as though she could will him to his own space just by looking.

He stopped at the doorway. "Don't lock me in, okay?"

"I thought your hero was the great escape artist Houdini."

Hap rolled his eyes and stepped through the door. "Just, you know, if there's a fire or something . . . I don't want to be locked in here."

She groaned. "I don't even know how to lock it, so give it a rest, okay?"

He nodded and turned back to the tiny bit of space that was to be his. There wasn't much to it—a boxy sort of coffin bed, a silver cupboard that revealed a few scant supplies inside, a funky tray at the ceiling that provided a soft light, but nothing more. Two pieces of silver in an entirely white room. Not even a porthole to look through at the universe surrounding him.

Hap sighed and looked at the cupboard. The sanitation box contained plastic gloves, some baggies, and a few hard containers with spouts and lids. He thought about reading the directions and decided against it. He knew what it was all for and wasn't really up for the details. It felt like camping.

Hap crawled into the coffin thing and pulled a wispy sort of white sheet over him. He shivered. Now that the adrenaline rush had subsided, he realized the ship felt cold. He shivered again and forced his eyes closed.

"Are you cold?" Nana asked.

"Yes." Hap's eyes popped open even though he couldn't see Nana. He pulled the wispy sheet tighter around him. He didn't like the ship spying on him. What if he *did* need to go to the bathroom? Gradually the sheet warmed under his fingertips.

"Is that better?" Nana asked.

Hap snorted in amazement. "Yeah, lots better. Thanks!" He snuggled into the coffin bed a little deeper and closed his eyes again, feeling dumb for thanking a—what? Did he just thank a computer?

A spying computer, he reminded himself. How would he be able to explain to Tara about his grandfather, Tolvan, and the thing Laney stole if the computer followed him all over the ship? How would he ever plan an escape to get back home when his every word was tracked by a machine?

"Hap?" Tara called from the other side of the wall.

"Yeah?"

"I can't sleep."

Hap rolled his eyes. She'd been the one to insist he leave her room. "Give it a minute. Sleep'll come."

"Why do people call you Hap?"

Hap smiled. "They didn't used to. It's kinda 'cause of my dad. He used to call me a little devil because of my red hair. But he said he started calling me Hap after the broken arm, the busted collarbone, the sprained ankle, the burned hand, and the final straw—where I'd climbed the sycamore tree to look into a bird's nest. I fell. Dad caught me and saved me from cracking my skull on the cement. My dad said I had a haphazard way of jumping into trouble. The name sort of stuck." He loved reciting his parents' words. Telling Tara the things his mom and dad told other people when they asked about his nickname sent a wave of sadness through him. What if he never got home? What if he never saw his parents again?

He heard the swish of her blanket and assumed she'd turned to face his wall.

"What's your real name?"

Hap hesitated. His parents never used his real name, and in his small town everyone knew him by nickname only, even on school records. If Tara told anyone, he'd—he rolled his eyes again. Being on the other side of who-only-knew-where, Tara wouldn't be telling anyone anything. "Fredrick Eugene Hazzard."

She snickered. "Are you serious? Who looks at a brand new baby and thinks, 'Yep, he looks like a Fredrick Eugene to me?'"

"Don't laugh. I was named after Grandpa Hazzard."

"So it's your *great-grandparents* who give big names to little babies . . . Can I call you Freddy?" Her tone sounded on the verge of more laughing.

Hap groaned. "Don't even go there."

"Hap?"

"Yeah?"

"I'm sorry about your dad."

Hap blinked away the sting in his eyes. "Yeah, me too. And I'm sorry about your dad too. Life stinks sometimes. What do you do?"

"You know, it's not like he was fun to have around anyway."

Hap laughed.

"What? Why is that funny?"

"You can say that again! Remember during the summer before fifth grade, and I crashed my bike into his car? I thought he was going to kill me."

Tara sighed. "He isn't always that intense. I mean, he has his good days."

"Hey, Tara . . . you don't need to defend him to me. If you say he was an okay guy, then he was. Case closed, right?"

She stayed silent on her side of the wall a long time before saying, "But he wasn't an okay guy. Not really. Not like your dad. Your dad always went to our plays and school stuff. My dad never went to those things."

Hap thought about that and blinked back more stinging in his eyes. His dad *had* gone to those things. He'd taught him to ride a bike—taught him to tie a tie and how to shave and then joked about the few hairs on his upper lip as not being worth the trouble. Growing up with a guy who knew when to joke and when to be serious had been the highlight of Hap's life. Hap's dad was seriously cool—which made losing him all the more painful. For Tara to compare her dad to his was hardly fair. No one compared to his dad. "Look, lots of dads don't make it to stuff, but it doesn't mean they're bad guys. It's not that they don't want to, but sometimes they just can't."

"If I don't have to defend him, then neither do you."

They both listened to the ship engines humming a moment before Tara spoke up again.

"Thanks for telling me your name." Her blanket swished once more, and Hap took that to mean she'd decided to finally go to sleep. He closed his eyes, feeling dumb for telling her his name. He hoped she didn't tell anyone.

With his eyes closed, he thought more about his family. He hoped his mom didn't cry. He hoped Grandpa Hazzard had seen the spaceships and found a way to follow them.

He thought about Tremble and shivered, though not from the cold. He wished Tara could lock his door, after all. The last thing he needed was to wake up and find a crazy twin-soul hovering over him.

* * *

"Landing in ten, nine, eight . . ." The countdown continued. Nana's methodical voice calmly paced their entry into this new world's atmosphere. Nana had told Hap and Tara to stay in their beds. Straps appeared from nowhere and basically cocooned them into their coffins like mummies. The roar of the engines reverberated off the metal and echoed around Hap's head. The ship vibrated, and he felt the sensation of plummeting.

Hap doubted King Tut ever had to deal with this sort of thing once he'd been wrapped in his coffin. Hap could tell when they hit real gravity. He felt the pull as though someone was trying to drag his whole body through his feet. The ship's fake gravity had seemed normal until he hit the real thing. Several moments passed before Nana readjusted the gravity on the ship.

"I hate this!" Tara wailed from the other side of the room. The wall and engine noise muffled her voice.

He agreed, but the new sense of gravity and the movement resulted in the worst elevator-drop-stomach feeling he'd ever had, preventing him from agreeing out loud.

The roaring rumbled through the ship louder than ever. When everything cut to silence, Hap remembered to breathe again. After several moments during which Hap heard only the sound of his own breathing and the blood rushing past his ears, the bands that held him snugly in his little coffin bed released and zipped back to wherever they came from.

Nana's voice startled Hap. "Svarta wanted to leave you wrapped in your beds, but I told her you wouldn't get into trouble now that we're docked. You won't, right?"

Hap nodded, not sure if Nana could "see" or just "hear" them. He couldn't have spoken if he'd wanted to. He'd lost his voice sometime during entry to this new world's atmosphere. He tried to move his legs up and over the side of his coffin bed, but they refused to obey his brain's commands. As it was, his brain still felt crammed against the top of his skull. He swallowed and tried to yawn to force his ears to pop. When they did, he grabbed at his head and yelped.

Several tries later, his legs wobbled under his weight as he stood.

A crash sounded from the other side of the wall. Hap hurried over to make sure Googool hadn't broken into the room. Tara lay on the floor in a tangle of arms and legs.

"Don't say a word!" Tara shouted from the floor.

"I didn't."

"I don't ever want to do that again. I swear I'm going to puke." Tara maneuvered herself so she could try to stand again. She used her bed to lean on.

"Don't get too used to being planetside. We'll only be here for a few rotations." Nana's cheerful way of saying everything was starting to irritate Hap.

"Where are we?" Hap asked Nana.

"Welcome to Stupak's Circle. We've landed on the Orissa, which, according to my calculations, you should find preferable to the actual Circle. Orissa lacks the fumes found closer to the Circle and therefore provides more favorable conditions for human existence."

Tara threw up.

10. One Small Step for Hap

Hap and Tara argued at the door for what felt like hours.

"You don't know that!" she said for the millionth time as she stood with her arms crossed over her chest. Everyone else had left before they arrived at the control room. Hap was a little bugged to be abandoned on the ship by themselves.

He blamed Tara, since he'd stayed to help her clean up the mess from her getting sick. Nana had guided them to a wall where they located a thing that looked like a dust vacuum. She called it a chemvac and said the contents they cleaned up would be expelled when the ship did a refuse dump.

"Everybody else went out. There has to be oxygen out there." Hap refused to let the argument drop.

Nana had already confirmed the air's breathability, but Tara stood resolute in not listening to anything Nana or Hap said about this world. Hap wanted to get to a phone. He wanted to get off the ship that watched and listened to their every move and word. He could not understand why Tara wanted to stay on board to wait for the people who kidnapped her. Besides . . . the idea of exploring a new world . . . what idiot wouldn't want to do that?

"How can you be so sure? Our faces will probably melt if we leave this ship."

"Aren't you even just a little curious? I mean c'mon, Tara. We're on an alien planet! How often do people get to do this?"

"Would you like me to run that statistic?" Nana asked.

"Er . . . no," Hap said. "I was being rhetorical." His mom asked rhetorical questions all the time. His dad liked to tease her about it.

Hap pushed aside the thoughts of his parents before he gave into his desire to bawl over his situation. Bawling in front of Tara would be embarrassing. Guys did not bawl. Guys found phones and figured out how to get themselves out of trouble.

"People *die* on alien planets." The quaver in Tara's voice betrayed her dry eyes. She was scared and likely worried over her mom.

But this was an *alien planet* they were talking about! This was something totally new and totally cool. Hap imagined being interviewed by all the TV stations and newspapers. They'd probably make a movie of him. He felt his face sliding into the silly grin his mom said he got when he wasn't focusing. He hurried to straighten it out before Tara noticed he'd stopped listening to her.

"This isn't a vacation we're on! Don't you even miss your family?"

Now she wasn't being fair. Making lemonade out of lemons didn't make him some heartless creep of a kid who didn't miss his family. "Of course I miss them. But we're kind of stuck in this situation, so we might as well make the most of it."

"I don't think getting myself killed is making the most of it." She was really ticked off.

"How is this getting killed?" He'd asked the same question twice already.

She tried a different line of reasoning. "If Laney thought it was safe, she'd have invited us to go with her."

Hap made a pshaw sound and leaned against the wall behind him. This wall had more of those funny-looking hieroglyphic characters etched all over it. The outline of their various shapes pressed through his shirt into his back. "Laney isn't our guardian. She totally doesn't care what we do." With Nana listening, he decided against adding the fact that Laney kidnapped them and couldn't be trusted.

"Okay, so if that's true, then she won't care if we're not here when she gets back. So then she'll leave us and we'll *never* get home."

Hap thought about asking Nana if this fear had any merit but worried Tara might be right and didn't want Nana confirming it.

If Laney left them, how would they get home? If they stayed with Laney, how would they get home? Laney ran from ICE. She'd stolen something important, something that concerned his grandfather.

Hap had to get on that planet and away from Nana's eavesdropping so he could talk to Tara and find a way to call home. If Laney left them, well . . . he'd deal with that if it happened. She had to stay long enough to deliver whatever she'd stolen. Two rotations . . . that had to mean two planet rotations. On the display in the control room, the planet looked pretty big. Two rotations would take a while. He had time to scout around.

He finally shrugged and shoved away from the wall. "Fine. I'll go alone. You stay here alone." He stood in front of the door waiting for Nana to swish it open. He had to clear his throat several times before she did open the door. A whoosh of hot, humid air nearly bowled him over as he peered down the tiny ramp to see where it led.

He looked back at Tara where she bit into her bottom lip as though making a snack of it. He shrugged and gave a wave before turning back to the ramp and taking the fateful first step onto an alien world.

Tara growled behind him before yelling out, "Wait!"

Hap grinned. He *so* knew she'd follow.

She had a good talking to Nana first about making sure not to leave them in case Laney got back first and then asking all kinds of questions about survival needs. Nana guided them to the same supply room where they'd been locked with the bugs.

Though Hap faltered at the door, Tara blazed ahead. "Don't touch anything, Hap."

He scowled. "I wasn't planning on it."

She rolled her eyes and gathered the mat-packs that Nana took forever to describe. Tara shoved a mat-pack into Hap's hands with a "You don't deserve this."

Hap eyed his new belongings suspiciously. After the bug incident, anything that came from the supply room was tainted in his eyes. "Don't deserve what? I don't even know what this is."

"It's food and water. Aren't you an Eagle Scout yet?"

"I'm only fourteen. I have until I'm eighteen," he said defensively. Suspicions of the supply room aside, Hap wouldn't have given the pack back for anything. His stomach felt like it had resorted to eating itself. His last meal felt like a million years ago—no, *two* million. He undid the magnetic snaps that closed the canvas top.

Tara smacked his hand. "It's for survival."

"Which is why we should eat some now. I'm starving. Starting a journey when we're already famished doesn't make any sense."

Tara agreed with his logic after a minute and took two more packs out of the supply room. They made short work of the tubes of nutty-flavored paste. Hap wondered about what might be in the tubes they sucked down. He couldn't read the funny lettering on the tubes and felt a little annoyed that his implant didn't let him decipher writing too. He almost asked Nana about the food, but Tara stopped him.

"Better not to know," she said with a shake of her head.

So Hap finished off the rations from the first pack and stared longingly at the second. He wasn't exactly hungry anymore, but he wasn't exactly full either. He followed Tara's example and slid his arms through two of the several holes in the pack. The pack looked as though it was made for Gygak's body, with all the available armholes. But it worked okay for them with their two arms.

Hap felt the weight of his own body as soon as his feet touched the ramp. He felt heavy and his body immediately broke into a sweat. Tara frowned but didn't mention the heavy air or the way every step seemed to take extra effort to make. Hap decided if she wasn't going to whine, neither was he. He led her off the ramp and onto a dirt path.

He furrowed his forehead at the landscape around him. He'd expected a spaceport with robots and other ships. But Nana was the only ship around, and it looked like they'd landed in a swamp.

Nana had given them instructions, and Hap had made a crude map from those instructions. Nana would have given them a map on what she called a link key, but Laney had locked that sort of access before she left. Nana made them take a link key anyway, just in case Laney came back and agreed to unlock it.

The ground squished under their feet, making a sucking sound every time they lifted a foot. And Gygak had been right about the smell. Everything smelled like Easter eggs that were never found until weeks after they'd rotted.

Water surrounded the place where the ship had landed. The water didn't look inviting so much as it reminded Hap of all those pollution ads he'd seen in school. Silver-and-pink-colored reeds pierced through the water's surface. Every once in a while the water rippled from something that had touched the surface from underneath. Hap craned his neck to glimpse anything beneath the water, wondering if he'd find another world underneath, but the murky water didn't allow him to see anything except the ripples.

"This is cool, huh?" Hap said every couple of feet as they walked. He wished he'd left his jacket on the ship, since the planet's heat made him feel like he was wearing a hot tub instead of a jacket. He took it off and tied it around his waist.

"It's a swamp, Hap. I've seen swamps before."

"Yeah, but never on a different planet. For all you know, we could be the first earthlings to have ever walked on this planet."

"Laney and Svarta are already here."

"Right. That's right." Tara's indifference muddied some of the excitement Hap felt, but he was still pretty excited. *A new planet. I'm on a new planet!* He stooped to pick up a black, mottled stone and deposited it into his pocket. He also took a few leaves from the reeds. *If I get home, I'll be famous. Scientists all over the world will want to talk with me.*

Hap stopped. *If I get home? No. I mean when . . . When I get home.*

Hap took a deep breath. No matter how deeply he filled his lungs, he felt like he took in more water than oxygen.

"We'll probably catch pneumonia before we ever get back." Tara scratched at her neck irritably. "And for all I know, I just got bitten by a mosquito carrying the West Nile virus."

"I doubt this planet has the West Nile virus."

"Well, then I'll get some other virus, and we haven't had any shots. Everyone knows when you leave the country you should get immunity shots. I bet leaving your planet requires way more shots than just a trip to Mexico."

They'd entered a place where the silver and pink reeds were taller than either of them, and the air became thicker, if such a thing was possible. The reeds had been joined by tall sticks that resembled bamboo.

Hap jumped back when one of the bamboo plants lowered to the ground and walked away on slivery legs he hadn't noticed it having before. He stole a glance at Tara, who hadn't noticed that a five-foot-tall stick just walked away. The stick freaked him out, but he knew if Tara saw it, she'd drag them back aboard Nana and never let him out again.

Once Hap felt they'd moved safely away from Nana's prying ears, he stopped Tara. "We need to call home."

She blew her hair out of her eyes impatiently. "No kidding."

"No, really. You know how I acted like a creep at the magic shop?"

She nodded and crossed her arms over her chest as though about to give him another lecture about that.

"I only acted that way because I'd had kind of a bad day—and I know that isn't an excuse, but listen. Just before you showed up, some weird guy came into the store." He described Tolvan and the fragments of overheard conversation in the back room.

"So you think that Laney is the person this magician told your grandpa about?" Tara no longer had her arms crossed, and she clicked her fingernails together while she listened.

"Exactly. And whatever this thing is she took, I think it's important."

"So what do we do about it?"

"We need to call home. Call my grandpa. He can help—I just know he can."

Tara looked around her, throwing her arms out wide to indicate their surroundings. "We're in a swamp! How are we supposed to call anyone?"

Hap looked at his crude map and turned it around. He wondered where Laney had gone with all her little shipmates. He wished that Laney had just taken them along to wherever it was she'd gone. Surely she'd have gone to civilization where some sort of long-distance communication would be available.

The reeds shuddered around them as though barely containing the wildlife hidden there.

Tara stopped. "I think we should go back."

Hap stopped too but only because he was right behind her and didn't want to run into her. "Why?" he asked, feeling a little resentful that she wouldn't let him be the leader.

"Something's out there . . ." Beads of sweat trickled down her forehead, but Hap didn't know if it was because of the physical exertion of just walking, the humidity and heat, or because she was freaked out.

After looking at her eyes, he chose the freaked-out option. Her chest heaved as though every breath hurt. Her eyes darted in every direction, trying to see everything, everywhere all at once.

Hap's movements were similar, but he wasn't scared. He wanted to search the planet, find a local restaurant or a gift shop or *something*—anything that might have people who could help him. "Of course something's out there. We're outside. Animals live outside. Haven't you ever seen a chipmunk in the canyon?"

"Let's go back." Tara's voice cracked.

"Aw, c'mon, we need to get somewhere to call home. And if we go back, that ship will listen to everything we say to each other. We'll never get another chance to escape."

"But what if escaping means we're trapping ourselves on this planet forever?"

"Tara, I need to contact my family. I need my parents to know I'm okay. This kind of stress could be the end of my dad, and I need my grandpa to tell us what to do. Besides, it's an *alien* planet. Don't you want to explore just a lit—"

A guttural noise came from the reeds behind him. He didn't have to turn around to know that something scary stood there. Tara's eyes widened, and she shook as though having a seizure. "I don't think that's a chipmunk."

11. Neubins

Hap should have just run, but his need-to-know mind forced him to whirl around to see whatever had freaked Tara out.

Twenty feet away, big eyes blinked innocently at him. Those eyes were set into a face of smooth, rust-colored fur. Big ears drooped down the sides of its face, making its face look longer and slightly forlorn. "It's just a big kitty."

"Big" certainly described the thing. It stood at least half as tall as Hap and quite a bit wider. The creature blinked its big eyes in a way that would have made his sister, Alison, get all mushy and say, "For cu-ute!" Hap took a deep breath of relief and turned to grin at Tara for being nervous over nothing, but he froze as the creature opened its mouth. Saliva dripped over rows and rows of razorlike teeth. The creature let out a shriek that sounded like a cry from a zombie off one of Hap's video games.

The creature, which had seemed so much like an adorable cat just moments before, now looked demonic as its body went into spasms. Layers of spikes jutted from its back like quills from a porcupine.

The quills shuddered and the animal's shoulders jolted and twitched.

Tara's instincts kicked in first. She grabbed Hap's arm and dragged him along behind her as she turned and ran. A horrible cry came from the animal as though someone were killing it. Hap glanced back to see it stomping in some weird sort of tantrum.

The quills rubbed against each other, making a chirping noise to add to the screeching. A sharp stab pierced Hap's leg. His leg buckled and he collapsed to the ground, dragging Tara down with him as he fell. He looked down to see a long, red needle poking from the fleshy place behind his knee.

The creature jerked and twitched as it slowly came toward them.

"I can't move! My leg's numb!" Hap yelled. The sensation of numbness tingled through his other leg as well. He couldn't stand, let alone run. "Tara! Run!"

But Tara didn't run. She spun around, searching for something. Hap wanted to kick her—anything to make her just get out of there! He knew he'd never be able to handle her getting hurt when he was the one who'd dragged her out of the ship.

Tara stooped down, finding whatever she'd been looking for. Her fingers wrapped around several stones and she sprang to her feet. She hurled the stones with more force than Hap ever guessed her capable.

One of the stones caught the creature full in the mouth, knocking against those terrible teeth with an awful sort of shattering noise. Its shoulders lurched as another volley of needles left its back.

They would die.

Hap was sure of it. He wanted to close his eyes so he couldn't see their doom lurching toward them, but he couldn't tear his gaze away from the needles hurtling through the air. In a last-second decision, he grabbed Tara's ankles and pulled her hard to the ground at the same instant he turned his back and ducked his head away from the needles. He felt multiple thumps against his backpack but no stabs of pain.

Another cry erupted from the creature. The way it lumbered forward tortured Hap. He knew he'd be able to outrun the thing if he could just use his legs. He shoved at Tara with his arm. "Go! Now!"

But she ripped off her backpack and wrapped the straps around Hap's neck to hold it in place over his head. She kneeled behind the little body shield she'd turned Hap into and flung more rocks.

With a squeal, she ducked as another volley of needles thudded into the packs.

He could no longer see the creature closing in on them. He wondered why his life didn't flash before his eyes. Wasn't his life supposed to flash before his eyes before he died?

Another chirp—more thumps against the packs. The time between the chirps and thumps was fleeting, which meant the creature was close and they'd be cat food any minute. Then a new sound interrupted the thumps—a clattering sound like nails being dropped into a tin can.

A blast shot out from somewhere to the side, and something thumped the ground just a few feet from where Tara and Hap huddled behind their packs.

Something moved around the pack, making Hap scream before he realized it was just Laney and Svarta. They stepped in front of him. Svarta pocketed her drubber and smirked at the black disc in her other hand. Sticking to the disc were dozens of the creature's red needles.

Hap felt the heat climb his neck into his face, and he really wished he hadn't shrieked like a little girl just a moment before.

Laney folded her arms over her chest and narrowed her eyes. "What are you doing out here?"

She looked madder than his mom the time he'd shown up at home with a rip in his Sunday suit pants from skateboarding on his stomach and using his knees as brakes.

Hap couldn't say which scared him more—the creature intent on eating them or the angry woman who'd taken them away from Earth.

Tara's eyes darted to the ground. Her face flushed even redder than it had been with the heat, humidity, and exertion. "Go ahead, Hap. Tell her why we're out here." The stutter in her voice reminded Hap of Tara's straight-A grades and teacher's pet status. She'd never be able to fib.

Hap dug his fingers into the spongy ground. "Exploring . . ." He held his breath to wait for their reaction.

Svarta laughed outright. Laney threw her arms in the air and paced energetically while ticking off all the dangers of this world. "There's the skrapligts, the hesten, the pustules. Do you have any idea how fast a pustule could kill you?"

"I'm gonna die from a blister?"

Laney snorted at him. "Sarcasm will get you in lockdown in your cabin for the rest of our journey back to Earth."

Hap shut up, keeping his thoughts about the scrap licks that hasten to himself.

Hap couldn't get over the way they acted. For Svarta to laugh . . . like his grandfather did when Hap got into mischief. For Laney to get blustery and act like a mother hen protecting her chicks, the way his mother would. He shook his head in confusion. These people were his abductors, *not* his family.

Tremble, Mosh, and Gygak didn't seem to care either way about the kids wandering off by themselves. Or about the fact that they'd nearly witnessed that creature—which Svarta called a neubin—have a double dinner of Tara and Hap.

Every member of the crew looked hot and irritable. Dark spots of sweat soaked through their clothes. Mosh and Gygak set the crate down between them.

When Laney stopped yelling, she busied herself with removing quills from Hap's legs. "You're lucky you had the packs to shield you or your whole body would be paralyzed for hours. Since only part of your nervous system was affected, it should wear off soon enough. We'll rest here until you can walk."

Svarta shrugged out of her pack. "I'll check the area and clear out any companions this one might have had. She kicked at the neubin's body, and with her drubber at the ready, she disappeared into a tangle of bamboo and reeds. Tremble ripped Hap's jeans to the knee to clean off the area where the needle had embedded itself.

"I'm allergic to bees," Hap said to anyone who would listen. "What if this sting kills me?"

"It *would* have killed you if we hadn't come along." Gygak seemed to take pleasure in the kids' misfortunes.

Tremble spoke matter-of-factly. "The needle won't kill you. It's nothing like a bee's stinger."

Hap had already figured as much but wanted to voice his concern anyway. He removed his hand from his jacket pocket where he carried the EpiPen among his pocket tricks. "I thought we were goners for sure. If that thing hadn't been crippled, we'd be dead."

"It wasn't crippled. Its entire body is almost magnetic. The minerals in the ground pull on its body with such force, it's hard for it to move at all. The quills it fired are nature's way of allowing it to catch prey. The neubin shoots the quills, which paralyze the prey long enough to let the neubin feed. You're lucky. Lucky to have the packs . . . lucky we came along . . . lucky."

"I don't feel lucky." Tara clicked her nails together. "I want to call home now." Her pert tone indicated she wasn't asking but insisting.

Laney stiffened and brushed a strand of dark hair back under her baseball cap. "We will as soon as we get back."

Gygak snorted and shot Hap an I-told-you-so look. Tara gave Hap a look of desperation.

"How did you find us?" Hap asked, trying to ignore Gygak and Tara. He worked hard not to stare at the crate either. Whatever Laney had stolen likely sat inside that crate. His stomach felt all knotted and pretzel-like. To be so close to the thing Tolvan wanted Grandpa Hazzard to save and not be able to do anything about it . . .

"Nana linked and said you'd wandered off. We were able to track you with the link key you took."

Hap grunted. Even when they weren't on the ship, the ship spied on them. Though he supposed he'd be more upset if they hadn't saved him.

"You'll have to come with us, I guess." Laney said.

"Where?" Tara asked.

"Orissa's settlement."

"But I can't walk." Relief that they didn't drag him back to the ship and lock him into his room flooded through him. Maybe he'd be able to make the call home from Orissa.

"We'll wait." Laney crossed her arms, looking as though she might glare at him for the entire wait.

* * *

They sat around waiting for Hap's legs to prick into feeling, but not a minute longer. Laney jumped to her feet as soon as Hap said he thought he could walk.

"Good. You can help carry the crate." She pointed to where Mosh and Gygak moved to pick the crate up.

Hap sighed.

Carrying the crate proved difficult. The planet's gravity seemed to pull back on anything you picked up. Even the stone in his pocket felt heavier than it should have. His mom would never visit a place like this.

After a bit, Laney enlisted Tara to help with the crate as well.

"Don't you have hovercraft to carry this?" Hap asked. He'd seen enough sci-fi movies to know that alien technology surpassed human technology, and therefore everyone had hover cars and things that made work easier.

"Some people might. Hovers are very popular in Stupak's Circle due to the dense minerals in the soil. But we don't have any hovers because such things are expensive and impractical. Where would we store such a thing on Nana?"

The lecture sounded like similar ones he got from his mom. *"We can't buy a projector for a home theater; they cost too much and we don't have space in the family room."*

Laney cast a sideways look at Mosh.

"Happy to be home, Mosh?" she asked after a minute. Hap strained his neck to turn and gape at Mosh. That big thing lived *here* in a place where the gravity felt like an anchor?

His bottom lip jutted out more in what looked to be a pout. He shook his head. Mosh didn't look happy at all.

"So what's in here?" Hap tried to sound casual, while working to keep from stumbling on the occasional rock on the path.

"The Piramida Hira," Tremble answered before Laney snapped out, "Nothing!"

Gygak growled a curse under his breath when Hap nearly dropped his corner.

"You have piranhas in there?" So much for this being some important item his grandpa needed to save. It was nothing but a bunch of sharp-toothed fish.

Tara growled too, but Hap didn't think she cursed. She wasn't like that. "Don't be so immature," she said.

"I'm a guy. It's my job to be immature. According to my mom, it's not even something I'll grow out of." And what did she care if he called the crate contents piranhas?

She grumbled something Hap didn't hear then said out loud, "And if you drop your side, I swear, Hap . . ." The threat hung in the air and Hap didn't want to know what it was she swore. He tightened his grip.

"They're just kids, Laney." Svarta walked behind where Mosh, Gygak, Tara, and Hap wrestled the crate down the path. Laney led the way.

"That means what to me?"

"I swear you didn't learn a thing in raising me. If you keep secrets, you only make them want to know more and they get themselves into trouble trying to find out more. If you tell them outright, they'll realize it wasn't all that interesting in the first place and will leave you alone about it. It's not like it matters if you tell them."

"They're better off not knowing. But if it makes you happy, go ahead and tell them." Svarta brightened. "Okay. It's the Piramida Hira."

"Sounds pretty," Tara murmured.

"It's like a miniature pyramid made of crystal. The name *Piramida Hira* is Hindi. Translated it means 'diamond pyramid.'"

The pyramid . . . Hap remembered hearing the word *pyramid*. He darted a quick look to Tara, who shrugged.

"Emperor Ashoka of India had it created in like 250 BC—so, a long time ago. He'd started a secret society of scientists, called the Nine Unknown."

"If they're unknown, how do you know there were nine?" Hap asked.

Svarta had moved to where Hap couldn't see her anymore, but he had the feeling if he could, she'd be glaring through her black bangs. "Do you want to hear the story or not?"

"Sorry."

Svarta continued. "Each of the nine wrote a book revealing mysteries of the universe."

"Mysteries?" Tara asked.

"What kind of mysteries?" Hap chimed in.

Svarta shrugged. "Oh, you know, the cool stuff—how to turn basic metals and rocks into gold, how to time travel, and how to heal any disease known to the universe . . . stuff like that."

Hap nearly stumbled, causing a few groans, curses, and general discord until everyone found their footing again. He didn't care. His mind had drifted away into the words *"how to heal any disease known to the universe."* He could save his dad with a book like that.

"Anyway," Svarta continued, "they found a way to glean truth through the Hira. Emperor Ashoka hid the Hira, and the books the scientists wrote, when his land went to war so that his enemies wouldn't use the knowledge against them. They had to be hidden all separate from each other since the Hira allows the books to be read like a translator. The nine left the planet, each one going to a different place in the universe, so if they were ever found, the mysteries of the universe could never be fully unveiled since they were no longer all together."

Gygak grunted, his breathing heavy and wheezy through his forehead nostrils. "Like it mattered."

"Wh—why didn't it matter?" Tara wheezed too. It annoyed Hap that he gagged for breath when Svarta walked and talked like she was on a stroll. But then . . . Svarta didn't have to carry the crystal thing either. It also annoyed Hap that his ripped pants flapped while he walked.

"They were all captured and tortured until they told their secrets," Gygak said. "The stick Svarta used to knock Tremble out when she was having her . . . issues is a tool made by one of the scientists. His book was on mind control. He didn't have too much control over his mind at the end with all that torture, huh?" Gygak laughed as though he'd said something funny.

"That's horrible!" Tara sputtered.

"He's exaggerating." Tremble broke in before Gygak said anything else. "The last of the unknown was never found. They never wheedled secrets from him. And none of the books has ever been recovered. The scientists never revealed anything important. They had control over themselves, regardless of torture." She said this with more than a little respect. Coming from someone whose whole life depended on self-control, Hap could understand why she'd feel a kinship to these scientists.

Hap tried to slow his breathing but ended up feeling like he was going to pass out. So much for being tough. "So what happened to the last guy?"

Tremble darted a quick look to Laney before answering. "No one knows. But it doesn't matter. The Hira will show us all."

"You won't use it if you know what's good for you," Gygak said. He looked like he might say more, but at one darkened glance from Tremble, he shut up. It seemed no one was up for another episode of Tremble's identity crisis.

Hap couldn't get the thought of something that heals disease out of his mind. What if such a thing were possible? What if he could save his dad?

They finally came out of the reeds, and Hap nearly dropped the crate again. They'd entered a forested place that looked like something Hap envisioned from the rainforests in Hawaii. The path had gone from squishy and brown with mossy green patches to hard like cement. The path had a dull shine from frequent use. Dark green trees lined the path, and wild grasses and thickly leafed bushes swayed in the breeze. Flowered vines tangled through half the trees and hung from the branches like long swings.

"Lava," Tara said, stamping her foot on the hard path.

The hardened lava swirled upward to a dome of flowered vines.

"It looks like a green beehive," Hap suggested to no one in particular. He'd heard about alien bugs. What if alien bees with stingers the size of his arm lived in those holes? He couldn't move forward another step, even with Mosh and Tara pushing against the back of the crate trying to urge him forward.

Gygak grimaced, his forehead wrinkling around his nostrils. "I hate Orissa."

Only Hap heard the Gygan mumble. Hap didn't like it either. The place looked creepy. The silence, which only made it creepier, made him feel as though someone had stuffed his head with cotton.

The rotten-egg smell was gone, though, replaced by the scent of the flowers and vines.

"And I hate the Rissans," Gygak muttered as a faint humming began within the wall.

Hap's legs felt frozen to the spot, even though everything inside his head begged for him to run. The humming reminded him of the time a swarm of bees chased him away from their hive. He'd only been curious, and hadn't meant to hurt the hive in any way. After several stings and swelling to sumo wrestler proportions, it had been determined that Hap was allergic to bees. That had been another time where he would have died if his mom hadn't found him so fast. He'd carried an EpiPen ever since.

Hap dug his fingers into the crate's slivery wood. Somewhere in his jacket pocket, the EpiPen rattled around with his flashlight and pocket magic tricks. He'd tied the jacket around his waist.

When a head emerged from the vines, Gygak made a noise that landed somewhere between a squeak and a whine as he dropped his corner of the crate.

Hap stumbled under the crate's shifted weight. Mosh worked to keep the crate from falling and by so doing made Tara lose hold on her corner as well.

The being coming from the hive was tall, taller than Mosh. It popped out of the hole and became a blur of motion as it flew straight to the crate. It landed on hind legs, the bottom of its bright green robe fluttering around its single-toed feet as it landed. The double set of wings folded behind it as it grabbed the crate with its four arms. Once the crate had been steadied, its head snapped around, and the almond eyes turned on Hap.

12. Mind Control

A BUZZING FILLED HAP'S EARS as though bees swarmed inside his head. The words formed in his mind, "Do not fear us."

But Hap *was* afraid, and the voice in his head only made that worse. How had it known he was afraid? He still had a hold on the crate and couldn't make his hands move to reach for his EpiPen. If the thing stung him, he wouldn't be able to do anything about it. Was the creature trying to take over his mind? Did the alien implant make that easier or harder? Hap felt lost amidst the buzzing and the strange words in his mind. *Get out of my head!* Hap thought.

The buzzing ceased immediately.

The thing tilted its triangular head like a bird observing a worm before turning to Tara. Tara seemed to calm down, and Hap could've sworn she nodded. *So . . . is Tara now under mind control?* Hap wondered.

Black flecks freckled down the sides of its milky white face like sideburns. The black flecks rippled up and down as though being bounced on waves. The creature stared directly at each of Laney's crew in turn, though it had to look down to do so. Gygak was the only one who looked away when faced with those eyes.

Everyone but Hap and Gygak acted all pleasant and happy with the dragonfly person. Hap would have high-fived Gygak but figured, with all those arms, Gygak could high-five himself. Besides, no matter what they had in common, Hap didn't like the leathery, four-armed bat.

He'd have to figure out a way to get Tara away from everyone. He'd hoped to be taken somewhere with other humans . . . somewhere he could communicate without something barging into his mind. This place was worse than being on Nana. At least with Nana his thoughts still belonged to him.

"This is Elriss," Laney said. "She is to be our guide and protector while we stay in Orissa's Neswar. If you need anything, you need only ask her."

Yeah, sure, Hap thought. *I'll ask her to add extra salt when she feeds me to her queen . . . Whatever, Laney.*

The sound of more buzzing came from the wall and several of the winged things glided down. They adjusted a net under the crate, then four of the creatures each took a corner and lifted the crate into the air. That impressed Hap, since it had been hard enough to just lift it a few feet off the ground to carry. Taking it that high meant the creatures were really, really strong. *Whose idea was it to come to Orissa?*

Laney led them to a stairwell cut into the lava rock. The black and green stairs blended so well into the black and green wall that the stairs were nearly invisible. The wide stairs easily accommodated Mosh's big feet, which made going up uncomfortable for everyone else. Hap had to take two steps on every stair in order to get to the next one up.

It felt like forever before they reached an opening in the wall. The stairs continued upward, but Laney led them through the opening where Elriss waited for them. She'd only taken a few seconds to reach that spot with her wings and had waited while the rest of them hiked to it.

Laney turned to Hap again. "She apologizes for not arranging transportation to the Neswar, but she felt you might be more comfortable walking."

Laney's way of speaking seemed as offbeat as a heart murmur to Hap. Laney hadn't once been polite when she said stuff. She was more often blunt. Weird. And Laney only seemed to speak to Hap and Gygak. The others nodded with understanding before Laney had the first word out.

They entered the Neswar through the hole.

Hap had seen *Mary Poppins* a lot when he was younger because his little sister wouldn't watch anything else. He'd loved the carpet bag—something that looked small from the outside, but inside fit anything and everything. He'd once written a short story for English class where he jumped into the carpet bag and found a whole new world inside with cars and traffic lights and, well . . . he never turned it in. Guys his age shouldn't admit to liking carpet bags.

Orissa's Neswar was like that carpet bag, though. There weren't cars or traffic lights or anything, but Hap had entered an entirely different world. He looked back from where they had come and was amazed at the difference. It looked pretty insignificant on the outside, but inside was another thing entirely. Hap scrubbed his hand through his hair, grateful for the cool air inside the Neswar—grateful, terrified, and . . . excited.

Orissa's Neswar hid a huge city inside its walls. The internal walls were all polished to a shining white, and lights embedded in the walls sparkled like interior stars. The entire place hummed as Rissans moved from one place to another in the soft light, their wings twitching and fluttering. The opening led into a wide courtyard of sorts with doors running along all sides.

"This is their core—the place where they gather for school and work. The personal quarters are on higher levels," Laney explained, as though she'd been transformed into a tour guide.

"It's like a really cool mall," Tara whispered.

"Or . . . not," Hap whispered back. Okay, he did think it was pretty cool in the weirdest way possible, but certainly not like a *mall*. Only a girl would compare something cool to something so lame. Tara stayed close and Hap was glad. If things got really creepy, he'd need to grab her and run. But run where? Would Nana take off with just them? Could Nana fly herself? He knew *he* couldn't fly a spaceship no matter how many movies he saw or how many times he read *Schlock Mercenary*.

Several of the tall bug people surrounded Laney. Svarta backed away to allow Laney room.

Laney swiveled her head so much that it looked like all the tall bug people were talking to her at once even though no one said anything.

Mind control. Hap knew it. They were all under mind control—well, everyone except him and maybe not Gygak either. He'd seen nearly every episode of *The Twilight Zone* and every episode of *The X-Files* in his grandpa's video library at least three times each. Hap knew about mind control.

Svarta disappeared for the short while that Laney nodded and did whatever she was doing with the bug people. Svarta looked suspicious when she came back. She walked with an overexcited bounce to her step. Hap pretended to ignore her but leaned in as she whispered to Laney, "The Hira is with the scientist. He wants to see us as soon as possible."

"We need to pay our respects to the queen or they won't let us anywhere near him *or* the Hira again."

Svarta nodded, hiding any emotion her eyes might have given away under her hair. Laney seemed to be hiding behind her calm and icy exterior, but Hap saw her eyes flicker with hope. Was she making the delivery to this scientist guy? Was *this* the delivery Tolvan warned Grandpa Hazzard about? And if they made the delivery, did he lose any chance he might have had to find a way to save his dad?

Gygak leaned toward the sisters as though trying to eavesdrop as well, but from the way his forehead wrinkled around his nostrils, he looked irritated, which meant he hadn't heard a thing.

"Let's get to it, then, but let's drop off the tagalongs first." Svarta flipped her head so her black pigtails streamed down her back.

"We'll take you to your rooms now," Laney said, as Svarta stepped aside, letting Laney go first. Elriss turned her head to look at Hap when he watched them all walk down the wide middle of the hallway. "I'm coming," he said and shuffled along behind them.

Hap peeked into the various spaces as they passed and felt surprised to see the variety of tall buggy people. They all wore long robes of all kinds of colors, and hats with veils. No two outfits were the same.

And no two rooms were the same. Many of the double doors stood ajar, allowing Hap to peek inside. One had what Laney called a multi-D display where the entire room was little more than twinkling lights surrounding colorful balls. Another room had several vendors selling what might have been food. It looked like a food court, only Hap didn't see pizza or anything else that looked familiar. His stomach rumbled with the thought of food. Another room was shelved like a library, but instead of books he saw thin, square plates of metal lining the shelves. Hap stretched his neck to see in farther and spotted a Rissan with a plate on the table in front of her. Above the plate, little figures glowed like a 3-D movie. He stretched his neck more and spied several other Rissans with plates and glowing figures in front of them too.

"It's their library. That's where their students go for study," Laney explained as she caught Hap by the scruff of the neck to drag him along so he didn't fall behind.

One room held a bunch of small Rissan girls turning and twisting around in time to a complex mix of noises made by some male Rissans standing in the center of them. "It's like ballet . . ." Laney murmured. It didn't look anything like the ballet recitals he'd had to sit through when his sister, Alison, decided to be a famous dancer.

Hap stared with open astonishment into another room where smaller female and male Rissans alike seemed to be pummeling each other.

"What are they doing?" Hap thought it odd that such dignified creatures were beating each other up.

"It's their version of wrestling. Everyone needs exercise. And it keeps them strong in case they are attacked."

"Oh. Attacked?"

"The Circle is in a state of political unrest right now. They've been preparing for attack for a long time. The Serviens want the Neswar back. The Rissans don't want to give it back. It's a holy war for them, but not for Nova, who's funding the Serviens."

Elriss began moving her arms and pointing to various things as they passed. Everyone bobbed their heads like chickens when she pointed, which irritated Hap to be left out of the conversation. Not that he wanted Elriss in his head again, but he felt Laney could spend more time translating.

They stopped for a long while in front of some sort of painting spanning the length of an entire wall. Finally, after Hap's legs had gone numb and he didn't think his companions were ever going to stop nodding and smiling at each other, Laney bowed her head to Elriss in what looked like a bow to royalty. *She's just a tall bug,* he thought sourly.

Tara fell back to walk with Hap. She exploded into huge smiles. "That was awesome! That was just beautiful . . . I hardly thought I'd be able to keep myself from floating out the window. Their whole history is just . . . amazing!"

As Tara mentioned her feeling of being able to float, Hap noticed that Tremble actually *was* floating.

"How exactly is having a bug invade your personal privacy beautiful?" Hap asked Tara, ignoring the fact that Tremble really could float. He'd thought she'd just been kidding around when she'd said she could.

"You didn't feel it?" Tara stared at Hap like he was the one with four arms or wings or like he was floating a foot off the ground.

Laney interrupted. "He closed his mind to her. The Rissans never stay where they are not welcome. So she left his mind."

"Why would you do that?" Tara seemed unable to believe that Hap would push Elriss out on purpose.

"She has no business in my head. It's my head and if I want to think something, I should be able to think it without anyone *bugging* me." He emphasized the word *bugging* in the hopes that Tara would realize how weird it was for her to accept this little bug meeting.

Laney rolled her eyes at Hap. Svarta snorted. "They aren't trying to invade your mind. It's just how they communicate. They are a species advanced far beyond humans. Their communications are instantaneous. They empathize with everyone they meet because they are able to put themselves into every other person's situation. That's how she described her history to us in a way we could understand. That's why it's beautiful."

"I don't like other people in my head." He pointed at Tremble floating happily along. "She might be used to schizophrenia, but I'm not."

Tremble dropped to her feet with a thump. Gygak wheezed what sounded like a snicker from his nostrils.

Laney shot her hand out to gently pull Tremble away from Hap. "Don't let him destroy your euphoria, Tremble."

Svarta snorted again. "Yeah. He's just jealous because he couldn't handle the experience."

"I could too," Hap grumbled under his breath. "I just didn't want to."

Hap looked back toward the painting, feeling a whole lot of annoyance. Had he just chickened out of something cool? He looked at Tara, who'd gone from scowling at Hap back to looking excited.

Hap sighed. Traveling to another planet wasn't as cool as he thought it should be.

It felt just like middle school.

13. STONEHENGE

HAP WANTED TO GO HOME and tell his grandpa that aliens were lame and totally not worth the mental energy it took to think about them. He wanted to make sure his dad was still okay.

"I want to call home," Hap said.

Laney hesitated. "Okay." She shared a look with Svarta that didn't convey very much, since Svarta's eyes were always covered by her bangs. "We'll take care of that back at the ship. But we're staying here tonight. Queen Kennriss has offered us last meal and a room to sleep. Beats protein rations and Nana's cramped beds any day."

"Does the call not work from a planet? Do you have to be on the ship in outer space to make the call?"

Laney hesitated. Svarta looked away altogether, fiddling with the utility belt hanging at her waist. Gygak jumped in as though he were some hero saving the day. "Not at all. Planetside links are actually cheaper to make than shipside links. The whole known universe always talks about the incredible advancement of the Rissan people, so they definitely have link capability."

Laney interrupted while slicing Gygak to ribbons with her glare. "Queen Kennriss has been more than hospitable. I don't think we should skid all over her kindness by bothering her with link requests. It would look rude. We'll do it from the ship."

"Right. And how would it look when she asked you to pay and you didn't have the credits to cover it?" Gygak grinned, showing too many of his crooked teeth. He had both sets of arms crossed in front of him. Hap wasn't an expert on alien body language, but right then Gygak looked like his dad when he thought he'd won an argument with Hap's mom. He looked smug. Hap wondered if he should tell Gygak that whenever his dad got that look, nothing but trouble followed.

Laney's icy stare could have frozen a volcano to silent inactivity. "I will not disrupt the queen with such requests. If you want to ask her, feel free to do so, Gygak. We all know how well she likes you."

Gygak's smile slipped into a grimace, but he didn't say anything else.

Hap didn't necessarily like Gygak—so it wasn't like he cared that Laney shut him up. But Hap did care that shutting up Gygak meant no one would stand up for him and Tara.

"You'll sleep here." Laney had taken on that polite hostess tone again. She spoke for Elriss. They'd already dropped off Tara and Tremble a few doors down. Laney looked in at her room but continued on with Hap, Mosh, and Gygak. Hap's room was wedged between Laney's and Svarta's. Hap wondered if Laney meant to keep an eye on him.

He acted as though he'd closed the door but lurked in his doorway, leaving the door ajar just enough that he could see out. Hap watched Mosh lumber into his room.

Gygak stopped before following Mosh and turned to ask, "Where are you two going?"

"To visit the queen." Svarta grinned wickedly. "Wanna come?"

"No." He rolled his shoulders as though getting ready for a boxing match. "A rumor back at ICE is floating around that the Rissans are hiding the last scientist. Do you know anything about that?"

Svarta jabbed a long finger at Gygak's chest. "Making accusations, Gy-*geek*?"

Gygak spread his four arms out wide in innocence, looking anything *but* innocent. "Not at all. If for some reason he was here and you tried to get him to help you, you'd likely be dead before the end of the rotation. You shouldn't push your luck is all I'm saying."

Svarta used the heel of her hand to shove Gygak into his room. "Don't you push yours."

Gygak took a brave step back into the hall. "If Nova hears you're *here* with the Hira, he'll have you steamed faster than a scourab beetle multiplies."

Svarta flicked Gygak in the forehead above his nostrils with a laugh. "Get ahold of your little-man syndrome, Gy-geek. The scientists aren't here. They're all dead. No one's using the Hira without them."

She turned and strutted away, her boots clicking along the smoothly polished floor. Gygak stood in the corridor, glaring at Svarta's back.

Hap frowned. Svarta had told Laney back in the courtyard they were going to meet the scientist after they met the queen. She had just lied to Gygak.

Laney raised her eyebrows at Gygak and cocked her head to the side.

"All right. Whatever." Gygak disappeared into his room. Once his door closed, Laney nodded to Elriss. Elriss nodded back and with her mouth in a grim line of determination, she fluttered down the corridor. She returned almost as quickly as she'd left, two Rissan men following behind her. They took up what looked to be guard duty at Gygak's door.

Laney nodded her approval to the new guards and turned to meet up with Svarta. "No need for spying, Hap," she said as she passed his door.

Hap jumped at her voice and stammered as he tried to come up with a logical excuse for why he was spying. "I'm not," was all he came up with.

"Don't make those guards look over your shoulder too. Go get cleaned up. I'll be by soon to get you for last meal."

She closed his door for him. Hap didn't much like the sound of "last meal," even if he was hungry. It had the sound of imminent doom. He quashed his impulse to throw open the door, grab Tara, and start searching for the Hira and any secret it might hold for saving his dad. The guards outside guaranteed he wouldn't get that far.

With a sigh, Hap turned to see his room, which at the moment felt more like a prison. The bed looked like a huge pillow right on the ground.

Silky pillows of every possible color adorned the bed along with a variety of furry blankets. A table sat in the corner with a large basin. Hap peeked into the bowl. A ring of tiny stone pillars encircled a second set of stone pillars in the shape of a horseshoe. The whole miniature stone ensemble was positioned in the basin in a way that looked like some Stonehenge model. Hap looked for handles to turn on water but found none readily evident.

"Grandpa would love this," Hap said aloud. "Stonehenge in a bowl . . ."

Closer to the sides of the bowl sat several smaller singular stones spaced at random places . . . seeming to have nothing to do with the rest. Hap picked up one of the singular rocks—or rather he *tried* to pick one up. He could lift it an inch or so from the bottom of the basin, but the rock seemed to reach out and pull itself back like a magnet. Hap yanked harder, determined to make the rock let go, but the harder Hap pulled, the harder the rock pulled back, until Hap's knuckles slammed into the stone, burning the skin off, so little spots of blood remained when Hap lifted his hand to shake it.

He didn't know why he always shook his hand when he hurt it. It only made him look stupid and never made it hurt less. But he still shook his hand and danced around until the initial shock of pain dulled to a throb.

Hap glared at the rock then pushed at it with the heel of his hand. When he shoved one rock, they all moved over one place. Outside the circle of pillars, a secondary circle of small holes appeared in the basin. Water flowed through these holes, filling the basin.

Cool, he thought. *I figured out how to work the faucet.* He felt pretty smug until he realized the water didn't stop when it reached the rim of the basin.

Water ran over the sides and over the table, slapping the stone floor in a steady stream.

"Holy Houdini! Just stop already!" Hap thrust his hand into the water to try to make the stones move back. They wouldn't budge. He may as well have been shoving against a mountain for all the good it did him. Water sloshed over his jeans and over the front of his shirt as he tried to catch it in his hands and pour it back into the basin.

"Holy stinking Houdini!" Hap hurried to the window, figuring he could start bailing the place out. He shoved the brightly colored curtains aside to open the window and growled when he bumped the side of his hand against the stone wall. He let loose another growl when he found a stained-glass window that didn't open. With a frustrated yell, Hap ran back to the cistern and noticed several things.

The light from the window fell onto the bowl, giving the water a golden sheen on top, but the water's surface glowed as though lit from underneath as well. Each of the individual stones glowed a bright electric blue. He sucked on the side of his fist and stared into the water in awe.

Water still dripped to the floor in a remnant echo of the chaos, but no more water came out. With his unwounded hand, he reached out to touch the light on the water.

A stinging zip arced through his fingertips and up his arm . . . like the time Nathan Davenport from down the street where he lived had dared him to put his finger in a lightbulb socket. That was the day that he and Nathan became determined enemies.

The water rippled its blue-gold light as though laughing at him for being dumb enough to try to touch it.

His pants stuck to his legs in that horrible itchy way wet jeans were prone to do. Hap grumbled and went to the window, the sliced flaps of his jeans slapping cold and wet against his leg. It had to open. What was the point of a window that didn't open?

Hap couldn't find any latches. The stained glass had a blurry image of the queen on her throne. Hap frowned and stepped farther from the glass to be able to make out the picture. If he tilted his head right, he could make out the image of a tiny stained-glass man standing in the corner. The man stood on a rectangle stone structure that looked like a part of Stonehenge.

In the man's hand was a triangle on top of a triangle.

Hap stepped back a little more to take the whole window in at once. The window itself was a big triangle. In the stone on both sides of the stained-glass pane were the same shapes and patterns that Hap had seen on the ship's control room wall. Hap moved closer to the window, touched his finger to the patterns and traced them.

"Interesting, aren't they?" The voice startled Hap enough that he tangled himself in the drapes as he tried to turn around to see who'd entered his room without permission.

14. The Scientist

Hap batted away the fabric until he freed himself enough to see a man standing just inside his room. He felt a degree of surprise that it was a man—a human man, and not some ten-legged, twelve-eyed alien standing in front of him. The man's brown skin contrasted with his perfect white teeth. His dark brown hair was cropped short. He wore pants of the same shiny blue fabric that Hap's pillows were made of. And he wore a shiny white shirt that billowed when he closed the distance between them.

"Trouble with the cistern?" the man said, but in a way that he seemed to be making a comment and not asking a question.

"You could say that." Hap's face grew warm when he remembered his clothes were soaked, and the room looked like it had experienced a monsoon.

The man walked a few steps closer to the puddles on the floor. "It's a marvelous replica of the Blue Stone Starport."

"It looks like Stonehenge in Europe." Hap had never seen Stonehenge up close—had, in fact, never left his own country before this insane ride into the universe—but his grandpa had posters of Stonehenge in his room. "On Earth," Hap added after a moment.

"Stonehenge? They gave the starport a new name?"

Hap shrugged.

"I would imagine it is no longer in use. I've been told my home planet stays rooted to its spot. No one there takes to the stars any longer."

"Your home planet?"

"And yours, I've been told."

"You're from Earth?" Hap wanted to shout for joy and break down crying all at the same time. Someone from Earth, someone who might know how to help him and Tara.

"It was . . . a long time ago."

Hap had a million questions, questions about how to get home, how to contact home, how to— "Wait a minute. Did you say no one takes to the stars? Are you saying they used to?"

"Of course. Interstellar travel was a great benefit to mankind. At least until the days of the blind, before the fall of technology."

Hap blinked. *The days of the blind? The fall of technology?* "Umm . . . okay . . . So you're one of those guys who believes *aliens* helped build the pyramids?" Hap couldn't help but smirk. He'd heard enough late-night coast-to-coast radio shows that he knew about the conspiracy theories and weird urban legends.

"Absolutely not."

Hap was surprised until the man continued. "They offered help. But the Egyptians flatly refused. They insisted they knew well enough how to build their own cities." The man shook his head and smiled ruefully as though turning down alien help had been a huge mistake on the Egyptians' part.

"And you know this because . . ."

"I attended the building council the day the Egyptians were offered help on repairs. They declined help with that too. Prideful people. It's a shame. The Sphinx would never have lost her nose if those stubborn Egyptians would have just listened to a few design modifications."

"That would make you like, what . . . a gazillion years old?"

"Yes. It would make me old, indeed, from certain perspectives. Were I to return to my home, I would weep for the millennia lost and marvel at my homeland's future."

Hap stared hard at the man. "You're . . . you're the—"

"I am Amar. The last of the unknown." The man's eyes misted over, but he cleared his throat and took a deep breath.

Blood rushed past Hap's ears as his heart rate went up. Laney took the Hira to deliver to someone . . . the scientist. Tolvan told Grandpa Hazzard that the person Laney stole the Hira for would bring danger to the *trust* and *ICE*. Hap stood in a room with the man Tolvan feared. Hap gulped and took a step back.

"But that was like . . . *thousands* of years ago. You should look like a zombie." Hap would have taken another step away except the window pressed against his back and there was nowhere left to go.

"Chronology. Humans always worry about chronology. Space travel slows some things down. To me your thousands of years have been an eyeblink. Were I to return, my family would lie low in the dust. Mountains can be raised and leveled in a moment when given the proper circumstances."

Hap shook his head, not at all understanding the nonsense. He wondered if his implant was broken.

"The Rissan tell of you, Hap. They say you are closed minded." Amar squinted as though trying to see into Hap's mind.

Hap scowled and looked away. *I am not closed minded!* He fiddled with the drapes without responding.

"Do not feel shame. Many choose to close their minds to the Rissans. It is a hard thing to control thoughts enough to feel comfortable with others listening in."

"I can control my thoughts. I just like them being my own." He felt stupid standing there in wet, ripped jeans.

Seeming to sense this, the scientist backed away and moved toward the Stonehenge model. "The Rissans made this as a gift for me, as it replicates the last moment I stood on my homeworld's soil."

"Am I in your room?" It would be just Hap's luck to have to share a room with the guy dangerous enough to make his grandpa worry.

"On occasion. I . . . am inclined to move from time to time. I seldom stay here for very long. I only recently arrived to help prepare the Rissans for battle against the Serviens."

"Why do you have to help them?"

"I am responsible for their troubles. Men of honor repair what they have broken."

Hap moved over to where the scientist stood by the cistern.

The replica looked newer and better designed than the broken ruins in Grandpa Hazzard's pictures. Hap wished he could figure out how to take the replica home with him. Grandpa would love it. "A spaceport, huh?" Hap snorted in open disbelief.

The man looked offended. "Of course. When solar energy fills the stones, the aqueduct floods with water. The energy from each of the stones carries through the water to the next stone, creating a circuit that allows the water to hold the energy. The energy allows certain types of starships to land safely on the roundabout." The man's eyebrows bunched in the center of his forehead over his deep-set eyes, which made him look seriously put out that no one knew this simple information.

"Right." Hap shrugged. "It's one thing to move little rocks around, another thing entirely to move the real ones."

Amar laughed. "They don't move in the actual starport. Imagine the instability of such a structure! The energy comes from the solar source. When I left, I had to use the Hira to falsify the solar energy to make it work."

"Then why doesn't it work anymore when the sun hits it?"

"Perhaps the stones were moved to break the circuit; whether on purpose or by simple erosion, I could not say. I have not been there for quite some time."

Hap shifted from foot to foot, his pants sticking to him and his mind grasping for ways to get information from Amar without making Amar suspicious that Hap knew anything.

The problem was, Hap *didn't* know anything.

They both stood in an uncomfortable silence. Well . . . uncomfortable for *Hap,* anyway. Amar seemed fine to stand there and do nothing.

But Amar wasn't looking at Hap anymore. His eyes were focused on the window and the etchings in the rock wall. He moved to the window until he stood in front of it. The multicolored stained glass threw a pattern of color onto the man's face that shifted as he moved. "Do you like to read?"

Hap shrugged. He liked reading comic books. And he loved the idea of audio books for when his family went on road trips. It kept his sister from whining about the fact that his parents refused to allow a DVD player in the car.

"Marvelous how a simple window can tell a story."

Hap looked at the window again. Was there a story there? As his eyes flitted from one picture to the next, he could sort of see a story.

Amar and Hap stood in silence a little longer, looking at the picture.

"Are you really the last scientist?" Hap asked.

"That depends a great deal on how you perceive life." He smiled and gave a slight bow. "It is good to make your acquaintance." Amar stuck out his hand. Hap hesitated, wondering if it would be like shaking hands with the devil to shake hands with Laney's delivery guy. Hap finally stuck his hand out too, but instead of shaking hands, Amar gripped Hap's arm. "I am honored." Amar didn't let go of Hap's arm. "Do you know why you're here?"

Hap shrugged. He'd determined it was Gygak's fault for trying to drop the crate. "Laney said it was an accident." Hap shrugged again. He shrugged a lot when talking to adults. It spared him from having to feel stupid when he gave the wrong answer. And from experience, he knew he was prone to giving wrong answers.

Amar chuckled and his dark eyes flashed as he tilted his head. "Accidental . . . Hap Hazzard, pricking your finger on a thorn while plucking a rose is accidental. Landing on a planet outside your known sphere to meet with a human from your home world is far more providential than accidental. Wouldn't you say?"

Hap shrugged a third time. It was the best answer he could think of. He was pretty sure Amar wanted him to agree, and if Amar was dangerous, it seemed wise to agree, but everything that had happened seemed like one huge, blundering accident. Providence was the capital of Rhode Island, not a manager of daily events in Hap's life.

"The water on the floor and soaking to your skin is accidental. But even this small accident may have purpose in your future."

"Yeah. It means my legs are going to get a rash from wearing wet jeans."

Amar smiled. "You are a clever boy. Look around and see if you can find an alternate option to your wardrobe." Amar released his arm and strode to the door.

Hap watched. As Amar reached for the handle, he asked, "Do you really know all the secrets to the universe?"

It was Amar's turn to shrug. "It is a big universe, Hap Hazzard." He pulled the door open and left without any further explanation.

"That's what people keep telling me," Hap grumbled. He stared at the stained-glass window a little longer before deciding it was worth it to snoop around the room if it meant finding something else to wear.

He searched until he found a little drawer tucked into a desk. The drawer held several items of clothing, one of which was a pair of pants like Amar's. These were bright green instead of blue, but Hap didn't care if his red hair and green pants made him look like a leprechaun; his own pants needed to dry out, and that wouldn't happen very fast if he didn't get them off.

Hap tugged the green pants on and cinched them at his waist, reminding him of the hospital pants he wore when they took his appendix out. He raked his fingers through his hair then sat on the big mattress on the floor that made up his bed and stared at the green pants. The kids from school would be laughing their heads off if they saw Hap dressed in silky green PJ bottoms. Hap had to admit, he felt like laughing at himself. He'd taken a long time to hit a decent growth spurt, and "leprechaun" was the name bullies liked to use for him—another reason why Hap *never* wore green.

But as dumb as he felt, at least he didn't feel like he'd wet his pants, and these weren't ripped up to the knee.

The last scientist . . . Hap thought hard to remember the exact words Tolvan said to Grandpa Hazzard before everything in Hap's life fell to pieces. *She has the pyramid. Once she delivers it, he'll search for the books. The trust is in danger.* "She's already delivered it, Grandpa," Hap said aloud. He stiffened, wondering if Amar had recording devices in his room. *Idiot!* He chastised himself for talking aloud and chastised himself even more for sitting around messing with sinks that looked like Stonehenge when there was a crystal pyramid to rescue and a way home to find.

Hap got up, ignoring the way the silky pants swished with the movement. He grabbed his jacket, tied the arms around his waist in a last-ditch effort to take attention off the green pants, and opened his door to peek out. The guards still hovered around Gygak and Mosh's door.

They literally *hovered.* Their wings seemed like vibrating guitar strings, moving so fast they blurred. They were looking at each other intently as though having a staring contest. Laney exited her room with Svarta. Hap hurried to ease his door closed enough that he could peek out but make the door still look closed. Laney didn't look his way, but Svarta turned her head his direction. He ducked back and waited several moments before peeking again. The hallway was clear.

The guards still stood by Gygak's room, but they now had their backs to Hap.

Hap slipped out his door and down to Tara's room. In his rush he tripped over the hem of his silky green pants and slammed into the stone wall. He fell farther than he should have since the wall split into a nook. Hap barely caught himself from landing on his backside. The sound echoed in a dull thud down the corridor. Hap turned back and his stomach sank into his toes. The guards had heard him.

15. Last Meal

HAP PRESSED HIMSELF DEEPER INTO the nook, which he realized he shared with a funky sort of statue. It reminded him of the modern art he'd seen at an art museum in New York when he went to a magic trade show with his parents. It was ugly, both the modern art in New York and the statue he now hid behind. He scraped the top of his head against the sharp corner jutting out of the statue. He clenched back a cry of pain. The guards flitted by, the maroon and orange robes swishing past Hap's hiding place. He felt a tingle in his mind and heard the beginning of a buzz, but the sound and feeling left as soon as the guards were past.

Hap stayed until the place in between his shoulder blades cramped from twisting himself sideways. He tried to duck, but there wasn't any room, so he had to scrape his head again in order to get out. Blood trickled a path through his hair and down his left ear.

He peeked out but couldn't see anyone. Hap bolted for Tara's door.

He didn't knock, fearing the two guards' return.

When Tara leaped to her feet and opened her mouth as though she planned on yelling at him loud enough to wake up the next galaxy, Hap bounded across the room and covered her mouth with his hand.

"SSSHH! You'll get us in trouble!" He kept his hand there until she calmed down. When he removed it, she slugged his arm.

Hap didn't care what people said about girls. A girl could throw a nasty punch. Girls had those little hands with those little knuckles that felt like daggers cutting between the muscles. He gritted his teeth to avoid rubbing the sore spot. If he rubbed it, he'd only be giving her the satisfaction of knowing she'd hurt him.

"Don't stick your hands over my mouth." She had her arms crossed over her chest. "How do I know when you washed them last?"

"What makes you think I wash them at all?"

She snorted. "Didn't your parents teach you to knock? And what did you do to your head?"

Hap ran his hand over his ear and through his hair. When he pulled it away, his fingers had a sticky sheen of blood covering them. The scrape stung a little still, but he had more important things to worry about. "It's nothing. I just hit it is all. And nobody knocks when they're doing top-secret work."

"What secret work? Are you trying to get us into trouble again?"

"I want to call my family. You want to call your family. I'm pretty sure Laney's broke, and there's no way she can afford to let us call long distance. Plus she's a kidnapper, a robber, and likely a terrorist."

"Faith and begorrah! And you've found a pot of gold to help us make the call?" She flipped her blonde hair over her shoulder and smirked at his green pants. Her accent didn't sound Irish at all.

Nice. Leprechaun jokes.

He took a deep breath, determined to ignore it.

"I think that crystal thing can make the call. I think if we find out where they're keeping it and just go use it, we can contact our families . . . both of us. Then we can take it and hide out somewhere while we wait for rescue." He didn't mention he hoped it might save his dad's life.

"What makes you think the Hira can do this?" She stopped glaring and uncrossed her arms. She clicked her fingernails, chewed on her lip, and for the first time since Hap greeted her in front of Hazzard's Magical Happenings, she looked interested in what Hap had to say.

"I have this window in my room." He described the story in his stained-glass window. "And I think the crystal can be used to call other people. I think that's how Amar—the last scientist—called the Rissan queen to come and get him."

"But Laney didn't say anything about using the Hira for that."

"I don't think she knows. But the scientist knows. And we're smart—well, you're smart. I can find the crystal, and you can figure out how to make it work. We can let our families know we're okay. We can call and get someone to rescue us."

"They'll never let us near it." Tara stopped clicking her nails, seeming to be defeated.

"That's why we're not asking." Hap tightened the jacket sleeves around his waist.

He turned to lead the way out of her room at the same time Tremble walked in.

Hap halted. Tara grumbled, "Doesn't anyone knock?" But she didn't say it loud enough for Tremble to hear. Hap suspected Tara feared Tremble as much as he did—which was a lot. Nothing in the universe was as scary as a mentally unstable nice person.

"It's time for last meal."

Hap's stomach growled at the mention of food, even if it did put off his plans a little. They had to eat. And someone stood in front of them offering food. Operation "Call Home and Get Rescued" could wait a little bit longer.

Tremble hovered over the ground and glided along in front of Hap and Tara. Tara kept casting guilty looks at Hap, who wished he could erase those looks so she didn't give away any of their plans.

They entered into a tall arched doorway completely covered by a gauzy curtain. Tremble eased the gauze to the side to reveal a small room with a long table in its center surrounded by backless stools.

Amar sat at the end of the table while some Rissan lady sat at the head. Laney and Svarta sat between them. Mosh and Gygak were nowhere to be seen.

Everyone turned to stare as Tremble entered with Hap and Tara in tow.

Svarta grinned. "Into Gaelic mythology, huh?"

"What?" Hap asked, trying to read what her smile could mean. He didn't approve of her bangs-covered eyes. Reading someone's body language proved impossible without the added benefit of seeing into their eyes.

"She's talking about your clothes," Tara said behind him.

"Oh." He glared at her. Another leprechaun joke. Not only did he feel absolute irritation in her making a joke but felt doubly stupid for needing Tara to translate it for him. How was it possible that an alien planet on the other side of the universe felt like junior high?

Hap determined to ignore Svarta when his stomach grumbled again at the scent of food. He hoped this would be an all-you-can-eat meal, since he could eat a whole lot. The nutty paste from that afternoon had done little in the way of quieting the growling in his gut.

Amar stood to welcome them. No one else stood.

Once everyone settled, Rissan workers served the food on clay plates that were painted as brightly as the clothing the Rissan people wore.

And on the plates were . . . well . . . Hap had no idea what lay on the plates.

He stared in front of him. The thing steaming on his bright pink plate looked like some sort of skinned squirrel. He swallowed down his disgust when he realized that it stared back at him through dead, blackened eyes.

Hap had never faced his meal eye-to-eye before.

He gulped, missing home more than ever. His mom had planned chicken cordon bleu—his favorite—for the Sunday meal. He wondered if it was Sunday already at home, or if Sunday had passed by and the school week had already begun. Would his friends miss him? Would they make a memorial for him where they'd all drop off flowers and burn candles? Were they even in school, or were they all out scouring the mountains trying to find any hint of him and Tara? Did news of his disappearance make his father sicker?

Hap had to get home.

Tara's tense body next to him made Hap feel better. At least he wasn't the only one not interested in eating something that stared back at you.

Everyone else had no trouble picking up their two-pronged forks and picking apart the meat. Hap grimaced and slowly picked up his fork. He plunged the prongs into his food. The meat fell off the bones almost as soon as he touched it. With a shudder, he closed his eyes as he brought it to his lips. If he couldn't see the thing watching him through those coal-black eyes, maybe it wouldn't bother him.

His taste buds accepted the salty, savory flavor, but as the meat made its way to the back of his throat, his mind overpowered his taste buds and his gag reflex kicked in.

Hap forced his throat to swallow and he tried to keep his desire to puke it all back up quiet, but Tara snickered next to him.

"At least *I* tried it," he said under his breath. She stopped laughing and stared at her own meal.

Indicating she understood the challenge in his voice, she straightened her back and steeled herself to eat the thing with eyes.

She took a deep breath and shoved a forkful into her mouth. Swallowing hard, she grabbed the red clay cup and took several gulps of the water.

Hap's chuckle was met by Tara's elbow in his ribs. Food was food, and since Svarta and Laney ate without hesitation, it wouldn't kill him to follow their example. He ate most of Rocky the Squirrel, though he avoided the head and hoped the second course wasn't Bullwinkle the Moose. The water tasted like he was sucking on pennies, but he was really thirsty and so ignored that too.

The second course was worse. Thick brown bamboo-like branches sagged over the sides of a blue plate. The server placed a branch in front of Hap.

He looked at Tara, who shrugged and looked toward the front of the table to see what everyone else did with the branches.

The Rissan at the head of the table grabbed a branch and snapped it in half. She put the open end into her mouth and sucked out the contents. The slurping and sucking sounds elicited a groan from Tara.

Feeling a little uncertain, Hap picked up his branch and snapped it in half. Breaking the branch wasn't as easy as the queen made it look. His muscles trembled under the strain of breaking it open. It felt and looked, in a weird way, like a crab leg. There were no eyes and Hap liked crab well enough to give it a try. The rubbery meat made his teeth bounce as he tried to chew, but not in any worse way than the time he'd been dared to eat escargot at his cousin's wedding dinner.

Tara wrinkled her nose at the branch critter on her plate and pushed it farther from her. She'd finished most of the thing with eyes but apparently had eaten enough exotic food for one night.

Hap started in on the other side of the branch when Amar spoke up. He raised his voice loud enough to be heard by everyone sitting at the table but quiet enough to tell a secret.

"You wish for me to use the Hira for your gain, yet you plan on removing it from me in just over one rotation." Amar spoke to Laney, but Hap believed that Amar directed the rebuke in his tone to all of them.

"I'm under contract. I keep my word." Laney's icy tone made deep space look like a tropical paradise.

"It will not be used honorably—or wisely."

Svarta hurried to Laney's defense. "We just need to use it to find our father. That's certainly honorable! He's been missing for eighteen years. Do you have any idea how desperate we are to find him?"

Amar's eyes brimmed with sympathy. "Do you not feel any obligation to the society he sought to protect?"

Laney's jaw worked. "ICE betrayed him! I owe them nothing! They owe me my father! All I have left of him is a ship I can't even afford to fly."

"Your alliance with Nova and the people he works for would shame your father."

"Do you think ICE is right? Do you think they should hold an entire world back from knowing about space travel and the rest of the universe?" Svarta ran her hand over her bangs, pushing them back so her eyes were completely visible. She must have been hot, because her damp hair stayed back. She looked furious.

Amar didn't react to her fury. He maintained his calm. "Earth was once a part of the universal communities. They made a collective choice to isolate themselves. The universe respects their choice. You should as well."

"That choice was made by people dead and gone. Shouldn't it be put to another vote?" Svarta asked.

"Earth is no longer my home. The society of ICE who rules there now is not my concern. My concern is that life in the universe continues."

"And my concern," Laney said, "is finding my father. Please help me use the Hira to find him. What happens with the Hira after that isn't our business." No one ate anymore. All eyes and ears zoned in on the conversation in the middle of the room.

"The welfare of sentient society is everyone's business."

"*Our business* is our business," Laney said. "I do what I'm paid to do."

Amar slapped his two-pronged fork onto his plate. "So the balance of life hangs on whether or not Elaine Sanchez profits?"

Laney flinched. He understood her flinching—or *thought* he did. He hated when people used his real name too. "I need the credits to get to my father. I'm on empty. I don't even have enough to leave this plan—" She cut off her own sentence, as if just barely realizing that Hap and Tara listened—realizing she'd promised them a very expensive call home . . . promised them a *way* home.

The Rissan stood, her wings fluttering in what seemed to be agitation. Hap felt the briefest touch of buzz on his mind before Amar also stood. "You are absolutely right. We should convene this conversation elsewhere." He turned to Hap and Tara. "Hap Hazzard, you and your companion are welcome to continue last meal. We will send an escort to take you back to your rooms soon." He nodded to Tara and followed the Rissan. Laney, Svarta, and Tremble trailed after them until only Hap and Tara remained.

Hap waited a full minute before jumping to his feet. "Let's go!" He started for the door.

She grabbed his shoulder to stop him. "Do you think we should?"

"I don't think we shouldn't. You heard them. Laney's making the delivery. She's apparently trying to profit off of it too with someone else, or Amar wouldn't be mad. Not only that, but think, Tara. If Laney can't afford something as simple as a call, how is she going to afford to get us home? I bet it takes tons of fuel to fly Nana. Laney said it herself, or she would have if we hadn't been there. She said she doesn't even have enough to leave the planet. That means we're *stuck* here. Let's just get it and figure out how to use it. My grandpa can come get us."

"We're going to get into trouble." Her nails were clicking again.

"Not if we don't get caught."

She looked hesitant.

"C'mon, do you want your mom crying herself to sleep every night for the next several months or longer wondering if you're dead?" He felt like a creep putting it to her that way. But he imagined his mom and grandpa caring for his dying father. They did this last round of chemo, but no one expected different results from it. His dad said after this one, he wouldn't do any more—no matter the results. He'd been so sick when Hap had left for the magic store. What if Hap didn't make it back in time to say good-bye?

He nodded sympathetically at Tara's horror-stricken face "I don't want your mom *or* my mom crying. Let's go do something to keep it from happening." He motioned for her to follow as he pulled open the door.

They both peeked out. There weren't any guards or escorts waiting for them in the empty hall. Not yet. He led the way, taking the first left.

"How do you know where we're going?" Tara asked.

"I don't. But when we got here, I saw the dragonfly people take it to the first level and go in the hole at the far left. We entered the one at the right. So if we head in that direction, we should eventually run into it."

"But these tunnels could run for miles."

"Not really. We entered on the front end and we walked to our rooms at the back. It wasn't that far. So really, it won't be that hard to find."

"Hap . . ."

Honestly, the girl worried more than any person he knew. Even his mom didn't worry the way Tara did. "I need to call my family, Tara. My grandpa will know what to do."

"You're basing all of this on an overheard conversation with some guy dressed for a circus. You don't know if your grandfather knows anything."

"Tolvan did not look like he was going to the circus. He looked like a magician. And okay, yeah—that's weird too, but I overheard a conversation that fits everything that's going on. Too many pieces fit for them to belong in a different puzzle." His dad always said that.

Tara closed her eyes and shook her head. She balled her hands into fists. Hap flinched when she opened her eyes, sure she planned on punching him. "Why would the magicians guild have anything to do with aliens? Have you asked yourself how stupid this all sounds?"

"The second we ended up beamed into a spaceship, everything that sounded stupid before has started to make sense. I'm going. You can make your own choice."

Hap was glad to hear her muttering as she followed close behind him. It meant that even though she thought the idea was lousy, she planned on going with him anyway. Hap thought about explaining magicians and how their guild had been around forever. They'd always kept secrets. So why wouldn't they know about aliens and keep that secret too? Before he could say any of this to Tara, heavy footfalls thumped along the hallway behind them, coming fast in their direction.

16. Books and Crystals

Hap hurried to round the bend and duck into a side room. They were back at the library with the rows of little metal plates lining the shelves. Hap scanned the room until he spotted a table with several backless chairs lined up next to it. He grabbed Tara's hand and dragged her to, and under, the table. She hesitated crawling in after him until she heard the footsteps just outside the door. She dove under, and they silently worked to space the chairs in front of them to block the view from the doorway. Tara pulled on the tablecloth so it hung lower and offered better protection.

Hap closed his eyes. *If only I could make us disappear.*

The footsteps stopped in front of the library. "There's no one there," Gygak's squawking voice declared. "You're hearing things again. C'mon, let's go." The footsteps faded away, and Hap remembered to breathe.

Tara shoved one of the chairs out of the way and crawled out from under the table. "Aren't those guys supposed to be guarded?" She ran her fingers through her hair and cast a nervous look around the library.

Hap headed toward the door but stopped as his gaze fell on something that caught his attention. "There's a book." He pointed to the corner where a thin leather book sat on a side table next to a chair that looked made for humans—a chair with a back.

"So?" Tara had already started toward the door and glanced out to see which way Mosh and Gygak had gone. "It's a library."

"There's only one book in this entire library."

Tara turned to see where Hap pointed. She shook her head before Hap had time to say what he thought the book might be. "It's not what you think it is," she said.

"How do you know?"

"Because it's in plain sight. Something that an emperor tried to hide thousands of years ago is going to be in a locked safe or buried somewhere only a secret map will lead to. They wouldn't leave it out where anyone could read it."

"But what if they did? What if the most obvious place is the one no one would think to look?"

"*We're* looking." Tara gave a sniff of disapproval.

"Yeah, but we didn't mean to." He walked over and snatched the book up.

Tara groaned but followed him. "Hey! Be careful with that. Old books are fragile."

Hap rolled his eyes and flipped the book open.

"I said be careful!"

Words filled every page of the book. But the symbols weren't recognizable. Hap bit back his disappointment. He didn't know what he'd expected to find inside the cover, but the scrawled words seemed a letdown, certainly not like he'd expected it to look.

But Tara was right. The chances of this being one of the nine lost books were astronomical. And what was the point of having a book in a different language anyway? Hap set the book down and shrugged. "Let's just find the Hira and call home."

Tara agreed and followed Hap back to the hallway. They made it twenty feet before Hap said, "But what if it *is* one of the scientists' books? There's a scientist here, and that looks like a chair made for humans. What if it *is* something dangerous? We should take it with us just in case. If we can't get the Hira out of here, then maybe we can destroy the book . . . you know, keep the scientist from using the Hira on the book and all that."

Tara frowned. "He doesn't seem like the bad guy you think he is . . ."

"Are you kidding me? The nice people are usually always the ones you gotta watch out for the most."

Her eyes continually scanned the hallways until she nodded in agreement.

Hap nodded along with her. "All I'm saying is that we don't know who to trust right now . . . let's not go burning any bridges."

They hurried back to the library.

Hap reached for the book, but Tara hurried to pick it up before he could.

"What?"

If she'd verbalized her eye rolling, the sentence would have contained the word *duh*. She hugged the book to her chest. "After the way you handled it before, I wouldn't trust you to carry it for two minutes. It's a very old book and might be the only one left in print. For all we know it's the only history book about this planet, and if we ruin it, we destroy a whole world's history."

Hap sketched a glance to the shelves of metal plates and doubted this would be the only copy of the planet's history, but he decided to humor Tara and let her hold it if it made her feel better. She carefully tucked it into the back of her pants and covered it up with her shirt.

Hap laughed. "You look like one of the kids I caught shoplifting at the magic store."

Tara didn't laugh. "I don't like taking this. I am *not* a thief. I'm only taking this because I'm afraid of what it might be."

"We'll mail it back to them if we find out it's nothing, okay?"

Tara narrowed her eyes and muttered something Hap was glad not to understand.

They went back to the door and looked around for several moments before determining the coast was clear.

They hadn't made it far before a loud buzzing broke into Hap's senses.

Tara halted, her eyes darting around trying to find the source of such an invasion of their minds. She looked panicked, which made Hap feel glad. At least this time she wasn't acting all happy over the beautiful presence invading her mind. "Close your mind!" Hap figured being closed minded was a good thing when one had secrets. Maybe these Rissan people were so boring, none of them had secrets.

"Something's wrong." She clicked her fingernails so hard and fast that Hap cringed. "There's panic and confusion . . ."

"Whatever's wrong hasn't got anything to do with us. Probably Laney and Amar are in some sort of argument."

"Do you think so?" She looked unconvinced.

Instead of answering, he grabbed her hand and pulled her along. Whatever the rest of the people around here were doing,

Hap and Tara weren't involved. They scampered toward where Hap remembered seeing the Rissans fly off with the crate. He led them to dead ends twice and had to backtrack a little to figure out where they were headed, but Tara didn't complain much. She was probably too scared to.

Hap was scared but pretended indifference, even though his heart thumped so loudly against his chest that he was sure everyone within ten miles could hear it. The white walls with the twinkling lights were eerie with no one else around.

The closer they moved toward the Hira, the farther off the buzzing seemed. Shouts seemed to come outside the Neswar. And every now and again, dull booms seemed to make the Neswar shudder, making the lights cast deranged shadows on the walls.

Hap halted at a place where the hallway split down two different directions. Tara breathed heavily behind him. He took the hallway to the right.

Tara asked, "Why this one?"

Hap shrugged. "My grandpa said when given a choice, you should always make the right one."

Tara snorted. "I think he meant morals, not directions."

"Yeah, well, whatever. I always choose the right; it makes it easier."

"You mean it makes it so you never have to make choices."

Hap hated it when people played psychologist with him. "No, I mean it's just easier. I can always remember which way I went 'cause I always go right. I don't get lost much."

She cleared her throat, clearly in reference to the fact that he'd been lost twice already today. He smiled and shrugged, not offering any apologies for getting lost.

Hap's pulse quickened as they arrived at a hallway that hummed.

He glanced around the corner, gasped, and pulled back.

"What?" The word was so silent from Tara's mouth that Hap felt the breath of it more than heard it.

When he shook his head and didn't answer, she scowled and pushed past him to see for herself. She hurried to back up and pressed herself tighter against Hap. "Do you think they're dead?" Her raspy whisper sounded like it held an avalanche of tears behind it.

Hap bobbled his head, not sure if he was nodding or shaking it. He peeked back around the corner and took several steps toward a door surrounded by Rissans lying on the ground. Their multicolored robes made them each look like funny, lumpy pillows scattered on the floor. Hap took several more steps and bent low to look at the Rissan man lying in front of the doorway. The man's chest rose and fell with rapid breathing.

Hap straightened and gave her a thumbs-up to indicate the Rissans weren't dead.

"What happened to them?"

"I don't know," Hap said, but then he squinted at the pale blue robes on the guard closest to him. A red needle stuck out from the guard's chest. Hap reached over and pulled it out, wincing as he did so.

"Sorry!" Tara said to the guard, even though he was unconscious. "Neubins? Here inside?" Tara's panic escalated as she scanned their surroundings.

"No." Confusion tumbled through Hap's mind. "No. Neubins would never make it up those stairs. Someone else did this."

Hap sidestepped the bodies to enter the room. Tara looked like she might stop him, but he'd already made it inside as she hurried to catch up.

"Oh!" Tara exclaimed. "It's beautiful!" She nodded toward the crystal then looked behind her toward the door. "But what happened to those guys out there?"

Hap wanted to sound confident, wanted to sound reassuring— after all, he'd led them to where bodies lay strewn across the floor. "Whatever happened to them, we can't worry about it. Let's just figure this thing out and get out of here."

The basketball-sized crystal pyramid sat on a dais of multicolored satin pillows. The room seemed to spin and twirl in color reflected from every facet of the crystal, though the crystal itself glowed white. Tara's blonde hair captured the light and reflected it too. She wrapped her arms around herself and grinned at Hap. "I feel like I just found the mines of the seven dwarves!"

"Yeah, well, for all the off-to-work they're doing, it seems pretty pathetic to have only one crystal to show for it. Besides, all the dwarves are sleeping on the job." He smirked, nodding back toward the door where the Rissans lay.

"That isn't funny."

"If it isn't funny, why are you smiling?" he asked.

She groaned, trying to erase the smile from her face. "I'm not smiling. But you're right. We should hurry and get out of here." She hesitated, making it obvious she didn't know what it was they should hurry to accomplish. She finally wandered over to the crystal, her hand hovering over one of the smooth facets without actually touching. "Didn't you think it would be bigger, with the crate being so big and weighing so much?"

Shelving lined the walls from the floor to the ceiling. Glass jars with stones in various colors stood neatly along every shelf.

Tara scowled at him when Hap went to pull a jar from the shelf. "They'll be missing us soon. We don't have time to mess with their stuff."

"What?" Hap reached out and pulled a jar down anyway. "Afraid the dwarves will wake up?"

"I'm afraid you're just getting us into trouble instead of accomplishing anything."

"I'm not getting anyone into trouble."

Tara crossed her arms over her chest. Hap put the jar down. He wiped his hands on his silky green pants and moved closer to the crystal, where the humming seemed loudest. He looked at the crystal from all angles, circling it to see if there were any buttons on it or a mechanism of any kind. By the time he'd circled back to Tara, she said, "Do you have any clues on how it works?"

"Nope." Hap hated admitting it, but she'd figure it out soon enough.

Tara shrugged. "Me neither." Then she reached out to touch it. Hap almost snatched her hand away but figured what harm could she do?

At her touch, the prismatic colors melted into white light.

Hap felt as though he'd gone through a spiral drop again, even though he was standing still. The crystal cast a long shadow as it rose into the air and began to spin.

"What's it doing?" Tara asked.

Hap stared and shook his head. "I have no idea."

The spinning slowed to a stop, then it dropped onto the padded dais.

White light burst from the pinnacle of the crystal pyramid, forming another pyramid. Only this one was upside down with the two tips balanced perfectly atop one another. The upside-down pyramid on top was like a projector screen. It looked exactly like it did on the stained-glass window in Hap's quarters.

Hap's mind tugged at the memory of something Svarta said as they carried the Hira to the Neswar of Orissa. *The Hira allows the books to be read, like a translator.*

"We need a book!" Hap held out his hand to take the book from Tara.

She lifted the back of her shirt to get the book but dropped it again when they heard familiar garbling and squawking outside the door.

17. A Change in Loyalty

Tara pivoted as though trying to figure out where to hide, yet the room offered no hiding places at all. Years of getting into trouble due to his curiosity taught Hap that acting like you knew exactly what you were doing—even when you didn't—and as though you belonged where you were—even though you didn't—saved a lot of extra trouble. He didn't bother trying to hide but leaned against the dais and waited for Gygak and Mosh to come in.

Gygak's step faltered when his gaze fell on the two teenagers. His feathery eyebrows lowered in suspicion. "What are you doing here?"

"Curious. We carried it all the way over here and wanted to know what it looked like." Hap hoped he looked indifferent and casual. His heart pounded hard enough Hap could barely hear anything else.

"Curious? That all?" Gygak sauntered toward the Hira. "You kids shouldn't be here. It's a bad place right now. The Neswar's at war, you know."

Tara took several deep breaths, started to say something, stopped, shook her head, and burst out with, "What happened to all the Rissans outside? What did you do to them?" Her whole body shook with anger and fear. "Are you going to do that to us?"

Gygak seemed to be thinking for several long moments. "Don't look like you swallowed a scourab box, girl. We didn't hurt the Rissans. A neubin needle straight into the chest turns off the mind too. They're just sliding on the Jovian rings of slumber. They might have to actually talk to each other when they wake up since their thoughts will be too foggy to understand. They're sleeping. They'll be fine . . . You're wanting to call home, huh? You finally figure out that Laney's got a traitorous streak in her?"

Hap opened his mouth and closed it again.

Gygak dry-washed his two sets of hands. "You know, I think we can help you. You can still link home."

"How?" Tara and Hap asked at the same time.

Gygak grinned, and his feathery eyebrows waved enthusiastically with the motion. "Nova."

Hap's stomach tangled into discomfort when he heard the name.

"Nova wants the Hira. He's offered a lot of credits. You help us get it to him, and he'll reward you." Gygak nodded toward the crate. "He'll reward you with more credits than your minds can comprehend. Just think about it. You could link home. You could buy yourselves a ship and a pilot to transport you home. You wouldn't need to wait on Laney and her nasty little sister, or that two-toned psychopath."

Hap straightened. "I think—"

Tara touched Hap's arm. "I don't . . . I don't know, Hap."

He lowered his voice, knowing that it didn't matter. Mosh and Gygak would still be able to hear him. "It's our chance to get it out of here. She can't make the delivery to the scientist if we take it."

Gygak hissed. "The scientist? He's here? She's gonna deliver it to *him?*"

Hap agreed with Gygak's concern—he couldn't allow the delivery to take place. Tolvan had said that everything Grandpa Hazzard held dear would basically be burned to ashes if she made the delivery, but if Hap could stop that . . . Hap had made some dumb mistakes, but he if could help his grandpa, somehow it would make every other dumb thing he'd done to this point okay. Hap had gotten Tara into this mess, and he planned on getting her out.

But he didn't trust Gygak. Why would Gygak want them along? Why wouldn't he just knock them out like he had the Rissan guards and take it himself?

Gygak kept his tone smooth and soothing. "You can't let her give it to him, Hap. The scientist knows too much, is too powerful. An object like this in his hands could never be for the good of anyone else. You have to help us. If she makes the delivery . . ."

Hap knew that bad things would happen if she made the delivery. His grandfather wouldn't have wanted this. Hap trusted his grandfather, even if he didn't trust Gygak.

"Why would you need our help?" Hap asked, knowing Mosh could carry the Hira without them. He'd stumble around a lot, and it would slow him down, but he could do it.

Tara gasped. "Oh, look!" She pointed at Mosh.

Hap redirected his attention to the big ape mountain and saw a jagged rip running down the length of the creature's left arm. The edges of the cut were blackened as though they'd been seared by fire. There wasn't much blood, but what blood did exist had blackened with whatever had burned Mosh in the first place.

"What happened?" Tara looked distressed and immediately glanced around the room. When her eyes settled on a silky blue piece of cloth that hung over a few of the shelves, she ripped it right off the poles it hung from. She spun around as though in a terrible hurry to help until she realized what she'd planned on doing.

She stared at Mosh for a long moment as he swayed a little from the pain in his arm. Finally, lifting her chin with renewed determination, Tara lowered her eyes to focus on his wound instead of the enormity of the creature who terrified her. While wrapping the cloth around Mosh's arm, she said, "I wish we had some antibiotic ointment," more to herself than anyone else. "This is going to get a bad infection if he doesn't get it cleaned up, but at least this will help."

Mosh cringed as Tara tightened the little bandage.

"What happened to your arm?" Hap asked.

"We had an accident." Gygak's feathered antennae quivered.

Hap narrowed his eyes. "Doing what?" With these guys, it could have been anything.

"Mosh here tried to make himself something in the kitchens. Laney hadn't invited us to dinner and we were starving. He slipped in some agoy oil he'd spilled and fell against the oven. He tried to catch himself with his arm and burned it. Could've been worse. If he hadn't used his arm, his face would look like that." Gygak grimaced. He scratched his neck with one of his upper arms while his lower arms remained folded in front of him.

"Oh." The explanation made sense. Laney hadn't invited them to dinner. Naturally they would be hungry. Hap felt guilty for automatically assuming the injury came because they were up to no good.

But they *were* up to no good. They planned on stealing the Hira. But so had Hap and Tara. Why not join forces with people who shared the same goal?

"So you understand, we need your help because Mosh here isn't in such good shape, right?"

Mosh ignored the conversation and stared intently at his arm where Tara had bandaged his wound. He looked at Tara. Since she stared at Gygak, she didn't notice his inspection.

"So if we help you, we'll get home?" Hap wanted to confirm this point. He didn't exactly trust Gygak, but he didn't trust Laney at all. Neither one of them played straight with him, but at least with Gygak, there was still a chance.

"Sure you will."

Hap nodded. Tara nodded too, though she looked as nervous and worried about it as Hap felt. Gygak's grin widened. "Welcome to the family, kid. Help me get this thing back into the crate."

The crystal responded to touch and seemed to close up once Gygak pressed his hands into the faceted sides. They made short work of boxing it back up in a way that wouldn't break it if they jiggled the crate around.

Hap hesitated before picking up the crate. His dad had taken him boating once, and a storm had come while they were still on the lake. The wind whipped the waves, making the boat dip and pitch. Hap had gotten seasick, and his skin felt cold and clammy even after they'd made it to shore. He felt that same way now—as if the world underneath him was pitching and rolling, turning his insides to mush. *Am I making the right choice?* But what other choice existed? *None.*

Hap shook off his reservations and picked up one end of the crate. Mosh used his one good arm to help on Hap's side. Gygak and Tara took the other end.

They'd hefted the crate to the door when Hap said, "How will we get it out without anyone seeing us?"

"The Rissans are busy right now. There was a disturbance out on the ocean side of the Orissa."

"What kind of disturbance?" Tara asked.

"The whole Stupak Circle is in a bit of unrest right now. That's why Laney landed us in the marshes rather than at the starport. The starport changes hands every few days due to some coup or another. Anyway . . . the Serviens admire Rissan handiwork. They like the cliff dwellings well enough to relieve the Rissans of ownership."

With his thick, rough voice, Mosh interrupted Gygak's interpretation of world events in Stupak's Circle. "It's not like that." He seemed to be clenching his teeth against the pain from his arm. "The Serviens were there first. They carved the Neswar cliffs."

Hap didn't really care all that much about who carved the cliffs or who wanted the cliffs back. He worried over whether or not they'd get out of the cliffs before civil war broke out. He worried over Laney finding him and letting Tremble/Googool blast him into space particles.

Hap tried to make them go right, but Gygak steered them left. "Wrong way, kid. You're acting like you're still stuck in the spiral."

"I thought you said you never got lost," Tara muttered from her side of the crate.

18. Out of the Frying Pan

"Can't we call someone to come pick us up?" Tara asked, and not for the first time.

Rather than give the standard answer of not having a link key on him, Gygak grunted in response.

They'd made it out of the Orissa without much difficulty. The attention of the Rissans was all on the attack from the ocean side. Hap had the feeling they were missing him and Tara by now and missing what he and Tara had taken, but he pushed the thought out of his mind. If he thought about it too long, he felt guilty.

Dumb to feel guilty with Laney being the thief and Tremble being the schizophrenic with a gun. If Laney let Amar have the Hira, bad things would happen. But that was just the thing. Hap considered himself an excellent judge of character, and Amar hadn't seemed all that threatening. Under different circumstances, Amar would have seemed like a great guy—the kind of guy his parents would invite over to barbecues.

And Laney hadn't exactly been horrible to them. She'd rescued them from the neubins, given them a place to sleep, and made sure they got dinner when she hadn't invited Mosh or Gygak.

He tsked to himself. No, Laney hadn't been horrible, but she made promises she couldn't keep, and she'd stolen the crystal to begin with. If it came to a question of his family or hers, his won every time. Her theft of the pyramid upset Grandpa Hazzard.

These were the arguments that went back and forth in his mind. He felt guilty that Laney had kind of helped them while he tried to bury his guilt by reminding himself of her crimes. But he could never bury his guilt very far. Laney and Svarta had real needs in Hap's estimation. They wanted to get to their dad, who'd been missing for a long time. He could relate to their need. He needed to get to his dad too. Was he so different from them? *Forget all that! My needs are more important!* He had a family who depended on him. His family was more important than anything in the universe. If he had to deal with a little guilt to get back to them, then he would deal with it.

His heart rate increased as his grandfather's soft voice came to his mind. *"That's not the Hazzard way, Hap. We're men of honor . . ."*

Men of honor.

But he didn't owe Laney anything. She'd been the one to take him away from everything he loved. She'd been the one who refused to take him and Tara back. And this Amar guy? He didn't owe Amar anything either. For all he knew, Amar was a fraud. Nobody lived that many years unless they were a vampire, and Hap didn't believe in vampires.

Except Hap did believe that Amar was the scientist from all those thousands of years ago. And a few days ago, Hap didn't believe in aliens either. Being wrong about one thing made him wonder how many other things he'd been wrong about. Was he wrong to help Gygak?

"Men of honor, Hap . . . We're men of honor . . ." His dad had said those words to him several times in his life too—like the time Hap stole a pack of gum when he was five and had to go confess to the store manager.

While he was struggling with what to do, his arms shook under the weight of the crate. Hearing the planet's night creatures rustling through the reeds near the path didn't help matters either.

Hap hated walking through the forest in the dark. What if the neubins were out? The fleshy part of the back of his leg itched with remembrance of the needle that numbed him. Hap's heart felt like it pounded up in his throat, making it hard to breathe. Laney had mentioned other things from this world that could hurt him . . . skrapligts, hesten, and pustules. Hap opened his mouth to ask Gygak and Mosh about them, but before he could spit out the first words, Tara interrupted him.

"Do you guys have guns?" she asked.

So . . . she worried over the night noises too.

Gygak's ears flattened against his head, his feather antennae drooping like wet noodles. "We lost our weapons to the twin-soul." He seemed reluctant about the admission of weakness.

"What happens if we're attacked by neubins?" Hap asked, totally alarmed by not having anything to defend themselves with and yet in some ways relieved. Would Gygak have shot the guards at the Neswar if he'd had his gun?

"They sleep at night," Mosh said, his garbling voice laced with worry, then added, "The hestens don't, though. We should be careful."

Tara moaned.

Hap's thoughts exactly.

"We'll be all right so long as we hurry." Gygak's voice sounded strained in the dark as he labored to speak between breaths.

They left the hardened black trail of lava and entered where the trail was on spongy ground. Hap smelled rotting eggs almost immediately upon the trail switch. He wrinkled his nose and swallowed hard, trying not to breathe any more than necessary.

Hap cringed every time his arms brushed against the reeds, remembering the reed that lowered itself and walked away on slivery legs. Should he have warned Tara about them rather than keeping that information to himself? What if one bit her? What would they do?

The moon finally emerged through the clouds. It looked like a harvest moon—fiery and golden. The light seemed to create crimson trails through the water. Hap hadn't realized they were walking so close to the water's edge until the moonlight reflected off the rippling surface.

A few moments after moonrise, Hap insisted they rest. Tara's labored breathing and the moans and grunts coming from Mosh proved that they could all use a break.

"Not too long. Standing still encourages predators." Gygak eased his side to the ground.

"What predators?" Tara turned her back toward the crate so she could face out toward whatever predator might be in the act of pouncing on her.

Mosh slid his back along the crate and fell down on his backside, creating a thud that shook the ground.

Gygak rounded on Mosh. "Are you trying to give away our position? Do you want us caught?"

But Tara knelt by Mosh's side. "He's sick. Leave him alone. He's likely got an infection in his arm." She shot back an accusatory look at Gygak, who fell silent under Tara's gaze. Hap almost laughed—the absurdity of Tara intimidating Gygak.

Tara could stare down anyone. As long as the guy she stared down wasn't Hap, Hap liked Tara's ability.

Mosh groaned again.

"I'm sorry, Mosh. I can't take the bandage off to see what's going on underneath, because it'll open it up to more infection." She held his hand, though, and cooed comforting words to him.

Hap slid down to the ground too. His head drooped under the cadence of Tara's voice speaking softly to Mosh, and for a moment he slept.

He woke up to the sound of Tara's scream.

19. Into the Fire

Hap jumped to his feet feeling dazed and disoriented. He blinked rapidly to clear his eyes and his mind so he could figure out where Tara was. When he finally focused well enough to see her, he could see Mosh holding her.

No. Not Mosh but someone who looked a lot like Mosh. This guy's clothes fit him better. His belly didn't have a basketball shape and didn't hang out of his clothes. He wore a mottled brown skirt that looked like an animal skin and a cloak made of reeds mingled with feathers and furs from various other animals. His bullfrog-pouched chin puffed as he tried to contain Tara's flailing arms.

Arms squeezed around Hap before he could react to the scene in front of him. He'd barely had time to shout out, "Leave her alone!" before a thick hand clapped over his mouth. He felt like the air had been compressed from him entirely.

Gygak struggled against yet another ape-frog man. His four arms were finally smashed into his sides to keep him from throwing any more punches. Mosh stood to the side, cradling his bandaged arm and gesticulating wildly with the other. He shook his head, making his pouchy bottom lip jiggle like a water balloon with a hole as spit flew from his mouth.

The gravelly voice that came from the arms holding Hap shouted loudly, making Hap's ears feel like they'd explode. The smell that came from the guy behind him was worse than anything Hap had ever smelled, which was really saying a lot considering the air around them smelled like huge sulfur bombs.

"Mosh! Stop!"

Mosh froze, his good arm still hanging in the air. His mouth hung open, though no more noise came out. The creature holding Hap back yelled out, "We'll take them to Nova. If he thinks they are as innocent as you believe them to be, we'll let them go. If not . . . their wings will be clipped."

Hap didn't like the sound of that.

The ape-frog holding him gave Hap a shove. He stumbled forward and for a brief moment considered running. But several other ape-frogs stepped out of the shadows carrying metal rods.

"You're hurting me!" Tara yelled as she struggled against her captor.

Hap reached his hand into the pocket of his jacket and slipped the buzzer onto his finger. He yanked his hand out and slapped the buzzer hand hard against the ape-frog holding him. The creature released him immediately with a yelp and a shaking of his arm. Hap ran to Tara to get her away too.

Another ape-frog barred his way, holding one of the long metal rods. The rod swung out toward Hap.

He raised his arms over his head in anticipation of a crushing blow, but the rod stopped a foot away from him. He relaxed briefly until a flash of blue light zipped out of the tip and into his chest.

His body seized up, crumpling to the ground. All of his muscles curled involuntarily as electricity arced through him. When his muscles finally relaxed again, sweat poured down his face.

"The prod carries for some distance. If you ran, we would not have to move at all to catch you. Do you understand?"

Hap nodded. He understood, all right. They had better buzzers than he did. "I'm sorry, Tara," he said.

"On your feet!" the lead ape-frog growled. His pouchy mouth had been painted a bright red and had black stains dribbling from the corners, as though he'd eaten black paint and hadn't had a napkin handy. His clothing was like the others'—a mottled array of animal skins, fur and leather, and some feathers too.

Tara's eyes leaked tears in steady streams.

Hap felt utterly helpless as he stood.

"Now. Walk."

Hap's feet moved without hesitation. He didn't want another zap from the frog prod.

Tara didn't need encouraging either. Watching Hap's example had been enough for her. Gygak and Mosh moved as well. Other ape-frogs took over the burden of the crystal.

These were Mosh's people, but none of them was as easygoing as Mosh. Their bottom lips jutted out in menacing snarls as they prodded Tara and Hap down a path hidden in the reeds. When they curled their lips enough to see their teeth, Hap couldn't stop himself from staring.

His body felt cold and numb whenever he looked, but he couldn't turn away from the teeth that were so cracked they looked like ragged knives. Because Mosh's teeth were yellow stumpy things, there was no way the razor-sharp fangs inside the mouths of these guys were natural. Hap couldn't imagine how they created such serrated edges on their teeth, short of chewing on bricks or purposely sawing their teeth apart, but who would do that?

Tara marched on, every now and again turning to glare at Hap. Hap instinctively knew that interpreting her looks would be a bad idea. Her fear seemed to match her anger. Her feet stomped into the squishy ground, her fingers rolling into fists and then out again, only to roll back up a moment later. But her breathing sounded like she held back sobs.

He'd tried speaking soothing words to Tara, but after a few sharp jabs of warning from the prod, Hap fell into silence.

He worked hard to pay attention to where they were going. The trail through the reeds interconnected with dozens of other trails. The reeds were a horrible maze of rotting egg smell and calls from the wildlife hiding where Hap couldn't see.

How did they get themselves into this mess? How did they go from getting paid for getting the Hira away from Laney and Amar, and getting to go home, to being prisoners of guys who looked like wild animals?

Hap glared at Gygak, all the while knowing that Tara glared at him. The leathery bat was a prisoner too, but that didn't make Hap feel better.

He darted a glance back at the ape-frog creature lumbering along behind him. The thing appeared dumb and slow, but Hap knew differently. The creature was as light on its feet as a ballet dancer.

At least Mosh appeared that way on the ship. Would the gravity difference make moving harder for them? The Serviens were strong. But they would have to be strong in order to maneuver their mass over a planet with gravity like this one had. Would the heavy gravity make it so Hap and Tara could escape?

No. Even if the gravity slowed the Serviens down, the prod would collapse him and Tara like puppets with their strings snipped, and the ape-frog wouldn't have to take one step to make it happen.

Hap felt like he'd be able to sleep for a year once they stopped—*if* they ever stopped! His feet felt like stone, his eyelids just as heavy. The monotonous sound of feet marching over the squishy ground made a slushy sort of rhythm that sounded like an odd lullaby.

But the creatures kept going—crisscrossing this path, turning down that one, and all the while it seemed they were going downhill. There was no way to really determine the slope of the path through the tall reeds. He only figured they were going down because his shins hurt.Occasionally a fiery glint of red reflected from the moonlight into the spotty pools of water peppered throughout the reeds, but mostly nothing but darkness and the sounds of night animals existed beyond the first rows of reeds along the path.

When they approached a huge hole that looked like a monstrous sink drain, Hap looked back again. The clearing was large enough to tell that yes, they'd been on a downhill slope, so to get back to the Rissan hive, they needed to go uphill . . . but which way uphill?

Hap couldn't believe he was trying to map out how to get back to the Rissan Neswar. Hadn't he wanted to get away from them? Hadn't he worried that he'd never escape the place where bug people tried to intrude on his thoughts?

And here he was trying to figure out how to get back to them. *I'm an idiot.*

At the hole, the sulfuric smell of rotting eggs overwhelmed Hap. It felt as though the stench actually coated the inside of his mouth and windpipe all the way down to his lungs. He grimaced in Tara's direction. "If breathing smoke causes cancer, what does breathing egg do? Rot our insides?" As soon as the words were out, one of the ape-frog guys clubbed the back of Hap's head with a meaty hand.

"Ow!" Hap grumbled, glaring at the ape-frog. He should have been grateful he hadn't been zapped by the prod, but he felt too tired to be grateful for anything.

Tara sighed and shook her head in pity, though she looked like she wanted to club him too. Hap didn't blame her. He wanted to club himself. He had no idea that his desire to contact his family would lead to his own death. Gygak had lied, plain and simple. This Nova guy would have them barbecued, not taken home. Otherwise, why treat them as prisoners?

If nothing else, that smell would do him in. He had an incredible desire to brush his teeth and gargle the toothpaste to get rid of the sulfuric slick layer of rot he just knew covered his entire mouth.

The sky had lightened in small degrees—a pink tinge now battling the black sky. They had walked the entire night.

The hole looked like one of the geyser holes in Yellowstone Park, only bigger—a lot bigger.

"Go." The lead ape-frog held the prod to warn them that they needed to keep moving.

"Go where?" Tara crossed her arms over her chest and narrowed her eyes as she flipped her hair out of her eyes. Being tired made her especially grumpy. Hap hoped she didn't get them pushed into the hole like some sacrifice to a volcano god.

The lead ape-frog's red pouch quivered as he kept his irritation in check. He pointed the prod toward the maw in the ground.

Tara looked toward the dark and shuddered. She shook her head, but the lead ape-frog stepped toward her, brandishing the prod. Hap hurried to jump in the way. "No! We'll go. That's not necessary."

Hap took Tara's hand. She didn't pull away—proving her fear to be exponential as they edged closer to the lip. He blinked several times as he peered into the dark and could just make out stairs carved into the walls. Hap's fingers rested close to Tara's wrist. Her pulse beat out a racing rhythm.

"It'll be okay," he whispered.

"I don't want to go into the ground." Her voice shook.

"We'll be okay." Hap didn't know how much of that phrase was a lie, but he had to believe they'd be okay—that everything would work out, even if they were going to be pushed into the hole.

Hazzard men are men of honor . . .

Hap wondered if he'd been adopted.

If he'd acted with honor, he and Tara would be home and completely oblivious to the terrible fate they'd avoided. Hap took the first step onto the stairway that spiraled into the belly of the earth.

20. Mob Bosses and Volcano Hideouts

Hap's legs wobbled with every step they took. His stomach lurched every few moments from the sick smell of egg slime. He worried about stumbling off the stairs because of the darkness, but with every step he took, lights embedded into the rock flickered to life, helping him take the next step.

Mosh had said that the Serviens had built the Neswar, which made sense since the similarity of light embedded in rock existed in both places. But Hap couldn't help but think the Serviens had done a better job with the Neswar than they had with this hole in the ground.

The wet walls appeared to be sweating, and Hap refrained from using them for balance. He felt like he was walking into a giant's nose during cold-and-flu season. The walls of the hole looked like they'd been sprayed in snot.

They arrived at the bottom much quicker than Hap would have ever imagined. Tunnels led off like mine shafts in almost every direction. Metal tracks crisscrossed the ground in a dizzying pattern. The lead ape-frog picked a tunnel and led them deeper into the earth. The interior of the tunnel wasn't what Hap expected. The walls were lined in metal sheeting, and the dirt and stone floor had been covered by a metal grating that ran the length of the tunnel as far as Hap could see. The lead ape-frog stopped at a door. "Into the tank." He held the prod aimed toward the captives in case anyone tried to argue.

Gygak, Tara, and Hap went in without argument. When Mosh made to follow, they stopped him and slammed the door. Gygak rushed the door. "Mosh!" he yelled, but no one answered him. Mosh was so sick from the wound on his arm that he likely hadn't heard Gygak's voice.

"Do you think they know about penicillin?" Tara whispered. She crossed her arms over her chest as if trying to hug herself.

Hap shrugged. He gave the room a cursory glance. Empty. No shelves with anything interesting to help them escape, no windows to climb out. Even Houdini would have been stuck in this one.

"Capo won't let him die," Gygak said, though his feathery eyebrows drooped. "He's one of them."

"Who's Capo?" Tara asked, but she didn't seem interested in the answer as she unfolded her arms so she could pace and click her nails.

"The leader. The one who kept watch over Hap."

So . . . the one with the red-and-black-stained pouch. Hap really disliked that one in particular. "If Capo will take care of him, why do you look like he's already dead?" Hap asked.

Gygak plopped himself down on the cold ground; both sets of hands moved to cover his face. "I've lost favor in Nova's family. I thought if I brought the Hira—I thought he'd forgive me. The Serviens aren't really Nova's people. They take care of their own. They follow Nova because they want their cliffs back. Mosh'll be fine because the Serviens will protect him."

Tara grunted in disgust. "But you're worried about *you*. Not Mosh, but *you*. You're worried because there isn't anyone who's going to cover your back. You're just like my dad—stupid, selfish creep." The silence that followed Tara's comment opened wide between them like a chasm. Tara's tennis shoes thumped against the grating as she walked one way, spun, then walked back.

"They aren't going to pay us for helping, are they?" Tara stopped pacing and glared at Hap and Gygak simultaneously. Both shrank a little under her scrutiny. "They're not going to help me contact my mom, are they? They aren't going to help me get home, are they?"

"Not likely," Gygak admitted.

Tara loomed over Gygak like a newly erupted volcano. "So you tricked us. You *lied* to us! And now here you are . . . in the same boat we're in. We'll likely be tortured and fed to some giant rat with five heads. And it *stinks* here! If we don't get killed, we'll die of some lung disease caused by that smell! If we'd have left the Hira where it was, that scientist guy—Amar—could've maybe helped us use it to call home. I don't care what your grandpa said about ICE and the Hira, Hap. That scientist guy didn't look too bad to me. He might've helped us if we'd asked him. I can't believe I let you talk me into this, Hap! I was right! The magicians guild doesn't know anything about aliens and ancient books from India! I can't believe I listened to you! And *you*, you big-eared, noseless, four-armed *thing*! If you hadn't *lied*, your buddy Mosh would still be with you! If you'd—"

She broke off when Gygak's head lifted. His eyebrows lifted. "Magicians guild? Tell me about this magicians guild."

She didn't respond but instead shot him her would-be-heat-vision glare and turned her back on Gygak.

His gaze swept over to Hap, who felt goosebumps rise up under the Gygan's measuring look. "Your grandfather's a magician, kid?" Gygak asked.

"No." Hap turned away too. Grandpa Hazzard studied magic, sold magic, taught magic, but he wasn't technically a magician. *What does it matter if the Gygan acts like the magicians guild is important?* It mattered because Hap thought the magicians guild was important to whatever this Hira thing was. It mattered because Gygak had gone from looking like a man mourning his own death to a man calculating new plans. Hap could feel himself being maneuvered into those plans. Hap took several steadying breaths and dropped heavily to the floor, so tired he was sure he could have slept for a million years.

He would not talk about Grandpa Hazzard to Gygak anymore, not ever again. Tara was right: Gygak had lied, and there was no way Hap planned on giving more information to a guy who had nothing but his own self-interest in mind.

Hazzard men are men of honor . . . Hap scrubbed his hands through his red hair, making the sides fan out like flames. Amar had said something about men of honor. How would Amar know to say something like that? Tara slumped down next to Hap, and in spite of her anger with him, she leaned over enough that their shoulders touched.

The door creaked open on rusted hinges.

"Geddup!" The gravelly voice intruded on Hap's fragmented thoughts. "You . . ." the guard pointed a thick finger toward Hap and Tara. "You stay."

Gygak stood in front of the guard and led the way out of their little prison cell.

Tara and Hap leaned into each other, neither saying anything. Really, what could be said? Hap could apologize, but apologies had started this whole mess, and he wasn't up to it. Hap allowed himself to fall asleep.

* * *

Hap's eyelids felt like sandpaper as they scoured his eyeballs. He blinked several times, and before he could voice the question on his tongue, Tara stretched next to him then asked, "What are we going to do?"

Hap pulled the jacket from around his waist to rummage through the pockets. He pulled out the deck of cards, the buzzer, the EpiPen, the flashlight, the fake vomit, and the scotch-and-soda trick. He was glad they hadn't thought to take the buzzer away.

She pointed to the EpiPen. "What's that?"

"EpiPen. I'm allergic to bees." He felt dumb admitting to such a lame weakness, but he hoped she'd finally understand why he wasn't all that excited about the Rissans. He'd mentioned it before after the neubin attacked, but Tara hadn't really been listening. Hap figured she'd gone into shock once Laney rescued them.

She eyed the rest of the stuff, her fingers sifting through the various pieces. "Does your grandpa know you shoplift from the store?"

"These are floor models. I'm supposed to use them to inspire more sales."

"Yeah, well, I'm inspired." Her flat voice and raised eyebrow belied her level of inspiration.

Hap shot her a withering look. "Let's just see if there's anything here we can use, okay?"

She picked up the flashlight, thumbed it on, and shone it on Hap's face. She flicked it off again. "Use? What are we going to do? Shine a light in their eyes and stick them with an allergy needle? This stuff isn't going to get us out of here." The flashlight clattered to the floor as she let it slip from her fingers.

"Don't break it!" He picked it up and flipped it on to make sure it still worked. If his grandpa had been abducted with him, they'd not only be free by now, but his grandpa would've found a ship and flown them halfway around the universe in it. He almost told her she was the worst abductee companion he could've ever asked for but closed his mouth when he saw tears brimming her eyes.

"I'm all my mom has left in the world; do you understand that?" She laughed as her voice cracked. "And I'm not even *in* the world!"

"I'm sorry." He didn't know what else to say. He'd seen Mrs. Jordan at the grocery store several times over the last month. She'd looked like a ghost walking through the aisles, picking up various pieces of fruit in the produce section and putting them back with a sniff that seemed to indicate she held back tears. Mrs. Jordan really didn't have anyone except Tara. Hap felt the sting of guilt. "I'm sorry," he said again.

"Me too." She sighed. "And I know this isn't easy for you either. I'm really sorry about your dad."

"Me too." He took it back—thinking she was the worst abductee companion. With all they'd been through, could he blame her for being mad? "And I know you probably don't want to hear this, but you've been a really good kidnap buddy."

She barked a laugh of disbelief. "Well, you don't get that compliment every day!"

"Seriously. I mean, I know this is weird and . . ."

"Terrifying?" she offered.

Hap smiled back. "Yeah, that. But you've been a lot stronger than most girls I know."

"Who are you kidding? I've spent more time crying and yelling at you than anything else."

"True. But you didn't leave me when that neubin attacked. You stayed and fought with me."

She bumped him with her shoulder. "I didn't fight *with* you. You were useless, remember? I fought *for* you."

"See, exactly. That's what I meant. You didn't ditch me."

She sighed and stared down at all the magic tricks in front of them. "Well, we're friends now, right?"

He grinned. "The best."

"Does this mean you'll give me a job when we get home?"

Hap laughed. "I dunno—you still need to work on that scarf trick."

Before Tara could respond, the door swung open, startling both of them. Hap swept the contents on the floor back into his jacket pocket and tied it firmly around his waist. Whether the items had use or not, they were all that remained of his life at home.

"Geddup," the ape-frog demanded.

They both scrambled to their feet and went ahead of the guard, who kept making stabbing motions with his prod. From the way Hap's muscles protested in agony with every step he took, he figured they'd slept for a long time. In the weird lighting of the tunnels, Hap had no way of knowing if it was still daytime or if they'd slept into the new night.

The guard herded them farther down the tunnel until they reached a door that looked as though it were made of gold. The ape-frog growled, "Open it!"

Hap reached toward the handle, scared he might break something if he touched it too roughly, and found himself surprised when the handle felt solid in his hand. He pushed against the door and then pushed harder since the door didn't budge. It took nearly all his weight to make the heavy mass finally swing open.

Hap didn't expect anything like what he saw.

The room looked like the hotel he'd stayed in the time his parents took him to New York for a magic trade show. They stayed at the Waldorf Astoria, his dad justifying the expense by saying he'd never taken Hap's mom anywhere really fabulous. This room was like that—only more.

The walls weren't the dull metal plating of the tunnels and the room Hap and Tara had come from but looked painted with gold leaf, just like the door. Framed pictures hung against the walls, but instead of normal portraits or paintings, all of them were 3-D holograms, like miniature stages where the performers practiced the same scene repeatedly. Tara snatched Hap's hand away when he moved to touch one.

Plush, overstuffed chairs and couches were arranged so that if anyone were sitting in them, they could converse comfortably. A large desk sat in a corner faced at a diagonal so that it offered a view of every part of the room. Several balls hung in the air close to the ceiling. They offered a soft golden glow that warmed the whole room, making the ambience almost friendly.

A long table stood toward the left with expensive looking overstuffed chairs all around it. The chairs were empty except one.

At the head of the table sat a human man with shoulders that would have put a linebacker to shame. His black eyebrows seemed to take up all the space where his forehead should have been. They hung heavily over his eyes making him appear menacing even as he turned a wide smile on the two teenagers. His dented square chin seemed more pronounced with the smile, and in spite of the room's grandeur and the warm light from the glowing orbs above, that smile looked anything but friendly.

The Hira pyramid hovered a few inches above the table in front of him, and a thin, catlike animal stalked around the crystal, the animal's tail lashing back and forth.

"It's nice to see other people from Earth. So . . . anything exciting happening on the home planet since I've been away?" The low, soft voice felt wrong coming out of this man's heavy form.

Hap heard Tara swallow hard. He squeezed her hand—whether to reassure her or to reassure himself, he couldn't say. Hap shrugged in response to the question.

The man stood as though to show off his substantial height. His wide shoulders narrowed down to a thin waist, making him look like a wedge of cheese. He stepped in front of a mirror and turned to take in his own appearance. He adjusted the flower-weed thing on his suit lapel and, while continuing to fuss with his own appearance, said, "So how do you like the universe?"

Tara looked at Hap as if to say, "Is this guy crazy?"

Hap looked back at her as if to say, "I wouldn't call him that to his face."

The wedge-shaped man stopped messing with the flower-weed, focused on Hap in the mirror, and cleared his throat.

Hap shrugged. He would have left his response as a shrug but understood that this man expected a verbal response. "It's fine?" Hap's response sounded more like a question than an answer, but it appeased the man.

"I'm Don Nova—originally from Chicago. My family had a pretty good import business back then . . ."

Don Nova turned from the mirror to gaze on Hap directly.

"Where are you from? My boys didn't have much personal information to give about you."

"Utah," Hap said. "We're from Utah."

Nova pursed the lips of his wide mouth. "Utah, huh? Never been to Utah. I wonder what the old homeworld's like now . . ." He raised an eyebrow, but from the way the eyebrows were connected, it looked like a snake going around an unseen bend in the road. "Seems I owe you a favor or two. You helped my boy Mosh with his . . . accident. You helped bring the Hira to me."

Alarms went off in Hap's mind. Even though Don Nova indicated he owed them a favor, the tone in his voice said he felt just the opposite was true. Hap shrugged. Tara clicked her nails. Hap wanted to reach around and take hold of her other hand to make her stop but felt frozen to the spot.

"So what do you want?" Nova asked. "What can I get you for the wonderful services you've done for me?"

"A . . . a ph-phone call," Tara sputtered.

Her nerve to still hope Don Nova would give them the thing they desired staggered Hap. Why would the guy who had thrown them into a prison help them with anything?

The door burst open before Tara could add to her request and before Nova could respond. "We got him!" A dark-haired human with a small scrap of fuzz on his upper lip strutted into the room. His short legs made the strut look almost comical. If Hap hadn't been terrified, he might have laughed.

Behind him came several ape-frog guards herding one more human into the room.

Amar.

21. DEALING WITH THE INTERGALACTIC MAFIA

GYGAK FOLLOWED BEHIND AMAR, LOOKING smug and satisfied, his eyebrows floating high above his face until he saw Hap and Tara, after which his eyebrows drooped to the sides.

Nova's smile turned into a sneer. "Amar. At last."

Amar didn't acknowledge Hap's presence in the room. "Don." Amar inclined his head.

"You come empty handed?" Nova edged closer to Amar but stayed far enough away to make him seem wary.

"I hardly had time to prepare." Amar moved farther from the guards and sat down in one of the overstuffed chairs in the center of the room as though he were a guest, not a prisoner.

Nova's eyebrows bunched into the center of his head, making it look as though the hairy snake on his forehead had coiled. After several seconds, he followed and sat in the chair directly across from Amar.

Tara's hand went to the small of her back where Hap could barely make out the shape of the book under her shirt. He'd forgotten about the book. He wondered at her ability to have walked all through the night in the sweltering heat with a book against her skin.

And she said *he'd* ruin the book!

Hap's heart slammed against his ribcage hard enough he was sure his heart was bruised. Amar and Nova acted like gentlemen having a nice discussion, but the tension underneath their words seemed like a plate of thin glass splintering under the weight.

"It's been a long time since we saw each other last." Nova's body remained tense.

"Yes, right before you set your dogs on poor Ehrich."

Nova chuckled, his wide shoulders bouncing. "Weiss deserved what he got. He knew the minute he found your book, his days were numbered. Let's not argue over the past."

Hap felt as though someone had stuffed him into a freezer. His whole body shook with cold. His teeth chattered. Ehrich Weiss? Ehrich Weiss—a name Hap knew as well as his own for all the time he spent reading about the man—Harry Houdini! Could Amar mean that Ehrich Weiss—Houdini—owned one of the books from the nine unknown scientists? Could they really be implying that? Could Nova really have been the one to cause Houdini's death?

Impossible!

"Killing the magician did you no good. You still do not have my book."

"Killing the magician did all sorts of good. I felt better, and I gave honor back to my family."

Amar leaned back on his chair comfortably. "How do you give honor to such dishonorable people? Your family were all rum-runners, profiting from the illegal sales of alcohol. Your mother made her living by preying on the desires and hopes of others. No honor can come from that."

"She gave people what they wanted. Weiss took that all away from those people she helped." Nova shifted in his seat, looking anything but comfortable. His lip curled upward into a snarl.

"Helped? Odd word to describe claiming to speak to the dead and taking money to help people contact loved ones who had died. She took their money and fed them lies. Ehrich exposed her for the fraud she was."

Hap thought back to his reading. Harry Houdini had made it his life mission to prove that psychics and mediums were frauds. He attended séances where the psychic claimed to be speaking to the dead. He showed all the people in the audience how the psychics used mirrors and tricks to make it look like they could speak to the dead. Nobody in the psychic business liked Houdini very much.

Nova's face darkened. He jumped to his feet, making all of his cronies stiffen as though preparing to shoot Amar. "But was he not a fraud as well? Claiming to be a magician, claiming power?"

Amar considered this. "No. He did the things he said he did. His only fraud was that he was more than the man he claimed to be."

"He was only the man your book taught him to be. Your book on how to control time and space made him the escape artist—the magician. Without you and the knowledge in that book, he wouldn't have been able to do any of that."

Amar didn't respond to the credit Nova gave him. "Killing him accomplished nothing. Your mother never reclaimed her business as a clairvoyant gypsy. Your family never regained honor. You gained nothing. You have nothing."

"But I have *you*." Nova leaned in, though he still maintained enough distance to make him seem paranoid. "And I have the Hira."

"You should have stayed on Earth, Don. You could have helped your family. Your mother died alone. You could have been a good son and been with her in her final moments."

"I couldn't stay. I couldn't watch—" Nova looked weepy for a moment but recovered quickly. "And I did help people! I saved those guys ICE was chasing. They'd have rotted in an ICE prison on Earth if I hadn't helped them."

"Yes, and there is an abundance of honor to be had by helping thieves whose sole purpose in coming to Earth was to rob the world of some of its greatest treasures. Those pirates you work for want the universe destroyed. Helping them does not add to your honor."

Nova straightened and adjusted his suit lapels. "I'm not going to battle you, Amar. You cost me a good employee. Convincing Laney to keep something I'd already paid her to deliver to me makes you something of a thief."

Amar's eyes darkened. "You paid that poor girl barely enough to make it to Earth and then limp back here to you. You kept her in poverty for a deadly job with little more than promises of credits, but you and I both understand you never would have completed your final payment to her. For you to have the Hira in your possession is a blasphemy to the souls of my eight brothers."

Hap's breath caught in his throat. "No . . ." Terrible understanding filled Hap. Laney was going to deliver the pyramid to Nova! THAT was the delivery Grandpa Hazzard didn't want. And Amar had tried to talk her out of it and would have probably succeeded if Hap hadn't gotten in the way and completed the delivery for her. Everything would have been fine if Hap had just stayed out of it. "What have I done?" Hap hissed through his teeth, his breathing coming too fast to provide decent oxygen to his brain. He felt as though he was going to pass out.

The delivery to Nova had been the danger. What had Tolvan said? *If he gets the books, everything you hold dear will be as parchment to candle flame—nothing but ashes.*

For all Hap's good intentions to get the Hira away from Laney and Amar, he'd done the one thing his grandfather would *not* have wanted. *I messed up. Idiot! Stupid, lame idiot!*

"Interesting how you've decorated the smelty." Amar kept his tone casual, and, with a glance at Hap, he raised an eyebrow.

Only Hap had no idea what the eyebrow raise meant. He tried hard to listen to the words the two men exchanged but had a hard time hearing over the roar in his own ears.

"I didn't do anything too permanent. I haven't been here long and don't plan on staying." The black eyebrows squiggled as Nova spoke—the hairy snake of an eyebrow looking like it might squirm away.

"I see. You're here to incite war between the Rissans and Serviens, and then you fly to another system and ruin *their* tenuous political structure."

"They were planning war long before I got here. And I don't care about their war. I'm here for the Nine Unknown—here for you."

Amar's eyes flitted briefly to the Hira hovering over the table. The catlike thing batted at the crystal with its paw as though trying to knock it out of the air.

Nova caught Amar's glance too. "Thinking of taking the prize?"

Reproving disgust tainted Amar's voice. "No. I'd planned to destroy the prize. Knowledge in the hands of the foolish is a waste. Yet the foolish always crave knowledge. They think it will make them powerful, when it will only reveal them for the fools they are."

Nova whirled on Amar. "Enough of this! You must realize that your brothers are dead. Now is the time to tell me where your book is."

"My brothers may have passed from their mortal bodies, but I know they did not tell you where to find their books. I will follow them in that path. I will not tell you where to find my book. I will cut out my own tongue before considering such a thing."

"Oh, you don't have to do that." Nova leaned over Amar, his dark eyebrows lowered over his eyes. "Not when I plan on doing it for you." Nova stood back and jabbed a thick jeweled finger at Gygak.

Gygak, who'd slouched and tried to seem invisible throughout the interchange, snapped up straight. "Sir?"

Nova snapped his thick fingers. "You heavy?"

Gygak's eyebrows drooped lower than Hap had ever seen them go. "I . . . well, I lost my drubber to the twin-soul on Laney's crew."

Nova spun, his wedge-shaped body reminding Hap of the Tasmanian Devil. "You lost it to a *twin-soul?*" He didn't raise his voice, yet Tara jumped a little at the intensity behind those words.

Gygak drew back when Nova pulled out a gun. Tara's eyes went wide as she shook her head and mouthed the word *no.*

Nova aimed the gun at Gygak. "So here we are, and you without your weight. How are you supposed to defend yourself?"

Gygak's feet shuffled as though he wasn't sure which way to go.

Nova holstered his gun in the strap at his side. "Don't ever come in here without weight again. There won't be another warning."

Gygak all but bowed in his professions of gratitude. Beads of sweat sprouted at his neck and poured down into his shirt, leaving dark damp splotches on his collar.

"Josset?" At Nova's command, a guard looked up. "Take our little scientist to the tank . . . We wouldn't want him overpowering our weak Gygak." Amar turned to Gygak. "Make yourself useful and ready the flare room. And help our guest up."

Gygak flinched at being called weak but hurried to bow his head and gruffly grab Amar's arm to pull him up. Amar jerked his arm out of Gygak's grasp, but Gygak's three other hands kept hold of him.

Nova moved close to Amar but stayed enough away that they never touched. "We'll search you thoroughly for anything valuable. Then you'll have the chance to finally commune with your brothers. Good-bye, scientist. Give my regards to Emperor Ashoka. You'll be seeing him soon."

He turned his back as the Servien guard took hold of Amar's other arm and Gygak helped drag Amar out.

Tara's eyes brimmed with tears as she whispered, "Stop them, Hap."

Hap couldn't stop them. What could he do? What did Tara expect a fourteen-year-old to accomplish? The gun holstered to Nova's side didn't exactly inspire thoughts of heroism. *Men of honor . . .*

Nova, as if sensing Hap's mutinous thoughts, spun back to them, reminding Hap once again of the Tasmanian Devil—reckless . . . scary . . . something to avoid. Nova leveled his eyes underneath those black furry eyebrows at Hap. Hap gulped.

"So you want to link to someone? Your parents probably—by the look of you. What is it, kid? You never stay out past bedtime before?" Nova ran thick fingers over his square jaw. "I think you deserve a link or two. You've been indispensable. Brought some of my boys back, brought me the Hira, and delivered Amar. You've been busy and need a break, huh?" Nova stared at them a long time then snapped his fingers at the last remaining guard. "Let 'em link, wherever they want. It's on me."

Hap knew he should feel grateful. He'd be able to call his family, talk to all of them, and explain what had happened. Maybe if Nova kept his word about the call, he would also help them get home.

But Hap didn't feel grateful; instead he felt guilty. Amar was a prisoner. Nova had the Hira. *My fault. It's all my fault.* Nova had killed Harry Houdini. Houdini had died of appendicitis. Some say his appendix burst because he'd been punched in the stomach. Was Nova responsible for that? And how did Amar know Harry Houdini? How had Houdini ended up with one of the books of the Nine Unknown? Would Nova really kill Amar? Would he really use the Hira for something bad enough to affect the people on Earth? And what could Hap do about it?

Questions and no answers.

Tara shook her head as though trying to break free from the moral degradation of the room and its occupants. The guard waved his hand, making the pouchy bullfrog underlip jiggle as he tried to shoo the kids out of Nova's lair. Hap and Tara walked forward, but Tara turned back suddenly. "What'll happen to the scientist? Are you really going to kill him?" Her shrill voice carried hope that Nova really wasn't as bad as he seemed.

Nova chuckled, his heavy eyebrows lifting and dropping with the motion. "Don't you worry about him. He's been around a long time. When a guy gambles in the universe for that amount of time, he's bound to roll snake eyes sooner or later."

"But to kill him?" Tara persisted, taking another step forward, her eyes pleading for some show of mercy.

"Wanna link home, kid?"

Tara straightened. "I—yes. Of course I do!"

"Then go do it. Forget about everything else. You take care of your own and let me take care of mine." Nova walked over to the Hira and looked down on it as it hovered over the table. He swept the little catlike creature out of the way with one swipe of his thick arm. It mewled a noise of protest and slinked away with its tail thrashing behind it. He snapped his fingers at the guard again without looking up.

"Out!" the guard demanded. Tara's shoulders slumped, but she followed Hap out of the gold-foiled room into the dank, darkened caverns.

"They're going to kill him." Her whisper sounded like a moan.

"I know."

The guard turned his ape-frog face to them. They fell silent and followed him into another section of tunnels. Their feet clacked against the metal grating on the floor, sounding as hollow and empty as Hap felt.

The walk ended in a room filled with wires. Gygak waited for them.

The guard shoved them in and left as though he thought himself to be quite above babysitting a bumbling underling and a couple of kids.

Nova called this the flare room, indicating there would be warmth, but the room's chill bit into Hap's skin immediately. Wires ran the length of the back wall from the high ceiling where they connected into a tangled mess at the bottom of what looked like a huge silver plate.

There was a recess in the wall toward the top that was partitioned off by a window. Several people sat at terminals behind the glass. They were human—like Nova.

Tara wiped angrily at the tears on her cheeks as she walked up to Gygak. "You!"

"What's your breakdown? I got you the link you wanted. And I know humans don't thank people with anger. Even the Nuturians abandoned that practice after the war with the Xemits."

"You disgusting little leather-wrapped insect!" Tara lifted her arm to take a swing, but Hap grabbed her from behind and pinned her arms to her side. He held her there for a moment and whispered, "Call your mom first," into her ear. "We'll fix this after we call."

She huffed and sputtered but gave a short jerk of her head that Hap took to be agreement as he let her go. He understood her anger with Gygak. But wouldn't she be more accurate to be angry with Hap?

"Is this where we call home?" she asked, her voice filled with enough acid to melt the whole planet.

"Yes." Gygak glanced up to the people behind the glass partition and nodded. "Get on the receiver." His voice mimicked Tara's in acidity. Hap wondered that Gygak still felt willing to help them call home.

Tara stared at him. "What?"

"There!" Gygak pointed at the silver plate. Tara took a hesitant step onto it.

"You have to stand in the middle." Gygak waved her forward with all four of his hands.

Tara walked forward, her footsteps clanging loudly on the metal. Hap felt shame for letting her be the guinea pig. "Wait! You sure you want to go first? Do you want me to test it out and make sure it's safe?"

Tara smiled, though her lips wobbled. "No, I need to talk to her. I'll be okay." She inhaled sharply and said, "Do I need something? I dunno, like something to talk into?"

Gygak snorted through the nostrils in his forehead. "Primitive. How did your planet ever figure out fire? Just stand there. Once you're linked, you'll know what to do."

"Okay, whenever you're ready!" Tara's nails clicked furiously as a high-pitched whine reverberated through the air. The room dropped several degrees, making Hap wrap his arms around himself to warm them up. He finally untied his jacket and put it on. The green silk pants didn't offer much protection from the cold.

Tara's teeth chattered, and her skin turned a light blue. Each breath she released turned into white vapor in front of her mouth, and she hugged herself furiously to retain her own heat.

Hap furrowed his brow. "She's freezing!" he told Gygak. "You're going to kill her with cold!"

Gygak used his lower right arm to wave Hap's worry away. "She's fine. The receiver's pulling her energy, but it also monitors her life support needs and won't take too much away. It's a very finely tuned machine. CME Links guarantees their products no matter what galaxy you link from."

"CME Links?"

"The corporation that makes linking possible. It's highly patented, but it has made space travel much easier to all planets mature enough to handle it." He cast a sideways glance at Hap as though to insinuate Hap's people weren't mature enough.

Hap ignored the jibe. He focused back on Tara, who seemed to turn bluer every second. Ice cracked along the metal of the big plate, snapping, frosting, and turning as blue as Tara.

Tara's body went into spasms, and a small cry erupted from her blue lips.

Hap took a step forward to pull her down, but Gygak wrapped three hands around Hap's arms. "She just made first link. If you pull her out while linked, you'll damage her mind."

"What's first link?"

"The receiver pulls her energy and then projects it out into the universe. Living energy is strong enough to cause solar flares in nearby stars. The flare catches her energy, consumes it, and spits it back out in the form of a coronal mass ejection. Get it? CME Links?"

Hap blinked at Gygak. He'd read about solar flares once when satellite systems were going down and a few cities had experienced blackouts back on Earth. It had been all over the news.

Gygak waved his fourth arm dismissively. "Anyway, the coronal mass ejection links to the next closest sun, and so on and so forth, until it reaches the person you want to link to."

"How does it know where she wants to link?"

"It's the thought in her head. It pulls out that information when it drains her energy."

Tara's body shook several more times while Gygak explained. Vaporous puffs of air spurted from her mouth as she gasped for breath.

"Are you sure it's not hurting her?" Hap felt alarmed at the process. She looked miserable. What if she didn't survive it?

"She's fine. It's a little difficult when you don't know what to expect."

"Well, why didn't you explain it before she got up there?" Hap wanted to rip the little creature's leather ears off—he felt so angry. Tara continued convulsing until Hap closed his eyes, fearing she'd never stop.

"She'd been rude, hadn't she? I don't owe her anything except to do what Nova told me."

Hap gritted his teeth to keep from screaming about what a loser he thought Gygak was. Hap would never have turned someone in for execution the way Gygak had turned over Amar. Hap would never have let someone get up on that big plate without at least explaining the discomfort that would follow. Hap would have punched Gygak's nostrils in if he could muster the strength, which was currently tied up in worrying about Tara.

Just as Hap felt certain Tara would collapse, the icy plate crackled, and hazy images appeared all around Tara. It looked like a kitchen. Hap had never been in Tara's house, but he recognized the woman sitting at the table.

Tara's eyes widened and brimmed with tears that seemed to freeze on her eyelashes. "Mom?"

22. Ghosts and Phone Calls

MRS. JORDAN'S HEAD HUNG IN her hands, her fingers tangled in her hair. Her grip on her hair relaxed as she looked up. Her eyes were puckered and red. And even in this faded sort of vision where everything looked translucent, Mrs. Jordan looked pale with grief. As she exhaled, her breath came out in a puff of white mist as well.

She blinked at Tara. "Tara?" The hazy Mrs. Jordan pulled herself to her feet using the table for support, though with the table looking transparent like it did, Hap didn't think it could offer much support. Mrs. Jordan stared at Tara for a moment before her hand flew to her mouth and she gasped, "Oh! You're dead!"

"What?" Tara blinked in surprise then waved her hands in front of her. "No, no, no, no, no. I'm not dead. I swear I'm not." Tara closed the distance between them and tried to give her mom a reassuring hug, but her arms only caught empty air.

Mrs. Jordan stumbled back in shock. "You're so cold! What happened to you?"

"I was abducted by—"

"And then he killed you? It was that Hazzard man, wasn't it? He killed you and his grandson, didn't he?"

"What?" Tara said.

"What?" Hap said. "Lady, you are so off. My grandpa didn't kill anybody!"

Mrs. Jordan's head jerked as she looked around. "Fredrick?"

Hap groaned. Who had told Mrs. Jordan his real name?

"Mom, we're here—together." Tara glared at Hap as she tried to bring her mother's focus back to her. "Mr. Hazzard is a very nice man, and he didn't do anything wrong. I'm not dead, Mom, okay? Neither is Hap. We're fine. We've just been . . ." Tara took a deep breath and tilted her head to the side. "We were abducted by aliens."

Mrs. Jordan looked incredulously at her daughter. "But look at you. You're a ghost! Your poor spirit's trapped." She circled the table, clicking her nails. Hap smiled. So that's where Tara got it from.

"Mom, please! Don't go crazy on me here. I'm not dead."

"But you were abducted by aliens?" Doubt filled Mrs. Jordan's voice.

"Yes, but . . . don't go telling anyone, okay? I don't want them to have you locked up for insanity. Just tell people you know I'm all right and I'll be home soon." Tara nodded as though by nodding her head she could force her mother to agree.

Mrs. Jordan shook her head in direct defiance to Tara's nodding. "When are you coming home? How?"

"It'll take a few months. The lady flying the spaceship says it won't be very long to me, but it'll be a few months to you." Tara hurried on to interrupt the growing agony on her mother's face. "But it'll go by fast. I'll bring you home something cool. And I swear I won't complain when you put meat in the spaghetti sauce for dinner. And you'll always get to hold the remote. Just don't be sad, okay? Everything's fine. I'll be home soon."

Mrs. Jordan's image flickered.

"Energy's waning," Gygak muttered.

"Mom!" Tara reached out again, trying to hold the fragmented wisps of her mother in place, but her hand caught nothing. "Mom! I love you!"

"I love you. Tara! Tara, don't go!"

"Mom!"

The hazy shadow of Tara's kitchen melted into the air. The ice on the big plate Tara stood on cracked as it melted off and dripped into a gutter leading out of the room.

Tara turned to Hap and Gygak, her face crumpling in tears. "What happened? I wasn't done!"

"It can only project the amount of energy it took from you. You must not be very strong."

Hap jerked his arm out of the loosened grasp of Gygak's three hands and got up on the plate. Tara collapsed against him and sobbed until Hap was certain no amount of time would dry his shirt out. He felt bad she didn't get to talk longer, but he also felt in awe about the whole experience. It seemed like her legs refused to hold her weight. So Hap held Tara up until she finally spent all her tears and straightened. She turned to glare at Gygak and stepped off the plate.

Gygak nodded for the technicians to start Hap's turn, and when he turned back to greet Tara, she punched him right in the forehead just above his nostrils. Hap figured she didn't want to get her hands snotty. His leathery, winglike ears and fluffy eyebrows folded forward over his face as he fell back. "I'm stronger than you'll ever be. You're a despicable, hairless weasel!"

Hap wanted to jump off the plate, whether to stop Tara or help her beat Gygak up, he couldn't say, but he felt the shock of cold and his energy being sucked away down through his feet and into the plate. He knew if he stepped off, there would be no second chance. A jolt of electricity arced through him. *The first link.*

Tara threw more punches. Gygak avoided most of them and finally caught her fists in two of his hands. With his other two hands, he started dragging her away.

"Tara!" Hap called out. He tried to take a step toward her, but another jolt of electricity arced through him and then another until he could no longer tell where one arc began and another ended.

Gygak opened the door, dragging Tara out. "Hap!" she yelled.

"Tara!" Hap could barely focus his mind to say her name, and then everything on the plate around him snapped into the hazy familiar shapes of Hazzard's Magical Happenings. His grandfather stood behind the front counter, his gaze out toward the windows.

Hap couldn't wrench his eyes away from the blurry image of his grandfather even as he heard Tara yell his name one final time.

At Tara's voice, Hap's grandpa jerked his head up. "Who's there?"

Hap didn't care that it wasn't cool to cry. He was so glad to see his grandpa, he didn't even wince when his voice squeaked as he said, "You won't believe what happened to me—but I'm not dead."

His energy wasn't very strong to begin with, stemming from bad sleep and not enough food for several days going. This meant his time, like Tara's, would be short.

Hap stammered a little and blubbered a lot when he realized his grandpa had tears in his eyes too.

"Hap . . ." he repeated over and over.

"Grandpa, we were abducted by aliens, Tara and I. And we're in some galaxy, or planetary system, called Stupak's Circle, and we went through this spiral drop thing, and some intergalactic police force attacked us and chased us out of Earth's atmosphere. And there are aliens, Grandpa, *real* aliens—the kind with too many arms and not enough fingers. And right now, one of the nine unknown scientists—who's, like, a gazillion years old—is about to get murdered by this space mafia guy, and I swear, I know Tara thinks we're getting home in a few months or whatever, but I don't think so. We'll be lucky to get off this planet alive! It was my fault, Grandpa. I gave the Hira to Don Nova. I told them where to find the scientist. It was all my fault!" Hap spoke so fast, his grandpa likely didn't understand anything he said. But Hap *had* to talk fast. What if the link dissolved or whatever it did when Tara used it?

"Nova?" Hap's grandpa whispered. "Hap, you didn't." His grandpa reached out a hand to try to touch Hap, but the hand went through Hap's shoulder. "The scientist . . . he's there?"

Hap nodded. "They're going to torture him and then kill him, Grandpa! I didn't mean to. I swear I didn't know. I heard Tolvan tell you some lady stole a pyramid. He said she couldn't make the delivery. I thought he meant she couldn't deliver it to the scientist. I didn't know he meant Nova. I was trying to help, but I totally screwed up. It's all my fault. I am so sorry!"

Grandpa Hazzard tried to grab Hap's shoulders and shuddered as his hands passed through. "Stop it, Hap. This isn't your fault. It's mine. I should've let you in, let you listen. The secrets . . . mum's the word . . . I've always told the MUM society that our secrets breed trouble. I'm sorry, boy. I should have trusted you."

MUM—Magic, Unity, and Might. The magician's magazine. Hap never had associated the word for Houdini's society of magicians with the phrase "mum's the word."

"Houdini found the box that hid one of the books of the Nine Unknown, and somehow through the box he contacted that very scientist, who was still alive and traveling the galaxy. They became friends, and the scientist shared some of his secrets with Houdini. When people from other planets showed up to take the box and steal the crystal pyramid, Houdini helped protect the pyramid and formed the trust—the MUM society. They were trusted to protect the scientist's secrets, and they have—for all these years."

"So the magicians guild is involved?"

"Oh, no. Not all of them. Very few of them, actually."

Tears froze on Hap's eyelids. The history of the guild seemed not so important compared to being face-to-face with a man he loved so much. "Is everyone okay? Are Mom and Dad okay? Is Dad still—" The word *alive* stuck in his throat.

"Your parents are both . . . fine. They're worried, naturally . . . we've all been worried, but they're holding up as well as they can. Your father is holding out as well as can be expected."

"I need to talk to them. I need to explain what happened. If you try to explain it, they'll lock you up in a nuthouse."

"We've already done the arguing over my theory. No one believes you were taken by aliens. I finally buttoned up before your mother punched me. I've been questioned by the police so many times, they've almost convinced me I'm guilty of something horrible." Grandpa Hazzard leaned in, his steel-gray eyes darkened with worry and fear. "You have to save the scientist, Hap."

"I don't think I can. They took him away a while ago to question him."

His grandpa hit the counter with his ghostly fist so hard the cash register jingled. "You can't allow that!"

Hap threw his arms up in the air in frustration. He felt the movement steal more energy, and his grandfather started to fade. Hap forced himself to hold still. "How am I supposed to save him? I'm fourteen; I don't have any kind of weapon. I thought I could fix things! I thought I could be the hero, but I made everything worse! We're talking the mafia here, Grandpa!"

"Hazzard men are men of honor."

"But—"

"No buts about that! Do you know who the Nine Unknown are?"

Hap didn't bother mentioning that the point of being unknown is that no one knows. Time was short, and the situation didn't allow for sarcasm.

His grandfather took a deep breath. "The books of the Nine Unknown contain secrets that—if in the wrong hands—would wipe out mankind entirely. Hap, no matter what . . . you must protect him."

"What if it isn't safe?" It sickened Hap to show his fear to his fearless grandfather.

His grandfather's eyes softened. "You're right, of course. Protect Tara and yourself first. You aren't a soldier. Come home to us. But if you can help the scientist while saving yourselves, then do it. At least try. In the meantime, I'll contact ICE. I'll contact MUM too. Together, we'll find a way to help you."

These were the words Hap had hoped to hear. Relief flooded through him.

Alison's hazy form sauntered in from the back holding a box of googly-eyed glasses and stopped short upon seeing Hap. The box clattered to the tile floor in a scattering of black and white. She blinked then screamed.

She fled to the back room, shouting, "Hap's a ghost! Mo-om! Hap's a ghost!"

Hap hurried after her. Or *tried* to hurry after her. His legs wouldn't leave the general vicinity of the front door. "Stop her, Grandpa! She'll make everyone think I'm dead!"

As soon as Hap's grandfather moved to catch Alison, the room changed, and though Hap stayed where he was, he felt like he followed his grandpa through the hallway, past the bathroom, and to the storeroom where Alison's shrieks could be heard.

The hallway flickered into the shapes of shelving, boxes, and the little sitting area his parents had made for him and Alison when they were really young. The worn couch was awash in blue light from the TV being on. Hap tried hard to see what was playing, but the screen looked like static snow. His mother sat on the couch, several invoices and a pen in her lap, with both hands on Alison's shoulders. "Talk slower, honey . . . I don't know what you're saying . . ."

Tears welled up in Hap's eyes again at the sight of her. His dad sat next to her, running his hand over Alison's head. A blanket rested over his legs, and a laptop balanced on his knees. On the laptop screen, Hap saw a website for missing children. His parents looked up as soon as his grandpa entered and saw Hap at the same instant.

Their gasps came out in the form of white vapor from the drop in temperature.

His mom broke into sobs. "No!" she yelled.

"I'm not dead!" Hap insisted. "I'm okay. I was—" He shot an apologetic look at his grandfather. "Tara and I were accidentally taken onto a spaceship. We were abducted by aliens." He hurried on before they could protest. "But we're alive. Tara already visited her mom. You can go ask her. But don't tell anyone else. They'll just think you're nuts. But, Mom . . . pretty cool that Grandpa was right about aliens, huh?"

His family flickered from view. "Wait! I love you guys . . . the call's ending. I have to go. I'll be home as soon as I can! Take care of each other! Dad! Hold on! I'll be home soon!"

Hap had no idea if they heard his last words or not. He wanted to mention he might have a cure, but he didn't know if he believed it or not and didn't want to give false hope. The ice on the plate cracked and melted into the gutters. Hazzard's Magical Happenings was gone. Hap collapsed where he was, drained of all energy.

When he lifted his head, he felt as though galaxies whirled past his vision. He saw Earth below him and sailed toward it until his feet touched soil in the middle of a city. People surrounded him. The city's buildings were all in disrepair. Hap stepped forward in confusion, his feet crunching on the broken glass littering the ground. Children cried. Men cried. The ground under his feet felt hot. Someone touched his hand beside him. Hap turned to see Tara, her eyes wide with horror. Her mouth moved as though she was yelling at him, but no sound came out. She pointed. Hap's eyes trailed in the direction she indicated. Hazzard's Magical Happenings stood in a clearing. His family stood in front of the store looking heavenward. Hap stepped forward to join them as they swung their arms over their heads to shield themselves. Hap glanced up in time to see the light right before everything exploded.

Hap's eyes snapped open as he drew a ragged breath. *A dream. Just a dream.*

But no dream had ever felt so real. His heart constricted in his chest with the realization he had just witnessed the earth exploding.

23. Magic Show

His mind whirled. His head felt like his brain had been slapped repeatedly against his skull.

Tara. He had to move. *Just a dream.* He had to find Tara. His legs barely twitched when he tried to get up. It was several minutes more before he finally felt normal and stood. His legs still wobbled, but they held him.

He looked up to see if the people at the desks were coming down to take him prisoner again, but they seemed entirely uninterested in Hap. He'd had a pretty direct conversation concerning getting the scientist away from Nova, yet the people at the desks seemed to pay no attention to him.

Hap hopped off the plate, his legs giving a little with the motion. For as cold as he had been, he now felt like he'd swallowed fire. Sweat rolled off his face. He forced his legs forward and left the room to go find Tara.

He went right.

The dark tunnel lit up under the grating as he moved forward, but even so, he couldn't see very well. He moved cautiously.

A few minutes into creeping down the tunnel, his body temperature stabilized. But because he'd sweated so much, the cool air in the tunnel nearly froze him to death. He passed one door made of bamboo and decided to check it for Tara.

He edged it open enough to peek inside. The room had a few humans and a few guys like Mosh in it. They played some sort of game on the table in front of them. Rumbling laughter filled the room as one of the humans won whatever it was they played.

Hap shook his head. Finding it empty, he eased the door closed and moved on. He checked several rooms: two had nothing in them aside from sparse supplies; one had a female Mosh. She sat at a control panel. She caught Hap looking at her and with a humph turned her back on him.

Another room smelled terrible—not that it didn't smell bad everywhere down in the tunnels, but Hap had almost grown used to the bite of heavy stink. Not until he reached for the door did he remember that every intake of air carried the rotted egg smell. And he only remembered it because from the door came a stench so much worse. How could he get used to such a stench?

A heavy throbbing bass shook the floor under Hap's feet as he nudged the door open. The huge room contained several pools of water that steamed and bubbled. Humans and ape-frog people, dressed in rags that seemed to be passing for swimwear, were having a party. The deep bass throb was music coming from a marble bowl at the table. Hap felt like he could *see* the music as it pulsed from the bowl. A man's voice sang out, "Riding a comet to the end of time, living the high life with you on my mind . . ."

Some people danced, and Hap shuddered, quickly shutting the door. Ape-frogs in swimwear redefined Hap's concept of nightmare.

In another room, Hap finally found Gygak and Tara. Gygak held one of his hands over his nostrils. Blood seeped down between his fingers as he glared at her. Tara glared right back. On a table behind her sat a human woman in a suit of plated red armor and two ape-frog men laughing at Gygak.

"Hit him again. You don't want to give him time to recover," the woman coached Tara. Her dark brown angular features contrasted against the red plating. She wore a helmet with a black fin across the top. A gun with a ten-inch barrel sat holstered at her thigh. At her wrists were thick black cuffs. A red ruby-like jewel in each cuff glittered as she moved her hands in a hitting motion.

Tara rolled her fingers into her palm and jabbed at Gygak. He barely moved out of the way in time.

"Good jab," the woman encouraged.

"What are you doing?" Hap asked, completely bewildered to find Tara taking boxing lessons from some buff woman in red.

"Proving I'm strong." Tara took another swing, which Gygak wasn't so lucky to dodge, and clipped him in the cheek.

The lady in red laughed and clapped her hand against her gun barrel. "Good one. You have serious potential."

Tara blushed. "Thanks, Meg."

Hap had been on the receiving end of several of Tara's punches, making him pity Gygak for a moment. She had way more than serious potential. He then took in the entire scene and realized that Tara wasn't being held captive and that no one seemed bothered by his presence.

"Tara?" At his saying her name, she turned. Gygak tried to throw a punch of his own, but the lady, in a blur of red movement, caught his fist. "Not behind her back." She pushed his hand away and moved to stand between them. "Never turn your back to your opponent," Meg said to Tara.

Tara nodded, acknowledging the advice, and walked up to Hap. "Meg's just been showing me how to defend myself. All my life, I've had to listen to everyone else, listen to adults fight and make decisions that have everything to do with me, but they never ask how I feel. Well, not anymore. I'm through getting walked on and pushed around!"

"Right . . . well, um . . ." He didn't know what to say. Hap wondered if she'd finally cracked under all the pressure. The fire in Tara's eyes as she tilted her chin proved she had enough anger in her to take on anything. Hap looked at the woman Tara called Meg. "Are we allowed to leave now?"

"Sure. But where you gonna go?" Meg folded her arms across the red breastplate, the hard material clacking as she did.

Hap shrugged. He didn't think it would be a good idea to confess he planned on going to find the scientist and then on getting back to Laney's ship, back to the Rissans. He wanted to go home and visit the burger joint by Hazzard's Magical Happenings and order ten burgers with onion rings and fry sauce. He wanted to drink soda pop until he floated away. He wanted to forget he'd had a terrible nightmare a moment ago. But instead of saying any of this—since the part about saving the scientist would likely get him killed—he shrugged again.

"Where you gonna go?" Meg repeated. "You need to think of this question in several parts. You need to think of it in its immediate sense. Where do I want to go right now? And its nearby sense. Where do I want to go tomorrow? And then you need to consider your long term. Where do I want to end up?" Meg took out a thin dagger from under the black cuff at her wrist and used it to pare her fingernails while Hap considered all the various answers he could give to her question.

Gygak had recuperated enough to growl his discontent with all of them and skulk out of the room, muttering something about a cold compress.

Hap sidestepped the question with a comment. "Thanks for helping Tara out. I thought he was going to hurt her."

"The quad? He's harmless. Nova considers you family now for bringing him the Hira and the scientist. He doesn't let the family fight amongst themselves. The quad was angry when I came upon them, but I straightened things out."

"By letting Tara hit him?" Hap's gaze dropped to the floor now spotted from Gygak's bloody nose . . . or forehead . . . or whatever those holes were. Hap frowned at the blood.

The scientist. Was the scientist already dead? Would they have already tortured him? Hap felt the weight of his guilt settle firmly on his shoulders. *If I hadn't told Gygak about the scientist, they never would have captured him. If I hadn't helped Gygak, Nova wouldn't have the Hira.* Hap felt like asking Tara to punch him out too. He and Gygak shared nearly equal responsibility for the horrible things happening. Tara was right to be angry.

Nova rewarded them with the links to their families because they had accidentally brought a man to his death—a man his grandpa said he had to protect if he could.

"She needed practice. We needed a target. And since he'd caused her grief, he owed her a debt."

Tara looked satisfied with having spent a moment pummeling the one person she considered to be at fault for all her troubles.

Meg snapped her fingers. "If the quad gives you any more grief, let me know. I'll remove his bottom set of arms." She pulled out another knife at her waist. "I've never really liked Gygans. A man with that many hands is always trouble." As she tucked her knives away and swaggered to the door, faint beeps emanated from the button-sized jewel at her black cuff.

She pressed the jewel, and Nova's voice rumbled through the room, demanding that Meg return to his office. In the background, another voice—female—shouted about her money, her payment, and her *kids*.

"Laney . . ." Tara breathed.

Meg snapped her fingers again, indicating for the guards to follow her.

Laney was there in the tunnels, in Nova's office. She'd come to rescue them, Hap just knew she had. Hap wanted to chase after Meg and her guards so they could take him to Laney.

But how could he face her when he'd stolen her crystal and given it to Nova, only after getting the scientist captured, of course? How could he face her and say he was sorry?

Hap wanted to kick something. *My fault. It's all my fault.* Events spun out of his control faster than he had time to think about them. Laney . . . the scientist . . . Tara . . . his grandpa. That weird dream. *The Hazzard way . . .*

Tara started to the door to follow Meg, but Hap grabbed at her sleeve.

"We need to get the scientist," Hap whispered.

"But Laney's here! Laney's *here* and we need to leave. Now! What if that Nova guy shoots her? You saw him draw his gun on Gygak—his own guy! He's insane. We made a mistake coming here, Hap. We shouldn't have given the Hira to the psycho with the unibrow. Huge mistake."

Her every word felt like daggers piercing him from all sides. "I know. And the mistake is mine. And I have to make it right. That's why we have to get the scientist first."

"We should get Laney first. She'll know what to do about saving the scientist. If we're lucky, Svarta'll be with her." Tara clicked her nails, and her body tensed like she planned on carrying out her own plan before hearing Hap out.

Hap grabbed her hand to make her stop. "That noise is driving me nuts," he said. "Svarta could probably take on a whole army by herself. I bet she'd beat Nova in a gun fight. Laney's got her back covered or she wouldn't be here."

"And maybe Meg would help her. Meg seemed nice . . ."

Hap wanted to roll his eyes but didn't want Tara punching him for it. She could be so naive. "Nice? Did you see the gun in her holster? That thing was bigger than my whole leg. She was helping you *hit* someone . . . And she works for Nova, who *isn't* nice."

"That little Gy-geek deserved to get slapped a few times. What a creep! Don't ask me to feel bad for hitting him. It's his fault we're here. He lied to us!"

"It isn't his fault entirely. It's my fault too . . ." Hap's voice sounded small, even in his own ears. He'd hoped Tara felt the apology behind his words, because he didn't know if he could say them out loud yet.

"You thought you were doing the right thing. But you know better now."

"I know better?"

Tara smiled. "You know to let me do the thinking from now on."

Hap smiled too. "Grandpa said he'd talk to ICE and MUM and see what kind of help he could get us. But Tara, he also said we had to save the scientist if we could. Laney will be okay. She wouldn't have come without a plan, but Amar . . . he's here because I told Gygak where he was. So our choices are Laney or Amar. What do you think, All-Thinking-One?"

She grinned. "It's not *all* your fault. I was with you when you made those choices. But you're right. Let's get the scientist—"

"You!" One of the guards who had been with Meg stormed into the room.

"What?" Hap asked, hoping he looked innocent. Meg said Nova considered them family, but he must have considered them more like the cousins who'd been in jail several times and were not to be trusted snooping around the house.

The second guard showed up a few moments later. He stood a whole head shorter than the first guy and had a bluish sort of zigzag pattern across his pouchy underlip. "What were they doing?"

"We weren't doing anything—" Hap started to say, but Tara interrupted.

"I was telling Hap that I could hold the stars in my fingertips. He doesn't believe me. That lame and way-stupid scientist Nova's got locked up doesn't believe me either. But I can." Her skinny chin jutted out in defiance.

Hap used all his effort not to say, "What are you talking about?"

The shorter guard looked interested. "Show us."

"It takes a lot of energy out of me. It makes me tired for days. I want to show Hap and the scientist at the same time. That way I don't have to use up energy I don't have. I can only do it once. You can watch too . . ."

The shorter guard's flappy lip curled upward into an agreeable grin.

The taller one shook his head, making his pouch jiggle. "The scientist is having last meal."

Last meal didn't sound like it meant the same thing as it did for the Rissans. It sounded like the death sentence it was. "Oh, good!" Hap exclaimed. "I'm starving! Let's join him. We can eat while Tara proves she can do what she says." Hap cupped his hand around the side of his mouth as though he were sharing a secret with the guards. "Personally, I don't think she can do it."

Hap hoped she knew what she was doing. He'd used the phrase, "I can hold the stars in my hands" tons of times when doing demonstrations in Hazzard's Magical Happenings. He figured she had a set of D'Lites in her pocket. D'Lites were a popular magic trick they sold at Hazzard's Magical Happenings.

He frowned at Tara. He'd shown her everything in his pockets that they could use to escape. But she hadn't shown him what she had. He wondered what else she had in her pockets. She didn't seem to notice his scowl. She focused on the guards, looking at them as though she held some sort of authority and fully expected them to take her to Amar's prison cell.

Hap almost laughed when they actually did. The big guard rolled his shoulders and turned with a sharp wave of his hand, indicating the two teenagers should follow. "C'mon, Blish!" the taller one commanded.

Hap nodded in appreciation. *Good job, Tara.* This would save them the time it would have taken to search the tunnels and possibly get lost—*probably* get lost. Hap considered all the different possible ways of getting Amar out with the guards there, but in most of the scenarios, they all ended up getting shot.

He shook the thoughts from his head, deciding his time would be better spent memorizing the passages they followed in case they needed to find their way back again. They didn't go far before they were at a door with a little barred window at the top.

Hap stood on his tiptoes to try to peer inside, but he was too short to see. Hap waited expectantly, but the guard didn't make any move to open the door.

Tara crossed her arms over her chest. "Well?"

"I brought you here. Now show us," the taller guard insisted.

"But I need *him* to see. He can't see me through a door." Tara flipped her blonde hair over her shoulder and leaned against the wall as though she had no intention of doing anything until they let Amar out.

The taller one did a raspberry with his huge mouth, spraying a light film of spittle everywhere. Tara grunted in disgust but didn't move.

The taller one turned and said, "I don't really want to see anyway."

Tara shrugged her indifference and looked at her fingernails. Hap wanted to stop the guard, make him come back. Hap saw their chance walking away, though he didn't know exactly how good a chance it really was even if they did get Amar out of his cell.

Blish growled in a way that sounded like a whine. He trotted to the tall guard and laid a hand on the guard's shoulder. "I want to see." The words came out as a definite whine. "Please, Oreg . . ."

Oreg grunted. "Why isn't the quad watching these two? How did we end up in charge?" But he turned in resignation. He stomped the few paces back to Tara. "Fine. Show us the stars in your hands."

She made no motion toward showing them anything, and Hap felt as impatient as the Servien guards.

Oreg grunted again and took out a thin rod maybe only an inch long from his utility belt. The rod slid into a hole in the door Hap hadn't noticed before. Oreg stopped and turned to Blish. "Get out your weight. Just in case."

Blish pulled out his drubber. Hap's plans that all ended up with them getting shot seemed far more likely now that a gun was already trained on the door.

True to Oreg's prediction, Amar had a tray of lumpy rolls in front of him. The rolls looked far better than anything they'd eaten at the Rissan dinner. Hap's mouth watered just looking at them. Amar hadn't touched any of it. He looked up, seeming uninterested in anything Oreg or Blish had to say. He suddenly took notice when he realized Tara and Hap were with them.

Amar focused on the two of them with dread in his dark eyes. His shoulders slumped, and Hap thought he heard the word *foolish* hiss from Amar's lips.

That wasn't a very nice thing to say about two people trying to save him, Hap thought, even if he did secretly agree with Amar. They were foolish. They had no plan, no ability to do anything about Amar except stare at him.

Besides, Hap had seen Tara's magical abilities when they were back on Earth, and hadn't been all that impressed.

"Show us!" Blish waved his gun in Tara's face.

Tara spread her hands wide to show they were empty, and with a flourish she plucked at something in the air seeming to have caught a red glow.

Blish gasped. Oreg grunted. Amar looked baffled by the whole visit. Hap took the opportunity to steal a roll off the tray. Who knew when, or if, they'd get another chance to eat? He stuffed it in his mouth and nodded appreciatively at Tara's trick.

Tara waved the red glow around until she made a tossing motion, and it disappeared from her right hand. She moved to catch it, and suddenly the red glow was caught between the fingers on her left hand. Blish let out an appreciative *ahhhh*. She threw the light up and "caught" it in her mouth then put her fingers in her mouth and fished the light out again.

Hap almost laughed out loud. She was really good! Her pantomime skills beat the heck out of anything he could do. He almost forgot they were there to help Amar.

Amar, in this time, started moving toward the door. Hap snagged another couple of lumpy rolls and shoved them into his jacket pocket. He was surprised they didn't taste like the egg-rot slime he inhaled with every breath. Hap then followed Amar's example.

Tara took sidesteps, forcing Oreg and Blish farther back into the cell so they could watch her show. She reached out and said, "Here. Let me give it to you so you can hold the star."

Oreg grumbled as though horribly inconvenienced, but his pouch flushed to an odd shade of pink. He held his hand out.

Tara stepped closer to him, waving the red glow between her thumb and forefinger in front of Oreg's face so he stayed focused on it. Her other hand disappeared behind Oreg's side as she placed the glow in the center of Oreg's palm. She held the red glow at his palm for several seconds and blew on it. She let go of the glow and it winked out, seeming to disappear with her breath.

"Hey!" Blish whined. "You blew it out!"

With the glow of Tara's star gone, Oreg noticed Hap and Amar at the door. His drubber came out, aimed directly between Hap's eyes.

24. PRINCIPLES OF FRIENDSHIP

"BACK 'ER UP!" OREG WAVED his drubber to the side, motioning Hap and Amar back into the room. Hap quickly complied, feeling his face flush with frustration, fear, and irritation for not getting out sooner. Of course, if he and Amar had made it out the door, what would have happened to Tara? Hazzards didn't leave anyone behind.

Grandpa Hazzard had been in the Army. His medals hung in a shadow box alongside a picture of the man Grandpa Hazzard pulled out of a torture camp. Hap could never have left Tara and gone home to face his dad and grandpa.

Tara didn't look worried. She winked at Hap. Winked! Dumb girl. They were all about to get shot and she was winking?

Amar didn't look worried either. Hap determined he was the only sane one of the three. He snagged another roll off Amar's tray and stuffed it full into his mouth. If he was going to die, he wanted a full stomach.

"Nova will want to know about your tricks, little scientist." Oreg trained his gun at Tara, likely fearing she'd throw stars at him or something. His pouch jiggled as he reached around his side for the little rod that locked and unlocked the door. Leaning his head closer to Blish, he said, "Do you have the key?"

"I have mine."

Oreg shook his head. "I need mine back."

"I don't have yours. You unlocked the door."

Oreg grunted and pointed his drubber on Tara. "She took it. Search her."

So that's what Tara's plan had been. She had taken the key once she had them distracted with her magic trick.

Blish pulled out a small horseshoe-shaped object that scanned over Tara.

Tara's smile vanished, and she no longer winked at anyone. She held her hands in tight balls at her side while he moved the horseshoe object over her several times.

"She doesn't have it." Blish let his arms fall to his side in defeat.

"Her hands! Check her hands!" Oreg's deep rumble boomed through the room.

Tara unrolled her fingers from her palm. She looked like she held her breath as she kept her fingers tightly together, palms out, flattened toward the ceiling.

Hap held his breath too.

"Nothing," Blish insisted. "You dropped it again."

Oreg's eye twitched. "Leave 'em locked here. Nova'll want to know what they've done."

Blish followed Oreg to the door. "But what *have* they done?"

Oreg turned and cast a cold, beady black eye on all three of them. Hap shuddered. "I don't know, but they're up to something."

The two ape-frogs left the room. The door shut, and Oreg's voice grumbled, "Use *your* key!"

"I imagine . . ." Amar seated himself on the cot behind the tray and glanced at the remaining food, casting a cursory glance at Hap's bulging pockets. "I imagine you came here to rescue me."

Hap shifted from foot to foot. He felt bad the rescue had turned out so poorly. He didn't feel bad for stealing the rolls, though. After the energy drain of the phone call, he really needed something to eat.

Tara eyed the plate hungrily until Amar shoved it in her direction. She plucked up several rolls and crunched into them. "We did."

"And now here you are, caught, and imprisoned with a man sentenced to die. Was that part of your plan?"

Hap shook his head and started to say no, but Tara interrupted. "Of course."

Hap looked at her. The girl had finally gone loony.

"Oh, stop staring at me like that, Hap!" she said as she sat next to Amar and swallowed another bite of roll. "Don't you know anything about magic?" Her smile confounded Hap.

Hap knew everything about magic. He knew about escape artists and ropes and illusions. Hap felt absolutely irritated that the girl who couldn't pull off a disappearing scarf trick dared ask him if he knew anything about magic.

"I know—" he began, but she cut him off as she stood with a little flourish.

"It isn't enough to make it disappear. You have to make it come back." She bowed to Hap, holding out her hand. In her palm lay a tiny metal rod.

Hap couldn't help it—he applauded. He snatched up the key rod in his fist and swung her around in a hug. "You're hired!"

Once he settled her on her feet, they hurried to eat the remaining bits of food under Amar's instruction. The scientist took possession of the rod and quickly unlocked the door.

"Which way out?" Amar whispered. Tara's expression went from excited to horrified.

She turned wide eyes on Hap. "We can't leave now. What about L—"

"We won't leave Laney."

Amar smiled faintly at Hap's comment. "How did Elaine come to be here?"

Both teenagers rolled their shoulders in shrugs. "We heard her on Meg's link key. She was yelling at Nova. She said she wanted her money and the crystal." Hap left off the part about her demands that Nova return Hap and Tara too. He didn't understand why her demanding their return made him feel protected, but it did.

Amar led the way back up to Nova's lair. Hap felt flushed with stupidity for telling Amar they'd made a wrong turn, but then flushed with satisfaction when it turned out Hap was right. They crouched low against the wall to talk. "You need to get out of here. Nova wants you dead and won't hesitate to have you killed as soon as anyone sees you. Tara and I are considered allies for the moment. They're watching us, but they haven't tried shooting us yet. Laney and Svarta are pretty tough. I bet they've got everything under control."

"You really do need to get out of here," Tara said to Amar. "The chances of us getting you out again are zero."

Amar chuckled and clucked his tongue. "I would have said the chances of you rescuing me the first time were zero. It's good I'm not a gambling man. I'd have surely lost that bet. I will take your advice."

Hap turned to get going but turned back when Tara pulled the book they'd found at the library from behind her back. The book didn't look too damaged in spite of the wear and tear of being stashed under Tara's shirt. "Is this one of the books?" She handed it to Amar.

Amar laughed outright. His whole body shook with the effort of keeping his mirth quiet. "No, Tara. It is not one of the nine books of my brothers. This is the only personal possession I had when I left Earth—belonging to my youngest daughter. It was all I could think to take with me when I fled my home to protect the society of my brothers. This book is Panchatantra—the five principles."

"Principles of what?"

"Friendship, of course." His fingers ran over the leather binding of the book. "My little daughter loved stories." He turned away from them, hiding his face. "Go save Elaine Sanchez. Tell her I have the credits she needs to get off the planet and to get you back to Earth. Tell her I will try to help her find her father. But if she wants my help, she must help me. Tell her there will be nothing done with nothing given. Tell her I will meet her at her starship."

Startled and elated, Hap and Tara whirled to do as directed by Amar.

"Did you hear that?" Tara squealed as quietly as she could manage.

"Yep. We're going home!" Hap felt good he'd done as his grandfather requested. He felt good that they'd managed to do everything they'd meant to do. He had a few pebbles and leaves in his pocket from this world and figured he'd sneak a few things from the supply room to offer proof that he'd been on an alien planet. Amar had credits. Hap was going home!

25. Rescue Plans

Finding Laney proved to be the easier part of the plan. Saving Laney . . . well, that was trickier than Hap imagined. Laney had the barrel of Meg's huge gun directly in front of her face. Three guards held Svarta pinned to a wall. Nova and the Hira were nowhere to be seen.

Hap pulled his head back into the hallway to avoid being seen by anyone inside the room. "Maybe we should've had Amar come with us," he whispered to Tara.

"You think?" Tara peeked around the corner. Svarta yelled something Hap was glad to not understand.

Tara pulled back. "What're we going to do?"

Hap's mind raced. He finally nodded as if confirming his plan to himself and jerked his head to the right. "We choose the right." He took off in that direction. Tara followed. Hap hoped his plan didn't end with them getting shot.

He peeked into the room with the ape-frogs. The music no longer blared from the stone bowl. A few people and ape-frogs still lounged in the bubbling pools of stinky-egg-rotten water. Hap left Tara outside the door . . . just in case these guys weren't the partygoers he thought them to be. He sauntered in.

"Hey, guys." Hap kept his voice casual and hoped that the knocking in his knees didn't echo out his mouth.

No one responded. Most didn't turn to see who spoke to them. There were two human men, one human girl, three ape-frog males, and three more ape-frog females. The human girl didn't even open her eyes. Her head rested against the side of the burbling pool. Every time one of the bubbles popped open at the surface, Hap held his breath.

The repulsive odors stung Hap's nose. His stomach churned, but he ignored the wave of sickness. "Nova can't, uh . . . sleep. He wants some music and asked me to come here to borrow your . . ." Hap looked at the bowl where the music had come from before. "Your player." Hap cringed. The probability of the bowl thing being called a player was beyond his ability to calculate.

"The sonico basin?" One of the humans lifted his head lazily. "Clort! Some kid wants your rhythm."

A huge ape-frog eased himself up over the side of the pool. A strip of grayish cloth clung to his midsection. Steam rose from his body. He didn't have the basketball-shaped belly that Mosh had—most of the Serviens kept in better shape than Mosh—but seeing him dressed in only the cloth made Hap feel queasier.

He strutted over to Hap, his large feet clapping against the stone floor. "Nobody takes my rhythm." He jabbed Hap's chest with a thick finger.

"Oh, I totally hear you. I'd be ticked too. But it's not for me. Nova wants it. And I was sent to fetch it for him."

"I don't know you," Clort slurred. His breath smelled worse than the odious steam rising off his body. Hap tried hard to breathe through his mouth, sure the entire place was giving him some airborne disease. The doctors would find he'd died of rotten-egg lung.

"I don't know you either." Hap shrugged. "But we both know Nova, and he said—"

Tara swept the door open angrily. "Haven't you got it yet? You're taking so long that he's decided that you're going to be shot. You and anyone who's detained you from getting the sonico basin. He's furious!"

Clort backed away several paces, waving his hands in front of him. "Hey, I didn't know he was in a hurry. Take it." Clort picked up the basin and pushed it into Hap's arms. "Hurry. And if you try to blame the delay on me, I have witnesses that'll say you wouldn't leave and I had to throw you out."

"I won't blame you." Hap backed up to the door. Tara held it open for him, and they exited with a wave and a thanks.

As soon as the door closed, Hap shot Tara a look of pure gratitude.

Once they'd made it to the end of that tunnel and turned the corner, Hap said, "You totally saved me. I really thought that guy was going to give me a swirly in that stinky pool."

Tara gagged. "It smells terrible everywhere down here, but that place was toxic! What are you doing? What would you need *that* for?"

"Distraction . . . I hope."

They settled in an alcove under a flight of stairs to test the thing. Spiderless cobwebs laced the corners of the alcove. Little things that looked like red potato bugs crawled over the fine strands of webbing. When they reached the top, they rolled into themselves, forming balls, and rolled all the way to the base of their web. Tara kept clear of the webs and the bugs. Hap did too.

Hap fumbled with the basin for several minutes, trying to get it to work. He finally realized he had to take the metal spoon thing out. As soon as the spoon no longer made contact with the basin, sound rolled around the sides until it escaped the top. The noise was deafening, and Hap hurried to replace the spoon. There wasn't time to figure out volume control, and the louder the basin, the better.

"So what's your plan?" Tara clicked her nails and darted furtive glances up and down the tunnel from the little alcove. She darted just as many furtive glances to the little red bugs to make sure they stayed on their webbing.

Hap considered. "Well . . . we take this and set it just outside the door. When they come out to see what all the noise is, we can konk them over the head or something."

"That's your plan?" Tara's fingers stopped clicking. "That's your *whole* plan? That plan stinks as bad as this hole in the ground. Did you see Meg's gun? Did you see how fast she moves? Konk her on the head? Are you insane? Now I know why your mother called you Hap Hazzard."

She ranted a few moments longer until Hap put his hand over her mouth. She tried to elbow him, but he tucked in his stomach so she'd miss. She stopped struggling against his hold when she heard Svarta's voice.

Svarta seemed to be struggling too. The clang of her booted heels echoed off the metal walls. She shouted, hollered, and beat her boot heels against the grating harder, but the guards didn't act bothered by her tantrum. Svarta and her two guards passed by the little alcove first. Meg and Laney were next.

"He owes me a ton of credits. Do you have any idea what it cost me to get that stupid rock for him? How can you not see how unfair this is? He owes me, Meg!"

Meg had her gun out, herding Laney from behind. "But you didn't bring it to him right away, did you?"

"I was going to get it to him. I still had a rotation before I had to be here with it. You know he's wrong to treat me like a prisoner! What if he did this to you?"

They passed the alcove. Blood rushed past Hap's ears, making Laney and Meg's conversation seem distant. With a cry of desperation, he pulled out the metal spoon and let it clatter to the grating. The music swirled around the bowl until it broke free. The metal walls rattled against the vibrations of the noise.

Meg turned in time to see Hap swing the basin around and thwack her directly in the face. She dropped her gun, spun a half turn, and stumbled a moment.

The music screeched to a halt on impact and the bowl went quiet.

On impulse, Tara grabbed the gun. "Sorry!" she yelled apologetically. She aimed the big barrel at Meg. When the two ape-frogs dropped Svarta and moved forward to take the gun away from Tara, she turned it on them. They stopped. "Sorry!" she cried again.

Laney and Svarta moved fast to get their weapons back from the ape-frog men. Hap was grateful when they were fully armed again because there was no way Tara knew how to shoot Meg's gun.

"Was that a better plan?" Hap asked Tara.

Tara smiled, though it looked like a wince. Laney relieved Tara of Meg's gun, which Tara happily relinquished.

The exultant pride of victory thrilled through Hap. They'd saved the people they'd meant to save, and Amar waited for them at the ship. They only had to get out of the tunnels, and they'd be home free.

Laney handed her belt to Tara. "Tie her up." She pointed at Meg with the barrel of the big gun. Tara kneeled down beside Meg and cinched it over Meg's wrists. "I'm so sorry," she said a third time.

Meg shrugged, but her eyes flickered like fire when she settled her gaze on Hap. If a woman's gaze could burn, Hap would have melted into the grating. He dropped the basin, and it clanged like the moan of death before falling silent again.

Laney pointed at Svarta's belt. "Let's get the big guys under wraps too."

Svarta shook her head. "No way. I won this belt in the tread races. Besides, do you think my belt is going to get you very far with those guys?" With no other options, they herded the new captives back to Nova's room. Svarta took the dagger from Meg's black cuff and used it to slice up the couches. She pulled several long strips of material free and used them to tie up the guards. Gagging Meg was easy enough, a small piece of material stuffed in her mouth doing the trick. The Servien guards required a much larger gag. Tara handed two pillows from the couches to Svarta, not daring—or wanting—to gag them herself.

"With the battle over the Neswar as a distraction, there shouldn't be too much of an issue getting out of here. Most of the Serviens left in the tunnels are underlings, housekeepers, cooks, people like that," Svarta said.

Hap thought about the guys in the pool room. It made sense. He felt a little annoyed that no one had bothered to thank him and Tara for the daring rescue. He'd risked his neck for them, but they didn't seem to care very much.

Svarta did a quick inventory of the room. "Hey, Laney, remember when Nova gave you the credits for taking this job the first time?"

Laney nodded absently as she checked the guards and Meg for hidden weapons. She pulled out all sorts of slender daggers and smaller drubbers hidden on Meg.

"He pulled it from the desk and tripped . . . remember?"

"Mm-hmm," Laney mumbled as she inspected the daggers hidden in Meg's cuffs and put them into her own utility belt at her waist.

"Something else opened when he fell against his desk. Maybe it's like a safe or something. Maybe we can collect our own payment." Svarta pointed to the corner desk. Hap moved to the corner, feeling kind of excited over the idea of a secret compartment. Svarta joined him, and together they pushed and pulled every knob and anything that looked like it could activate something. Hap noticed a knothole that looked suspicious and pressed it.

Nothing happened. He exhaled a breath he hadn't realized he'd been holding and looked up with a shrug to Svarta.

Out of the corner of his eye, he saw the catlike thing disappear in a flash of fur through the wall. Literally *through* the wall. "What the . . ." Hap straightened and put his hand where he saw the creature last. The wall looked firm, but his hand disappeared through it. "Hey, guys . . ." he started to say, but Svarta had already caught up to him. She edged him behind her and pulled out her drubber. With a deep breath she eased her head through the wall, giving Hap the creeps to see her headless body, but soon her body followed after and she disappeared entirely.

Laney frowned at the place where Svarta had been and grunted in irritation. "Doesn't she know we're in a hurry?" Laney muttered, pulling out her own drubber and putting a finger to her lips. Meg's eyes widened when Svarta's arm appeared back through the wall and beckoned them to follow.

Hap hurried to comply. Secret passages were exponentially cooler than secret compartments. And a secret passage in the bad guy's lair could only lead to something totally and completely awesome.

It wasn't until after they started climbing the winding stairs behind the "wall" that it occurred to Hap that Nova might be waiting for them at the end of those stairs. He sighed. His parent's really had been right to nickname him Hap Hazzard.

The stairs ended at another gold door, left ajar. Laney waved Tara and Hap behind her as Svarta peeked around the edge. Laney nodded and opened the door wider to reveal a room similar to the one they had left, only this one had windows. Nobody but the cat-thing occupied the room.

Hap looked longingly out the windows toward fresh air—well . . . *fresher* air. Freedom lay on the other side of those windows. Hap looked around for something to break one open when he saw the Hira.

Laney, Svarta, and Tara must have all seen it at the same time he did, because they all moved forward as one toward the glowing crystal.

A closed book with metal bindings lay underneath it. A red disc hung suspended over the crystal pyramid. Soft blue light shone from the disc in a single vibrant stream on the Hira, glinting off the faceted sides. Hap reached out to take it, his heart thumping hard against his ribs. He would be able to make everything right. He couldn't wait to call his grandpa back to say that not only did he get the scientist out of a death sentence, but he'd recovered the Hira.

Laney tried to snatch his hand away, but his fingers touched the light before Laney could stop him.

Pain flooded every cell in his body. He fell to the floor, curling up against the immense pain snaking its way through every vein and pore. The pain lasted several minutes before stopping abruptly.

"Light locks," Svarta said. "They're like a force field and are impossible to open unless you have the combination. I was going to suggest we throw something at it to test it before we started sticking our own body parts on the line."

"You could've suggested it sooner," Hap grumbled as he used a chair to help him stand up.

"Would my telling you not to touch it really have stopped you?" Her mouth quirked into a smile, and her eyes, partially hidden by her hair, stared straight through him.

He didn't answer. Her telling him might have stopped him. It *might* have. She didn't have to look so smug.

Another book, similar to the one under the crystal pyramid, lay on the table next to the crystal. No blue light shone down on it. The catlike thing mewled as it wrapped itself around his legs. He had to step carefully so he didn't step on Nova's pet and managed to make it over to an end table where he saw a metal square like the Rissans used in their libraries. He picked it up and threw it at the place where the book lay on the table. Nothing happened. Svarta laughed at him when he still timidly put his hand out to touch the book.

"There's no light, leprechaun boy. No light, no light lock, no pain. You can pick it up just fine."

Hap glowered as he swept the book off the table. *What if this is the book on healing,* he wondered. He opened it carefully and stared up in confusion to Tara, who'd crossed the room to look into the pages of a book that had caused so much trouble. "It's empty."

"It's not empty." Laney crossed the room to take the book from Hap. "It's just not readable without the Hira. Nova's had these two books for a long time. Hap, you and Tara work on figuring out how to get outside through this room. Svarta, help me break the light lock's combination."

"Can't we just bust a window to get out?" Tara asked, on the same wavelength as Hap.

Svarta laughed. "Go ahead and try, but it'll rattle your teeth for hours after you bounce anything off those windows. The glass isn't breakable—not without special tools we don't happen to have on us right now."

Hap hurried to the window and climbed onto the wide windowsill, wanting to do anything to escape the smell. He'd likely need his lungs surgically scraped after he left this planet and got home again.

Hap traced his fingers over the window frame to look for screw holes or something that might come undone when Tara yelled behind him.

26. Gygak's Moment of Glory

Hap whirled around to see Gygak standing just inside the door, yanking Tara close to him while shoving the barrel of a new drubber into her neck hard enough that she cried out.

"I will not be dismissed so readily!" he shouted, his shrilly voice sounding manic. "I will not be reduced back to nothing in the family when *I* found the Hira. *I* brought the Hira forth. *I* brought the scientist to Nova. *Me*!" He took several ragged breaths, his feathery eyebrows quivering with rage. "He demoted me to nothing. Then promoted me again. And now you want to run off with the one thing that grants me status?" Gygak nodded toward the book in Laney's hands and gave another sharp nod to where Svarta had already climbed on a chair and had started messing with the red disc in an effort to turn off the light lock.

"Get over your little-man syndrome, Gy-geek!" Svarta growled. She climbed down from the chair, bringing her own gun up to aim at him.

"Uh-uh." Gygak pressed the drubber harder into Tara's skin. "You don't want to do that."

Svarta growled, but Laney put a hand on Svarta's, forcing her to lower her gun. Gygak kept two hands on Tara and one on the drubber. With his last free hand, he motioned for Svarta to hand over her weapon. She growled again as she, quite unwillingly, released it to his outstretched fingers.

Mosh lumbered into view from the doorway, gnashing his yellowed, stumpy teeth. "What're you doing?"

"They're escaping." Gygak edged to the side to make room for the Servien and held Svarta's gun out to Mosh.

Mosh took the offered weapon. But when he turned, he pointed it at Gygak, not the others. "I know they're escaping. I had to tell the home crew I saw them all exiting out the lava tube once the home crew realized the scientist was missing. Otherwise, they'd all be caught already." Mosh nodded to Svarta and Laney. "I had to shut down the witness links."

Gygak's feathery eyebrows stood up straight. "What? Why would you do something so stupid?"

Mosh looked down at his bandaged arm. "I've had some time to think—"

"Well, that's the problem right there! You imagined you were capable of thinking!" Gygak backed away a couple of steps to the door, tightening his grip on Tara while tightening the drubber to her neck.

"Don't do that, Gygak." Mosh looked pleading, his pebble-black eyes watering and his pouch wobbling.

"If you hadn't ruined the witness links, Nova'd know *I'm* loyal. He'll take me with him once I deliver these traitors to him. I'll be rich and respected. He'll take me with him while he searches for the other books, and I can get off this STINKING planet! Away from the Orissa, the Neswar, and *away* from the Circle!"

Rather than take one of his hands off Tara, he waved his drubber hand to accentuate the idea of leaving the planet.

Hap used that second to leap from the windowsill into Gygak.

He had no idea what came over him. As soon as his feet left the sill and he was sailing into the air, he thought better of what he'd done. He closed his eyes, preparing to be shot before he ever reached Gygak.

No shots rang out, but a hiss of air shot from Gygak and Hap as they collided and fell to the ground—slamming the door open wide—and onto the landing just outside. Another foot and they would have taken a tumble down the stairs. Tara had been thrown out with them. She jumped to her feet and kicked the drubber from Gygak's many reaching arms.

Mosh picked the drubber up and leveled it between Gygak's eyes—right at his nostrils. Mosh waved the gun to indicate Gygak should go back into Nova's room. Hap hurried to get up in case Mosh wasn't a very good aim. Gygak's feathery antennae flattened against his face as he struggled to his feet. They all moved back into the room. Laney kicked the door closed, bolted it shut, and shoved a chair in front of it, though the chair wasn't very big and wouldn't hold off anyone for more than a moment.

"You gonna clip me, then? After all we've been through together? You'd clip me?" Gygak snorted through his nostrils, a light mucous spray coating the barrel of the drubber. "You might as well. Nova'll have me clipped anyway."

Mosh's eyes concentrated hard on Gygak's face. His hand shook, and his thick, sausage-like finger twitched at the button.

"No!" Tara hurried to push Mosh's arm and the gun away from Gygak's face. "No more!"

"Let him do it, kid. Gy-geek'd do it to you." Svarta took her weapon back from Mosh's other hand. Laney and Svarta kept their weapons trained on the Gygan.

"What is *wrong* with you people?" Tara circled so she could face each of them. Hap blinked at her, surprised at her outburst. Hadn't they just rescued her? Shouldn't she be thanking him? Why didn't anyone say thank you when he rescued them?

She shook her fist. "You don't just pull a gun out whenever something doesn't work the way you want it to! You talk about it. You figure it out. You *work* it out. You guys are as bad as my parents—always fighting, always wanting something more and whining because you think you have to hurt each other to get it." She whirled on Gygak. "Did it ever occur to you that if you wanted to leave this planet, you could *help* us? Well . . . did you? But no! You kept making everything worse!" She pressed her fingers against her temples in frustration. "You guys make me crazy! Just get a divorce and split everything up if you have to, but STOP hurting each other!"

Her voice cracked, and she started to cry. She turned her head away so no one could see.

Laney and Svarta didn't lower their guns in spite of Tara's meltdown. "She's just in shock over having someone threaten to blow a new hole through her windpipe. She'll be okay," Svarta said as though Tara's words hadn't meant anything.

"He's Nova's man. We can't just let him go," Laney said. Pity laced the edge of her words, whether pity for Gygak or for Tara, Hap didn't know.

Gygak raised his skinny chin as if acknowledging her words and accepting them. "Nova's a great man!"

"Nova's a great bonehead," Hap muttered. He walked over to Tara and put a hand on her shoulder.

She shrugged it off but turned puffy eyes and a red nose toward him. "Thanks for helping me."

Once she said thanks, he felt stupid for wanting her to. They were in this alien abduction thing together. That made them friends. If she said thanks or not, they would still be friends.

Hap glanced around, remembering they should be escaping and feeling intensely grateful to Mosh for sending others the wrong way to look for them. Tara must have felt the same thing because she put her hand on Mosh's arm, looking as though it took her some effort not to wince at the drubber he maintained his grip on. "Thanks," she whispered.

"Yeah. Thanks," Hap echoed.

Mosh nodded and handed Gygak's drubber to Hap. Hap tried to shove it back to Mosh, but Mosh shook his head. "You keep it. I have my own."

Hap frowned and kept the drubber.

Light and heat burst through the window on the left. Amar appeared from within that light, stepping out as though he were stepping off an elevator.

"Whoa!" Hap whistled. "Even Star Trek never made that look so good. How did you do that?"

"It's a gift of my eighth brother. I am not so skilled as him, but I manage where I can find light in abundance enough to move myself within it."

"So the books are real?" Hap felt light-headed. "They really do all those things Svarta said?"

Amar sidestepped the question. "I am sure some rumors are exaggerated."

Laney nodded toward Gygak and gave a meaningful look to Amar. Amar shook his head. "I cannot. He is not intelligent enough."

"You can't what?" Hap asked.

Amar looked at Gygak while answering Hap. "I've studied all the books. One is the book of communication—mind control, if you'd rather—but, in truth, there has to be some mind *to* control in order for it to work."

Gygak's protest about his intelligence was cut short when Svarta made a noise low in her throat. "Time to move. Someone's coming." Footfalls echoed at the bottom of the winding stairs outside the door. Laney shoved an end table in front of the chair.

Gygak opened his mouth to shout out for help, but Amar took the quad's head in both his hands. Amar mumbled something, and Gygak went limp.

Laney pointed her gun to the Gygan. "I thought you said you couldn't."

Amar shrugged while he lifted Gygak in a fireman hold. "I cannot. As I said, in order to control a mind, a mind must exist worth controlling. But I don't need intelligence to shut down a mind. No, this is basic physiology." Amar shifted Gygak's body on his shoulders and looked toward the windows. "I am quite talented at the death touch."

"You killed him?" Tara's wail elicited a stern look from Laney and Svarta.

"Oh no. The death touch is just a name. He is not conscious. I put his mind deep into itself, and it will not wake until I call it back."

"Too much talking, not enough moving." Svarta looked at Amar. "Can you take us out the way you came in?"

"I am not that strong. I cannot move another. I don't have the gift and I've not seen the book for a long enough time to study it well."

"A plan? Someone?" Svarta looked ready to beat up all of them for standing around when there was escaping to be done.

Amar pulled out a thing that looked like a candle taper and pointed it at the glass. A thin beam of light shot from the wand into the glass. The light seemed to bounce along the surface of the window until the entire pane came shattering down in a shower of shards. Hap and Tara covered their heads with their arms. Hap felt the shards hit him, but nothing cut into his skin.

A spark of fire burned a dime-sized hole in the door, whizzed past his head, and singed his hair on the right side. *So much for being considered part of Nova's family.*

27. Hunting Packs

Looking at the door melting into a hundred dime-sized burn marks that zipped into the room made Hap shudder with outright terror. "Holy Houdini!" Hap fell against the wall, dragging Tara with him to avoid the tiny flames. He moved toward the now-open window where Amar shouldered the Gygan out into Mosh's waiting arms.

Hap tightened his grip on Gygak's drubber with absolutely no intention to return fire. Engaging the enemy was something adults did . . . something heroes did. He was Hap Hazzard, fourteen-year-old-would-be magician. He wished he could disappear like magicians did.

"Why does everyone shoot at us?" Tara yelled. Hap pushed her in front of him to hurry her up. She clambered onto the window sill and leaped out.

Laney and Svarta returned fire but weren't successful in hitting anyone they could see since no one had yet crossed the threshold.

"The Hira!" Hap yelled. He edged along the wall to reach the crystal pyramid, glowing steadily behind the light lock. Hap jumped onto the chair Svarta left and tried to pull at the red disc, thinking if he moved the disc, the Hira would follow along.

The red disc refused to budge an inch.

"Forget it, Hap!" Laney yelled over the sound of fire blazing through the door. "Get out of here, now!"

"But the Hira!" Hap shook his head. And the book under the Hira . . . what if that was the one he needed?

Laney raced past the flames spreading throughout the room and grabbed Hap by the waist, pulling him back down to the floor and upending the chair in the motion.

"What good does it do anyone if you're dead?" she hissed in his ear as she pulled him along to the window. They joined Svarta on the sill. Hap jumped out at the same time flame caught Svarta full in the back. Her clothing lit up like a torch. She fell forward and rolled on the ground in a desperate attempt to smother it.

Hap looked back into the room that seemed alive with fire. He could make out the faces of several Serviens as they shoved through the door.

Mosh hurried to Svarta, rolling her against the ground. He spit into his free hand, hocking up a huge wad of slimy spit, and wiped the front of her clothes with it, keeping the flame from spreading. Then he hocked up some more and wiped it over her back. His spit extinguished the fire immediately.

"I'm going to throw up." Tara looked green and seemed to sway a little as she stared at Svarta's slimy, sticky clothes. Hap pushed at her to make her keep moving away from the windows and the guards. Tara sped along the ground and around the corner—out of Hap's view.

Hap raced past Amar. Laney stopped to shoot through the window at the door where Serviens poured into the room. She shot her gun repeatedly into the small cluster of people chasing them, buying the necessary time for Mosh and Svarta to douse the flames covering her body.

Hap didn't stick around to see if she hit anyone or not. He rounded the corner, scanning the landscape of marshland and bamboo for any sign of Tara. He spotted her on the ground trying to use her arms to crawl. He stopped, wondering why she'd crawl when they were being chased by men with big guns. Running seemed much more efficient in cases like these.

He squinted and could just make out the faint outline of red quills poking out from the back of her legs. Off in the distance, Hap heard a shriek. He turned toward the noise, dread shivering up his spine.

The rust-colored neubin stood at the edge of trees and shuddered. Rows and rows of spike-like quills jutted out from his back. The quills chirped as they rubbed against each other; the animal's shoulders jolted and twitched. The volley of quills whistled toward Tara.

Hap turned his head in horror to Tara as her eyes widened in sheer terror at the quills coming at her. She pulled herself forward with all her might and managed to escape most of the quills. But one caught her in the arm. She screamed out in pain and fear as the needle barbed her skin.

She tried to keep moving forward with only the strength of her right arm, but soon it froze up, and she couldn't move anymore.

The neubin lowered its quills, making them look like soft fur at its shoulders. It sensed the defenselessness of its prey.

The neubin spasmed forward, its mouth hanging open to reveal the rows of jagged teeth. Saliva dripped off in a rhythmic stream from its teeth and down its rust-colored fur. Tara's sob carried in the wind to Hap's ears.

The others were engaged in battle against the Serviens just around the corner, but Hap couldn't wait for them. He lifted the drubber and took aim. He pressed the button at the same time he squeezed his eyes shut and hissed, "Holy Houdini!"

The little drubber kicked back much harder than Hap had expected, and he ended up on his backside. He clambered to his feet to see the neubin fall at the same time Svarta clapped a slime-coated hand on his shoulder. "Nice aim, kid." She shoved him forward. "But no time to admire it. We need to get outta here. Grab the girl. Let's move!"

Hap ran to Tara, who wasn't able to even lift her head. She screamed when Hap stood over her and then started crying at the relief of it being him and not the neubin. He put the drubber in the waistband of his green pants, like he'd seen people do in the movies, and hoped with all his heart it didn't accidentally go off.

Hap picked her up, refraining from telling her she was a lot heavier than she looked. He had a mom and knew that such a comment to a girl would get him into huge trouble.

As he straightened, the chirping of quills rubbing together sounded behind him.

A cry escaped Tara's lips as Hap whirled to see the neubin behind him. His eyes widened when he realized he faced not one neubin but a whole pack of them. Some of them had their attention drawn to Mosh, Svarta, and Amar, who had just come around the corner. But most of them stared hungrily at Hap. Their shoulders jolted as the quills convulsed into their firing position.

Svarta let out a stream of words Hap didn't understand as she opened fire at the herd. Laney turned to shoot at the Serviens shooting at Svarta.

Once the shooting started, most of the herd had their attention on the people shooting, but three skirted around the edges in slow, shaking movements. They kept their eyes locked on Hap and Tara. It was as though they sensed Tara's debilitation. And they knew Hap wouldn't get far while carrying her.

Hap ran as the quills shot from the backs of these monsters that had every intention of making Hap and Tara dinner.

Running while holding Tara proved to be difficult, but adrenaline pushed him farther from the building and into the reeds. His feet kicked up water from the marshland as the mud sucked at each step as though abetting the neubins. Hap yanked his feet free with every step. He heard the quills thud into the mud and water around him, but he didn't feel any sink into his skin.

"Hap!" Tara sputtered, her eyes rolling around as she tried to see what was going on. "Hap. I don't want to die here."

"You won't." He made the mistake of looking down and trying to smile reassuringly, but he tripped in his exhaustion.

Water splashed up all around them as their bodies made a sickening splat into the mud. The second volley of needles whistled over their heads.

Hap laughed with a gurgling sound at the luck of it all. "Sorry! But they'd have got us if I hadn't been clumsy!" He pulled the drubber from the waistband of his pants and spun around to face the neubins. But before he could press the trigger, a violet light from above Hap's head sizzled as it hit the neubins, crumpling them. Hap looked up to see the entrance hatch in Nana dilating above him.

Everything stopped exactly where it was. Hap felt blinded by the light all around him. The light's heat dried him until he felt the mud shrinking and flaking from his face and hands.

Nothing in the light moved. The throbbing like a giant's heartbeat—slow and heavy—pulsed through Hap's ears and providing counterbalance to his own heartbeat. The giant's heartbeat came louder and faster until it finally matched his own.

It stopped. A zipping noise like static snapped over them. The light winked out.

28. Books, Magicians, and Decisions

Hap blinked in the darkness of Nana's cargo hold, but his eyes didn't adjust. "Tara?" His voice caught at saying her name. "You okay?"

"You mean other than I can't move anything from my chin down? I'm just perfect." Her voice caught too, and Hap felt something wet hit his hand, loosening up the tight feeling of the dried mud. She was crying.

"We're okay. We're okay now." Hap repeated these words several times until he felt a charge in the air. Light flashed, and he heard noises in the dark. He hoped Nana hadn't accidentally picked up one of those neubins.

"Who's there?" Hap demanded.

"Amar—with the Gygan and Elaine."

Another flash. More noise. This time from Mosh and Svarta.

Laney didn't waste time talking. She jumped to her feet and charged out of the cargo hold. Svarta followed right behind her.

Nana left the door open so that light from the hall entered the room, while also quickly suggesting, "You better get Tara strapped in her bed. I need to leave this area before Mosh's relatives decide to shoot me down."

Hap stumbled to his feet and carried Tara to the little room with her bed. He placed her in the silver coffin and was glad to see her smile faintly.

"Thanks, Hap."

"For what? For talking you into leaving the ship so we could get attacked by predatory kitties? Or for talking you into delivering the Hira to a criminal? Or do you mean for—"

"For jumping into some guy with a gun so he didn't shoot me. And for carrying me away from the kitties with big teeth. For being clumsy at just the right moment. And for making sure I got to talk with my mom."

Hap wriggled his shoulders uncomfortably. Praise from a girl who was not related to him had never happened before. In fact, praise from a girl who *was* related to him was pretty rare. Hap felt the heat rise from his neck to the tips of his ears.

He made sure Tara was strapped into her bunk, where she could wait out the effects of the needles, before heading to the control room.

Out the port windows he saw what looked like a city. "This must be the other side of the planet?"

"This is the city of Stupak—the opposite side of the Circle," Tremble answered when it became apparent everyone else had other things to do.

He stared out longingly. "I bet the gift shops are all on this side of the planet."

Tremble landed the ship at a platform where Nana refueled.

Amar put a heavy hand on Hap's shoulder. "Come with me, Hap Hazzard. I need to speak to the Rissan queen before I depart."

"The Rissans are here?" Hap asked.

Amar nodded. "They lost the battle for the Neswar and had to take shelter in the city. Nova had armed the Serviens too well. He is a very bad influence on decent society."

Hap didn't want to leave the ship ever again, but he couldn't argue with Amar, not after all the trouble Hap had caused.

He walked out into the alien city, feeling only a little of the wonder he should have felt when walking into such an amazing place.

Many of the people he saw were human, like he had hoped to find in the beginning; some were Rissan; others looked . . . well . . . odd. There were some with huge lightbulb-shaped heads held up by braces that hooked onto their shoulders because those bulbous heads were simply too big for a neck to support in this gravity. They had little fringes of skin that hung over their mouths like long mustaches.

There were Gygans like Gygak, though Hap only saw two. They were female and considerably taller and prettier than Gygak. More of the catlike things that Nova had as a pet crawled around the city streets, looking for stray scraps of food.

"Cannot abide those animals," Amar said, pointing at one of the catlike creatures as it pounced on a butterfly in a corner garden. "They are a pestilence to this city. Sneaking, plotting little creatures . . . sentient enough to be more than animals but not enough to take their place in the normal avenues of society."

"Sentient?" Hap said as he avoided collision with a lightbulb-headed person who shouldered his way through the crowd.

"Intelligent," Amar answered.

Most of the people walked with little boxes in their hands. Shadowy images of other people walked along with them, a little cloud of mist trailing from the box to the ghostlike people. Hap turned to stare at one as he chattered on to the girl holding the box.

"Was that a ghost?" Hap whispered. He'd never believed in ghosts before but now wondered if such a thing might be possible.

Amar turned to see what Hap pointed at and laughed. "No, Hap Hazzard. The dead have better things to do than haunt the living. Those are link boxes. They are talking to the images of live people on the other end."

They veered onto a side alley to the left until they came to a huge park. Little tents had been set up all over the huge expanse of green grass. "It's like a city of tents . . ." Hap stared at the Rissan children racing alongside small birds whose wings blurred as they zipped around the camp.

"They are the Neswar refugees."

Hap looked closer. Most of the bright, colorful robes the Rissan people wore were dull and faded with dust and stained with black marks. The marks looked like dried blood, and Hap hurried to look down.

Amar left Hap outside the tent while he went to speak with the queen. Hap stubbornly remained what they called closed-minded, and the queen didn't allow closed-minded people in her assembly.

He watched the children enjoying their playtime in spite of all the horrors of fleeing their homes the night before. They'd likely had to leave all their toys, all the stuff they loved, yet they didn't seem to mind playing with the birds. They didn't seem to mind what had happened to them.

"How can they be like that?" Hap asked Amar when he folded back the tent flap and hurried Hap back the way they had come.

"Like what?"

"They're happy. Look at them . . . they're *playing*. They got kicked out of their homes. They just lost a war, and they're acting like everything's *fine*."

"And you think they are wrong?"

Hap frowned and weaved his way through the people. "Shouldn't they be worried? Shouldn't they be scared? What if the Serviens attack the city? *I'm* worried. I'm scared. They should be worried and scared too!"

"And yet they have found joy in a moment, and you feel this is wrong. Perhaps it is not wrong. The Rissans have an ability to empathize and see the other point of view. For this reason they could never have won their battle for the Neswar. They saw how their assailants needed the Neswar. This is why they gave up without much of a fight and chose to move on. Perhaps their joy in this moment allows them to rebuild themselves. To find happiness in the moment allows them to have hope. That hope will feed them, help them to grow, to repair what is wrong. Consider a flower blossoming amidst the storms of spring. One day the sun comes out and spreads its love over the flower's petals. The flower accepts the gift of the sun's love and grows. It uses the storm's moisture to feed its roots and uses the sun's love to feed its soul. The flower cannot reject the gift in favor of worry over whether storms might return. It merely accepts and rejoices in the moment of warmth and, by so doing, thrives. Without joy in the moment for nothing more than the sake of the moment, surely the Rissan people would all fall to complacency, despair, or destruction."

"Joy in the moment . . ." Hap considered the idea of joy in the moment. He'd had a pretty rough day yesterday too. Yet he was alive. Tara was alive. They'd freed the scientist and had one of the nine books from the unknown scientists. Couldn't joy be found in any of that?

Of course it could.

"But I would imagine that for a growing boy, a full belly makes joy a bit easier to find. You will feel better with some food on your stomach." Amar walked into a little shop filled with people holding link boxes. Hap twisted through the crowd to the front. He couldn't read anything on the menu, so Amar ordered for him. He ended up with a stick skewered through several colored chunks of food that tasted like salty hamburger meat. After nothing but lumpy rolls, it tasted awesome. Hap felt a lot better after eating and asked if Amar could get one for Tara.

Amar nodded and paid for several more for the rest of Nana's crew. They continued back toward the ship. And Hap, with a full belly, found a lot of joy as he moved through the streets. *I'm alive. Tara's alive. Laney, Svarta, Amar, and Mosh are alive.*

Hap looked up to see where Amar led them and stopped Amar from turning right when they needed to turn left. "For being a smart scientist, you have a terrible sense of direction."

"Our talents cannot always be the same," Amar said with a laugh. His laughter died quickly on his lips as he turned to face Hap. "I brought you along that we might discuss our futures. Do you remember what I said about Providence?"

"Yeah . . ." Hap did *not* like the way this conversation started.

"Nova still has one of the nine books. He has the Hira to read and understand . . . and *implement* his understanding. After our escape, Nova will feel the urgency of collecting all the books, including the one we took from him."

The hair on Hap's neck rose. No. No, no, no, no. He'd had his adventure. Plus he'd told his parents he was going home. Lying to parents—never a good idea.

"If we visit Earth first, Nova will beat us to at least four books before we could ever hope to catch up." Amar's voice carried a hint of urgency. He clasped his hands together, almost pleading, his step slowing as they came into view of the ship.

"I just . . ." Hap picked at the loose threads in the green, silky pants he still wore, though after the mud, they had a more camo-army look. "My dad is . . . dying. He has cancer. If we're too late . . . I just . . . I need to be home."

"But consider, Hap Hazzard. To what home would you be returning? If Nova wins this race, he will alter the very fabric of the universe. Do not think Earth to be so far removed that Nova's plans will not affect you or your family. Nova is from our home planet and has revenge in his heart for the disgrace of his family name. Consider what would happen if such a man unlocks the power that controls everything."

Hap stared up at the sky, the blue of it not too dissimilar from the sky at home. "What's in these books that make them so powerful?" Hap wanted to hear Amar say it. He wanted Amar to say that one of those books would heal his father.

"The first is Propaganda. It teaches how to control the people and use them to do your bidding. The second is Physiology. It teaches one to control all components within their own body until they are indeed the master of their body. It teaches how to kill with touch— how to mend with touch—but you can be sure Nova will never mend anyone. This is my book, and its knowledge is what allowed me to put Gygak to sleep—how I lessened the burns on Svarta's body. The third is Microbiology. Again . . . its purpose was for healing. The microbiology book could heal any sickness, but the knowledge allows nefarious actions as well. With this he could poison the waters of every world; he could taint food and kill off populations, billions of people at a time."

Hap blinked. "Heal? Heal *any* sickness? Any sickness like what?"

"It can heal anything, Hap Hazard. In many ways, it could keep a body from the damaging effects of aging. It is what some call the fountain of youth. No matter the sickness, the knowledge in this book could heal that sickness."

It's true! And that was when Hap decided. He needed that book. He would not go home without it.

Amar continued his explanation. "The fourth is Alchemy. With this he would be able to create his own tradable currency. With this he could learn to transmute metals into gold. He could create metals and technology that could overpower that of the superpowers of this universe. The fifth is Communication. He would learn to get into the minds of anyone . . . this grants the user the ability to communicate across time and space with all sentient beings. The sixth is Gravity. It teaches one how to control the gravity of the many worlds. The seventh is Light. He would learn how to direct—how to be one with the light, how to travel in the light. He would learn how to focus all light to one place and obliterate entire planets in mere seconds. The eighth is Sociology. This teaches you to understand the evolution of society and, by understanding, predict how to lift it to the fullest potential or trample it into the dust. The ninth . . . The ninth is Cosmology. It would teach him to travel instantaneously through the space-time fabric. It would teach him to time travel. He could also journey throughout our entire universe and into others as well."

Hap considered the list of awesome books. He briefly wished that school books had cool stuff like that in them. "How long will it take to get the books?"

Laney stood outside the ship. When Amar gave her a nod, she strode forward to join them.

"Not too long. Not really."

The dream-vision he'd had when his link had ended came back to him like punches to the stomach. Hap's mind felt like it would explode in the same way Earth had exploded. Grandpa Hazzard's voice chanted in his head, *"Hazzard men are men of honor."*

Men of honor . . .

I'm only fourteen! What if I die getting these books?

Men of honor . . .

He knew the dream had been real—a vision of things to come, unless Hap stopped them.

"It is your choice, Hap Hazzard," Amar said.

Hap breathed in and out . . . deciding. He had to have that book for healing. He had to save his dad no matter what else might happen, even if he died trying. But he couldn't drag Tara around the universe against her will. "No."

Amar's face fell. Laney gasped at his response. She looked like she planned on whipping his backside until he agreed to do exactly what she asked him to.

"No, it isn't my choice," he quickly added. "It's *our* choice. This is Tara's life too. She should have a say."

"Then let us ask her." Amar motioned for Hap to lead the way.

"Yeah," Hap said, "You do the asking, though. That way, if she gets mad, she can punch you instead of me."

Hap knew she'd say yes and delay going home a little longer. Tara's moral compass always pointed to the-right-thing-to-do.

Hap chose right as a direction. Tara chose it as a way of life.

How long would it take? Could his dad hang on that long?

A few extra months and he'd be home. No big deal. Like being a foreign exchange student at a school in someplace really exotic. When he closed his eyes, he could still feel the crunching of shattered glass at his feet; he could see the flash of white as the earth exploded. Would it matter if he got home in time to see his dad if the earth blew up anyway?

And it wasn't like he'd get shot at again. That only happened because he'd been stupid. He'd be smarter from here on out.

In Tara's room, they handed her the multicolored shish kebab. She ate and listened while Amar explained everything in much clearer terms than he'd ever explained them to Hap. It turned out that because of Gygak, Nova had access to the same maps Laney possessed, which lead straight to the books.

Tara listened as he explained the books, the dangers, and the need—not that she could do much else since she was strapped, half-paralyzed, in her bed. "Which book do we have?"

"Gravity."

"Which one does he still have?" Hap asked, hoping it hadn't been the book of healing he'd been forced to leave behind in the light lock.

"Alchemy."

Hap exhaled in relief. "So it could be worse." Hap thought about that weird dream he'd had after he'd linked to his family and was glad Nova didn't have the light one where he could blow up planets like the Death Star. Or the one that Hap needed to save his father—the one that would allow Nova to poison the waters of every world or create supermutant soldiers . . .

"Worse? None of them are fit for improper use. In the wrong hands, they are all deadly. So, Tara Jordan, will you join us?"

Tara's eyes met Hap's briefly. "I've spent my whole life living with the choices other people make for me. Thank you, Amar, for letting me make this choice for myself. Yes. I'll go with you."

Amar smiled. "It is a true friend who makes the selfless decision when the choice is given them."

"I'll need to call home again and tell my mom. I don't want her to worry."

Amar nodded. "I will see to the link myself."

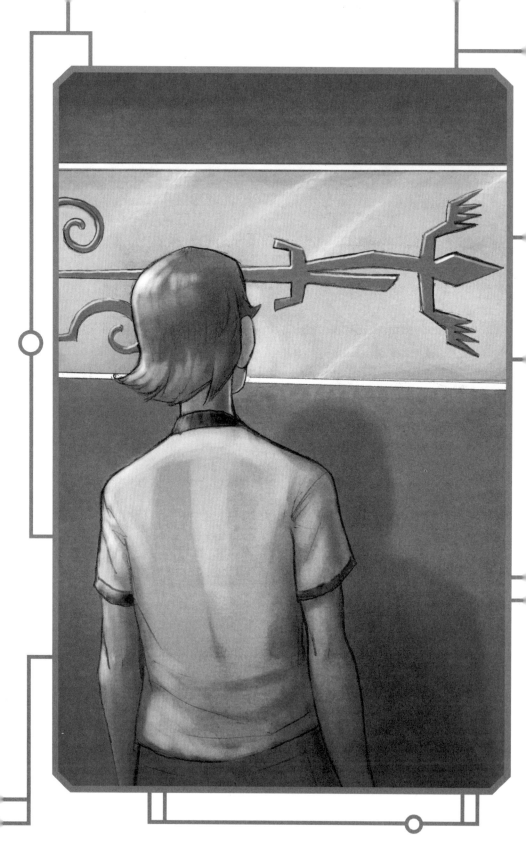

29. The Truth About Aliens

They finished refueling, and Svarta released the scourab box to the ship's hull before they took off. She wanted to make sure crettles didn't slow down their travel time.

"Where are those maps you told me about? I'm pretty good with directions and finding things. Maybe I could help you find the books," Hap said as Amar helped Laney tighten down a few things in the control room.

Amar nodded toward the low wall in front of the seats. "You are leaning on the map."

Hap looked down at the wall he leaned against and stepped back, noticing again the swirls, animal shapes, and triangles. "So it really is a map!"

Laney grunted around several of the screws in her mouth and turned her back on Hap. Hap spent a lot of time staring at the lines and shapes on Nana's wall. He finally looked up. "Who makes a map out of lizards and monkeys with swirled tails?"

Laney finished screwing in a panel on the wall and turned around. "You ever heard of the Nazca Lines?" Before Hap could even shake his head, she was shaking hers. "Of course you haven't. They never teach anything important in schools. The Nazca Lines are geoglyphs in the deserts of Peru. The Peruvians helped some of the scientists to make them when the scientists fled their own lands to hide their books."

Amar nodded and wiped the grease from his hands on a rag. "Each of my brothers commissioned a portion of the map so it could be readily seen from the sky but not seen by our enemies. The only part of the map I truly understand is the part I created. I know where my book is, and I know where my twin brother's book is because he left me a message before he died. And I believe there is one here." Amar pointed to the image of a lizard with a long tail.

"Where is that?" Hap asked.

Laney joined them at the wall. "It's hard to say because every minute . . . it's somewhere new. It's the Lizard Comet. The rock or head of the comet looks like a lizard. The tail of the comet . . . well, it looks like its picture."

"The book's on a comet?" Hap stared at the picture of the lizard.

"Yes." Amar looked apologetic. "My younger brother had a fondness for the bars and entertainment on the comet. Although now, there's a certain singer on that comet whose music I simply can't abide." Amar's mouth twisted around the word *singer* as though it was something distasteful.

Svarta came in just then. "Hull's clean. You guys talking about the rockstar Bo Shocks?"

Amar just shook his head in disgust.

Svarta started bobbing her head as though she could hear the music. "I like his rhythm. It speaks to me."

Amar gave Svarta a withering look. "Regardless of our opinions of his talents, or lack thereof, we will begin our search there. But the others . . . I do not know. I have ideas, but I do not know for certain."

"Where is yours?"

"The dead planet."

That didn't sound too bad to Hap. A dead planet meant there was no life on it, which meant there was no one to shoot at him or try to eat him.

"Where is your twin brother's book?"

"Still on Earth—the only one remaining there. Erich hid the book for Avkash."

"Erich? You mean Houdini?"

"Yes. Your Houdini."

Hap couldn't keep the confusion out of his voice. "If you left Earth thousands of years ago, how would you know Houdini?"

Amar smiled, his eyes looking past Hap as though he was involved in recalling a tender memory. "My link box. My twin,

Avkash, controls space and time. He could travel within space and time, be anywhere, anytime. He kept my link box with him, and the box allowed me to see all he saw in his travels. Houdini discovered his book, which compelled Avkash to go back to the book's location to retake it from Houdini. But they became friends, and Houdini's illusions and grand escapes amused Avkash. The dark ones discovered my brother had returned to Earth and journeyed there to find him, his book, and the Hira."

"Dark ones?" Hap asked.

"Ones who value no life but want their own lives to last forever. They want the books very much. ICE caught them on their entry to Earth. Nova rescued them, not truly understanding the evil they represented. Nova led them to Houdini and Avkash. Avkash gave my link box to Houdini's wife and begged her to contact me and inform me what happened. The dark ones killed Avkash. Nova poisoned Houdini and his wife—his revenge for the dishonor of his family. Houdini died. His wife, Bess, survived and contacted me with the link box. She told me where Avkash and Houdini hid the book." Amar sighed and refocused on Hap. "Since Earth is farthest from us than the other planets harboring the books of my brothers, we will claim Avkash's book last and will take you home at the same time."

Earth. Hap never realized how much he loved that word until that very moment.

They discussed the map until Nana interrupted to let Laney know she was ready to leave the planet. Hap decided to be strapped in his bed rather than strapped in the chair for takeoff. He needed sleep.

Hap snuggled down into his coffin bed and waited for the straps to zip out and cocoon him securely in.

They'd be heroes when they got home. He imagined being interviewed by Noory on *Coast to Coast.* Hap smiled and called over to Tara, "Do you have any idea how famous we're going to be when we get home?"

"As long as we're home, will it matter if we're famous?" Her voice sounded thick with sleep and irritation at him for disturbing her sleep.

"I'm just saying . . . we know something a lot of other people don't know."

"And what's that, Hap Hazzard?"

He thought about the pebbles and bits of leaf he'd tucked away from Stupak's Circle. He planned on collecting a whole lot more in the way of actual artifacts before he landed on his home planet again. Hap grinned at the wall separating them. "We know aliens really *do* exist."

"Hap! Please tell me that's not all you're thinking about right now. Go to sleep."

Hap smiled again at the wall, closed his eyes, and did as Tara instructed—drifting off into sleep.

He took a step forward and felt the crunch under his foot.

"No! Not this again!"

Hap looked around him in a panic, trying to pick out his family members from the people running from the city center. He knew they were here. They had been last time. He didn't recognize the city this time, though. He didn't recognize anything except the mortal terror on the faces of the people rushing past him. Screams. He couldn't hear them screaming, and he couldn't hear the sobs. Only the sound of static roared in his ears like wind. Yet he knew they were screaming and sobbing by the way their mouths hung open and their shoulders shook.

"My family! Where is my family?"

He closed his eyes, and when he opened them again, he stood in front of Hazzard's Magical Happenings, and his mom, grandpa, and Alison all huddled together by the front door. Their eyes were focused heavenward. Tara yelled Hap's name. Hap couldn't see her, though he looked everywhere. When he turned back to his family, he found his dad standing right in front of him. Hap stepped back, shaking his head. "No! I'm too late!" His dad's eyes peered out from a decaying skull. He looked up—like everyone else. Hap didn't look up, because he knew what was coming. His dad's decayed face glowed bright in the light before everything exploded.

Hap tried to sit up in his panic, but the straps held him down. Just a dream. The same dream he'd had after the CME Link. He wondered if Tara's link had caused her nightmares. The world—gone. His dad—gone. "Hang on, Dad," he whispered. "I've found out how to make you better. And we'll fix the world too. Hang on. I'm coming home soon."

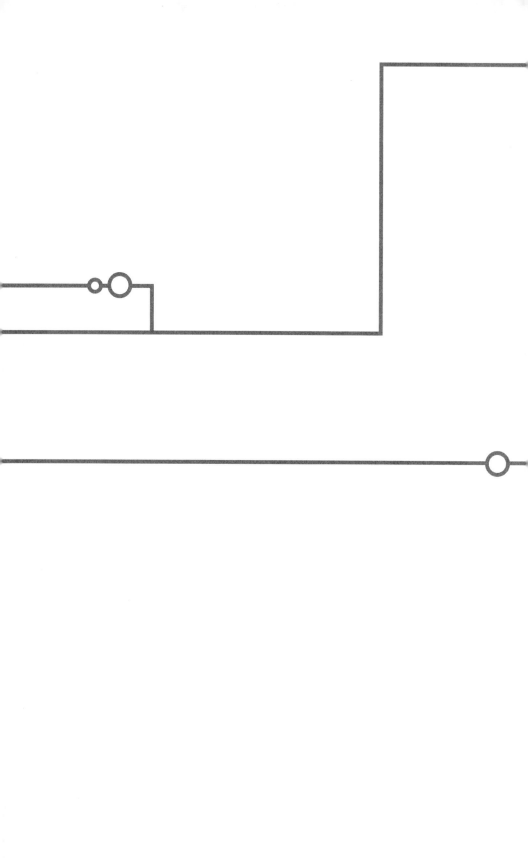

ABOUT THE AUTHOR

ABOUT THE ARTIST

Julie Wright has written over a dozen books, but especially loves writing about the fantastic. She strongly supports the cause of literacy for everyone.

She enjoys speaking to writing groups, youth groups, and schools.

She loves life and everything life has to offer except mayonnaise and mosquitoes. She especially loves reading, eating, writing, hiking, playing on the beach with her kids, and snuggling with her husband to watch videos. Julie's favorite thing to do is watch her husband make dinner. She has a profound respect for ice cream.

Visit her at her website:
www.juliewright.com

Kevin Wasden has an overactive imagination, is unable to sit still through meetings without drawing, and tends to be silly at the most inopportune moments.

He is an advocate of art and creativity in education and enjoys speaking to youth, writers, artists, and educators. He studied illustration at Utah State University and has studied figure drawing and painting from the exceptional figure artist Andy Reiss, in New York City. He is creator of the independent comic Technosaurs.

You can hang out with Kevin at
www.kevinwasden.com.

Visit Hap and Tara at
www.hazzardousuniverse.com

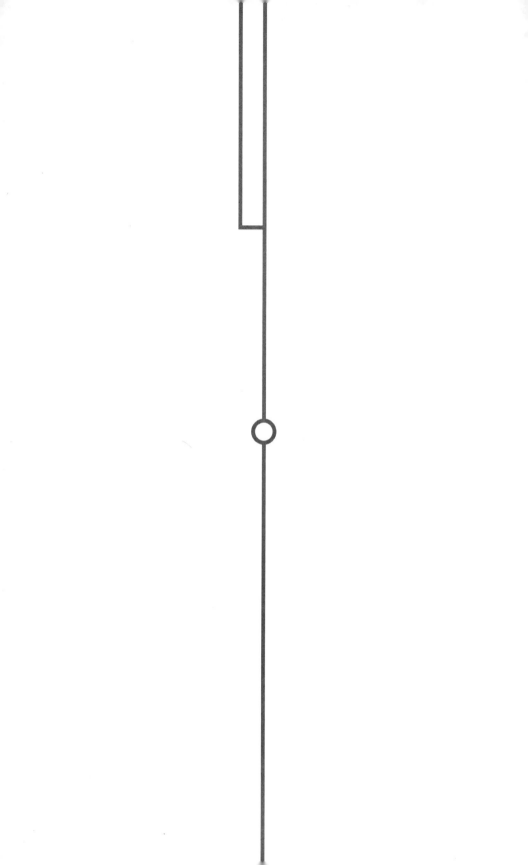